THE WAIF
OF THE
"CYNTHIA"

THE WAIF OF THE "CYNTHIA"

JULES VERNE
&
ANDRE LAURIE

TARK CLASSIC FICTION
AN IMPRINT OF

MANOR
Rockville, MARYLAND
2008

ISBN: 978-1-60450-305-0

Published by TARK Classic Fiction
An Imprint of Arc Manor
P. O. Box 10339
Rockville, MD 20849-0339
www.ArcManor.com
Printed in the United States of America/United Kingdom

CONTENTS

1

Mr. Malarius' Friend

There is probably neither in Europe nor anywhere else a scholar whose face is more universally known than that of Dr. Schwaryencrona, of Stockholm. His portrait appears on the millions of bottles with green seals, which are sent to the confines of the globe.

Truth compels us to state that these bottles only contain cod liver oil, a good and useful medicine; which is sold to the inhabitants of Norway for a "couronnes," which is worth one franc and thirty-nine centimes.

Formerly this oil was made by the fishermen, but now the process is a more scientific one, and the prince of this special industry is the celebrated Dr. Schwaryencrona.

There is no one who has not seen his pointed beard, his spectacles, his hooked nose, and his cap of otter skin. The engraving, perhaps, is not very fine, but it is certainly a striking likeness. A proof of this is what happened one day in a primary school in Noroe, on the western coast of Norway, a few leagues from Bergen.

Two o'clock had struck. The pupils were in their classes in the large, sanded hall—the girls on the left and the boys on the right—occupied in following the demonstration which their teacher, Mr. Malarius, was making on the black-board. Suddenly the door opened, and a fur coat, fur boots, fur gloves, and a cap of otter, made their appearance on the threshold.

The pupils immediately rose respectfully, as is usual when a stranger visits the class-room. None of them had ever seen the new arrival before, but they all whispered when they saw him, "Doctor Schwaryencrona," so much did the picture engraved on the bottles resemble the doctor.

We must say that the pupils of Mr. Malarius had the bottles continually before their eyes, for one of the principal manufactories of the doctor was at Noroe. But for many years the learned man had not visited that place, and none of the children consequently could have beheld him in the flesh. In imagination it was another matter, for they often spoke of him in Noroe, and his ears must have often tingled, if the popular belief has any foundation. Be this as it may, his recognition was unanimous, and a triumph for the unknown artist who had drawn his portrait—a triumph of which this modest artist might justly be proud, and of which more than one photographer in the world might well be jealous.

But what astonished and disappointed the pupils a little was to discover that the doctor was a man below the ordinary height, and not the giant which they had imagined him to be. How could such an illustrious man be satisfied with a height of only five feet three inches? His gray head hardly reached the shoulder of Mr. Malarius, and he was already stooping with age. He was also much thinner than the doctor, which made him appear twice as tall. His large brown overcoat, to which long use had given a greenish tint, hung loosely around him; he wore short breeches and shoes with buckles, and from beneath his black silk cap a few gray locks had made their escape. His rosy cheeks and smiling countenance gave an expression of great sweetness to his face. He also wore spectacles, through which he did not cast piercing glances like the doctor, but through them his blue eyes shone with inexhaustible benevolence.

In the memory of his pupils Mr. Malarius had never punished a scholar. But, nevertheless, they all respected him, and loved him. He had a brave soul, and all the world knew it very well. They were not ignorant of the fact that in his youth he had passed brilliant examinations, and that he had been offered a professorship in a great university, where he might have attained to honor and wealth. But he had a sister, poor Kristina, who was always ill and suffering. She would not have left her native village for the world, for she felt sure that she would die if they removed to the city. So Mr. Malarius had submitted gently to her wishes, and sacrificed his own prospects. He had accepted the humble duty of the village school-master, and when twenty years afterward Kristina had died, blessing him, he had become accustomed to his obscure and retired life, and did not care to change it. He was absorbed in his work, and forgot the world. He found a supreme pleasure in becoming a model instructor, and in having the best-conducted school in his country. Above all, he liked to instruct his best pupils in the higher branches, to initiate them into scientific studies, and in ancient and modern literature, and give them the information which is usually the portion of the higher classes, and not bestowed upon the children of fishermen and peasants.

"What is good for one class, is good for the other," he argued. "If the poor have not as many comforts, that is no reason why they should be denied an acquaintance with Homer and Shakespeare; the names of the stars which guide them across the ocean, or of the plants which grow on the earth. They will soon see them laid low by their ploughs, but in their infancy at least they will have drunk from pure sources, and participated in the common patrimony of mankind." In more than one country this system would have been thought imprudent, and calculated to disgust the lowly with their humble lot in life, and lead them to wander away in search of adventures. But in Norway nobody thinks of these things. The patriarchal sweetness of their dispositions, the distance between the villages, and the laborious habits of the people, seem to remove all danger of this kind. This higher instruction is more frequent than a stranger would believe to be possible. Nowhere is education more generally diffused, and nowhere is it carried so high; as well in the poorest rural schools, as in the colleges.

Therefore the Scandinavian Peninsula may flatter herself, that she has produced more learned and distinguished men in proportion to her population, than any other region of Europe. The traveler is constantly astonished by the contrast between the wild and savage aspect of nature, and the manufactures, and works of art, which represent the most refined civilization.

But perhaps it is time for us to return to Noroe, and Dr. Schwaryencrona, whom we have left on the threshold of the school. If the pupils had been quick to recognize him, although they had never seen him before, it had been different with the instructor, whose acquaintance with him dated further back.

"Ah! good-day, my dear Malarius!" said the visitor cordially, advancing with outstretched hands toward the school-master.

"Sir! you are very welcome," answered the latter, a little surprised, and somewhat timidly, as is customary with all men who have lived secluded lives; and are interrupted in the midst of their duties. "But excuse me if I ask whom I have the honor of—"

"What! Have I changed so much since we ran together over the snow, and smoked our long pipes at Christiania; have you forgotten our Krauss boarding-house, and must I name your comrade and friend?"

"Schwaryencrona!" cried Mr. Malarius. "Is it possible.—Is it really you.—Is it the doctor?"

"Oh! I beg of you, omit all ceremony. I am your old friend Roff, and you are my brave Olaf, the best, the dearest friend of my youth. Yes, I

9

know you well. We have both changed a little in thirty years; but our hearts are still young, and we have always kept a little corner in them for those whom we learned to love, when we were students, and eat our dry bread side by side."

The doctor laughed, and squeezed the hands of Mr. Malarius, whose eyes were moist.

"My dear friend, my good excellent doctor, you must not stay here," said he; "I will give all these youngsters a holiday, for which they will not be sorry, I assure you, and then you must go home with me."

"Not at all!" declared the doctor, turning toward the pupils who were watching this scene with lively interest. "I must neither interfere with your work, nor the studies of these youths. If you wish to give me great pleasure, you will permit me to sit here near you, while you resume your teaching."

"I would willingly do so," answered Mr. Malarius, "but to tell you the truth, I have no longer any heart for geometry; besides, having mentioned a holiday, I do not like to disappoint the children. There is one way of arranging the matter however. If Doctor Schwaryencrona would deign to do my pupils the honor of questioning them about their studies, and then I will dismiss them for the rest of the day."

"An excellent idea. I shall be only too happy to do so. I will become their examiner."

Then taking the master's seat, he addressed the school:

"Tell me," asked the doctor, "who is the best pupil?"

"Erik Hersebom!" answered fifty youthful voices unhesitatingly.

"Ah! Erik Hersebom. Well, Erik, will you come here?"

A young boy, about twelve years of age, who was seated on the front row of benches, approached his chair. He was a grave, serious-looking child, whose pensive cast of countenance, and large deep set eyes, would have attracted attention anywhere, and he was the more remarkable, because of the blonde heads by which he was surrounded. While all his companions of both sexes had hair the color of flax, rosy complexions, and blue eyes, his hair was of deep chestnut color, like his eyes, and his skin was brown. He had not the prominent cheek bones, the short nose, and the stout frame of these Scandinavian children. In a word, by his physical characteristics so plainly marked, it was evident that he did not belong to the race by whom he was surrounded.

He was clothed like them in the coarse cloth of the country, made in the style common among the peasantry of Bergen; but the delicacy of his limbs, the smallness of his head, the easy elegance of his poise, and the natural gracefulness of his movements and attitudes, all seemed to denote a foreign origin.

No physiologist could have helped being struck at once by these peculiarities, and such was the case with Dr. Schwaryencrona.

However, he had no motive for calling attention to these facts, and he simply proceeded to fulfill the duty which he had undertaken.

"Where shall we begin—with grammar?" he asked the young lad.

"I am at the command of the doctor," answered Erik, modestly.

The doctor then gave him two or three simple questions, but was astonished to hear him answer them, not only in the Swedish language, but also in French and English. It was the usual custom of Mr. Malarius, who contended that it was as easy to learn three languages at once as it was to learn only one.

"You teach them French and English then?" said the doctor, turning toward his friend.

"Why not? also the elements of Greek and Latin. I do not see what harm it can do them."

"Nor I," said the doctor, laughing, and Erik Hersebom translated several sentences very correctly.

In one of the sentences, reference was made to the hemlock drunk by Socrates, and Mr. Malarius asked the doctor to question him as to the family which this plant belonged to.

Erik answered without hesitation "that it was one of the family of umbelliferous plants," and described them in detail.

From botany they passed to geometry, and Erik demonstrated clearly a theorem relative to the sum of the angles of a triangle.

The doctor became every moment more and more surprised.

"Let us have a little talk about geography," he said. "What sea is it which bounds Scandinavia, Russia and Siberia on the north?"

"It is the Arctic Ocean."

"And what waters does this ocean communicate with?"

"The Atlantic on the west, and the Pacific on the east."

"Can you name two or three of the most important seaports on the Pacific?"

"I can mention Yokohama, in Japan; Melbourne, in Australia; San Francisco, in the State of California."

"Well, since the Arctic Ocean communicates on one side with the Atlantic, and on the other with the Pacific, do you not think that the shortest route to Yokohama or San Francisco would be through this Arctic Ocean?"

"Assuredly," answered Erik, "it would be the shortest way, if it were practicable, but all navigators who have attempted to follow it have been prevented by ice, and been compelled to renounce the enterprise, when they have escaped death."

"Have they often attempted to discover the north-east passage?"

"At least fifty times during the last three centuries, but without success."

"Could you mention a few of the expeditions?"

"The first was organized in 1523, under the direction of Franois Sebastian Cabot. It consisted of three vessels under the command of the unfortunate Sir Hugh Willoughby, who perished in Lapland, with all his crew. One of his lieutenants, Chancellor, was at first successful, and opened a direct route through the Polar Sea. But he also, while making a second attempt, was shipwrecked, and perished. A captain, Stephen Borough, who was sent in search of him, succeeded in making his way through the strait which separates Nova Zembla from the Island of Waigate and in penetrating into the Sea of Kara. But the fog and ice prevented him from going any further.

"Two expeditions which were sent out in 1580 were equally unsuccessful. The project was nevertheless revived by the Hollanders about fifteen years later, and they fitted out, successively, three expeditions, under the command of Barentz.

"In 1596, Barentz also perished, in the ice of Nova Zembla.

"Ten years later Henry Hudson was sent out, but also failed.

"The Danes were not more successful in 1653.

"In 1676, Captain John Wood was also shipwrecked. Since that period the north-east passage has been considered impracticable, and abandoned by the maritime powers."

"Has it never been attempted since that epoch?"

"It has been by Russia, to whom it would be of immense advantage, as well as to all the northern nations, to find a direct route between her shores and Siberia. She has sent out during a century no less than eighteen expeditions to explore the coasts of Nova Zembla, the Sea of Kara, and the eastern and western coasts of Siberia. But, although these expeditions have made these places better known, they have also demonstrated the impossibility of forcing a passage through the Arctic Ocean. The academician Van Baer, who made the last attempt in 1837, after Admiral Lutke and Pachtusow, declared emphatically that this ocean is simply a glacier, as impracticable for vessels as it would be if it were a continent."

"Must we, then, renounce all hopes of discovering a north-east passage?"

"That seems to be the conclusion which we must arrive at, from the failure of these numerous attempts. It is said, however, that a great navigator, named Nordenskiold, wishes to make another attempt, after he has prepared himself by first exploring portions of this polar sea. If he then considers it practicable, he may get up another expedition."

Dr. Schwaryencrona was a warm admirer of Nordenskiold, and this is why he had asked these questions about the north-east passage. He was charmed with the clearness of these answers.

He fixed his eyes on Erik Hersebom, with an expression of the deepest interest.

"Where did you learn all this, my dear child?" he demanded, after a short silence.

"Here, sir," answered Erik, surprised at the question.

"You have never studied in any other school?"

"Certainly not."

"Mr. Malarius may be proud of you, then," said the doctor, turning toward the master.

"I am very well satisfied with Erik," said the latter.

"He has been my pupil for eight years. When I first took him he was very young, and he has always been at the head of his section."

The doctor became silent. His piercing eyes were fixed upon Erik, with a singular intensity. He seemed to be considering some problem, which it would not be wise to mention.

"He could not have answered my question better and I think it useless to continue the examination," he said at last. "I will no longer delay your holiday, my children, and since Mr. Malarius desires it, we will stop for to-day."

At these words, the master clapped his hands. All the pupils rose at once, collected their books, and arranged themselves in four lines, in the empty spaces between the benches.

Mr. Malarias clapped his hands a second time. The column started, and marched out, keeping step with military precision.

At a third signal they broke their ranks, and took to flight with joyous cries.

In a few seconds they were scattered around the blue waters of the fiord, where might be seen also the turf roofs of the village of Noroe.

2

The Home of a Fisherman in Noroe

The house of Mr. Hersebom was, like all others in Noroe, covered by a turf roof, and built of enormous timbers of fir-trees, in the Scandinavian fashion. The two large rooms were separated by a hall in the center, which led to the boat-house where the canoes were kept. Here were also to be seen the fishing-tackle and the codfish, which they dry and sell. These two rooms were used both as living-rooms and bedrooms. They had a sort of wooden drawer let into the wall, with its mattress and skins, which serve for beds, and are only to be seen at night. This arrangement for sleeping, with the bright panels, and the large open fire-place, where a blazing fire of wood was always kept burning, gave to the interior of the most humble homes an appearance of neatness and domestic luxury unknown to the peasantry of Southern Europe.

This evening all the family were gathered round the fire-place, where a huge kettle was boiling, containing "sillsallat," or smoked herring, salmon and potatoes.

Mr. Hersebom, seated in a high wooden chair, was making a net, which was his usual occupation when he was not on the sea, or drying his fish. He was a hardy fisherman, whose skin had been bronzed by exposure to the arctic breezes, and his hair was gray, although he was still in the prime of life. His son Otto, a great boy, fourteen years old, who bore a strong resemblance to him, and who was destined to also become famous as a fisherman, sat near him. At present he was occupied in solving the mysteries of the rule of three, covering a little slate with figures, although his large hands looked as if they would be much more at home handling the oars.

Erik, seated before the dining-table, was absorbed in a Volume of history that Mr. Malarius had lent him. Katrina, Hersebom, the goodwife, was occupied peacefully with her spinning-wheel, while little Vanda, a blonde of ten years, was seated on a stool, knitting a large stocking with red wool.

At their feet a large dog of a yellowish-white color, with wool as thick as that of a sheep, lay curled up sound asleep.

For more than one hour the silence had been unbroken, and the copper lamp suspended over their heads, and filled with fish oil, lighted softly this tranquil interior.

To tell the truth, the silence became oppressive to Dame Katrina, who for some moments had betrayed the desire of unloosing her tongue.

At last she could keep quiet no longer.

"You have worked long enough for to-night," she said, "it is time to lay the cloth for supper."

Without a word of expostulation. Erik lifted his large book, and seated himself nearer the fire-place, whilst Vanda laid aside her knitting, and going to the buffet brought out the plates and spoons.

"Did you say, Otto," asked the little girl, "that our Erik answered the doctor very well?"

"Very well, indeed," said Otto enthusiastically, "he talked like a book in fact. I do not know where he learned it all. The more questions the doctor asked the more he had to answer. The words came and came. Mr. Malarius was well satisfied with him."

"I am also," said Vanda, gravely.

"Oh, we were all well pleased. If you could have seen, mother, how the children all listened, with their mouths open. We were only afraid that our turn would come. But Erik was not afraid, and answered the doctor as he would have answered the master."

"Stop. Mr. Malarius is as good as the doctor, and quite as learned," cried Erik, whom their praises seemed to annoy.

The old fisherman gave him an approving smile.

"You are right, little boy," he said; "Mr. Malarius, if he chose, could be the superior of all the doctors in the town, and besides he does not make use of his scientific knowledge to ruin poor people."

"Has Doctor Schwaryencrona ruined any one?" asked Erik with curiosity.

"Well—if he has not done so, it has not been his fault. Do you think that I have taken any pleasure in the erection of his factory, which is sending forth its smoke on the borders of our fiord? Your mother can tell you that formerly we manufactured our own oil, and that we sold it easily in Bergen for a hundred and fifty to two hundred kroners a year. But that is all ended now—nobody will buy the brown oil, or, if they do, they pay so little for it, that it is not worth while to take the journey. We must be satisfied with selling the livers to the factory, and God only knows how this tiresome doctor has managed to get them for such a low price. I hardly realize forty-five kroners now, and I have to take twice as much trouble as formerly. Ah, well. I say it is not just, and the doctor would do better to look after his patients in Stockholm, instead of coming here to take away our trade by which we earn our bread."

After these bitter words they were all silent. They heard nothing for some minutes except the clicking of the plates, as Vanda arranged them, whilst her mother emptied the contents of the pot into a large dish.

Erik reflected deeply upon what Mr. Hersebom had said. Numerous objections presented themselves to his mind, and as he was candor itself—he could not help speaking.

"It seems to me that you have a right to regret your former profits, father," he said, "but is it just to accuse Doctor Schwaryencrona of having diminished them? Is not his oil worth more than the home-made article?"

"Ah! it is clearer, that is all. It does not taste as strong as ours, they say; and that is the reason why all the fine ladies in the town prefer it, no doubt; but it does not do any more good to the lungs of sick people than our oil."

"But for some reason or other they buy it in preference; and since it is a very useful medicine it is essential that the public should experience as little disgust as possible in taking it. Therefore, if a doctor finds out a method of making it more palatable, is it not his duty to make use of his discovery?"

Master Hersebom scratched his ear.

"Doubtless," he said, reluctantly, "it is his duty as a doctor, but that is no reason why he should prevent poor fishermen from getting their living."

"I believe the doctor's factory gives employment to three hundred, whilst there were only twenty in Noroe at the time of which you speak," objected Erik, timidly.

"You are right, and that is why the business is no longer worth anything," said Hersebom.

"Come, supper is ready. Seat yourselves at the table," said Dame Katrina, who saw that the discussion was in danger of becoming unpleasantly warm.

Erik understood that further opposition on his part would be out of place, and he did not answer the last argument of his father, but took his habitual seat beside Vanda.

"Were the doctor and Mr. Malarius friends in childhood?" he asked, in order to give a turn to the conversation.

"Yes," answered the fisherman, as he seated himself at the table. "They were both born in Noroe, and I can remember when they played around the school-house, although they are both ten years older than I am. Mr. Malarius was the son of the physician, and Doctor Schwaryencrona only the son of a simple fisherman. But he has risen in the world, and they say that he is now worth millions, and that his residence in Stockholm is a perfect palace. Oh, learning is a fine thing."

After uttering this aphorism the brave man took a spoon to help the smoking fish and potatoes, when a knock at the door made him pause.

"May I come in, Master Hersebom?" said a deep-toned voice. And without waiting for permission the person who had spoken entered, bringing with him a great blast of icy air.

"Doctor Schwaryencrona!" cried the three children, while the father and mother rose quickly.

"My dear Hersebom," said the doctor, taking the fisherman's hand, "we have not seen each other for many years, but I have not forgotten your excellent father, and thought I might call and see a friend of my childhood!"

The worthy man felt a little ashamed of the accusations which he had so recently made against his visitor, and he did not know what to say. He contented himself, therefore, with returning the doctor's shake of the hand cordially, and smiling a welcome, whilst his good wife was more demonstrative.

"Quick, Otto, Erik, help the doctor to take off his overcoat, and you, Vanda, prepare another place at the table," she said, for, like all Norwegian housekeepers, she was very hospitable.

"Will you do us the honor, doctor, of eating a morsel with us?"

"Indeed I would not refuse, you may be sure, if I had the least appetite; for I see you have a very tempting dish before you. But it is not an hour since I took supper with Mr. Malarius, and I certainly would not have called so early if I had thought you would be at the table. It would give me great pleasure if you would resume your seats and eat your supper."

"Oh, doctor!" implored the good wife, "at least you will not refuse some 'snorgas' and a cup of tea?"

"I will gladly take a cup of tea, but on condition that, you eat your supper first," answered the doctor, seating himself in the large arm-chair.

Vanda immediately placed the tea-kettle on the fire, and disappeared in the neighboring room. The rest of the family understanding with native courtesy that it would annoy their guest if they did not do as he wished, began to eat their supper.

In two minutes the doctor was quite at his ease. He stirred the fire, and warmed his legs in the blaze of the dry wood that Katrina had thrown on before going to supper. He talked about old times, and old friends; those who had disappeared, and those who remained, about the changes that had taken place even in Bergen.

He made himself quite at home, and, what was more remarkable, he succeeded in making Mr. Hersebom eat his supper.

Vanda now entered carrying a large wooden dish, upon which was a saucer, which she offered so graciously to the doctor that he could not refuse it. It was the famous "snorgas" of Norway, slices of smoked rein-deer, and shreds of herring, and red pepper, minced up and laid between slices of black bread, spiced cheese, and other condiments; which they eat at any hour to produce an appetite.

It succeeded so well in the doctor's case, that although he only took it out of politeness, he was soon able to do honor to some preserved mulberries which were Dame Katrina's special pride, and so thirsty that he drank seven or eight cups of tea.

Mr. Hersebom brought out a bottle of "schiedam," which he had bought of a Hollander.

Then supper being ended, the doctor accepted an enormous pipe which his host offered him, and smoked away to their general satisfaction.

By this time all feeling of constraint had passed away, and it seemed as if the doctor had always been a member of the family. They joked and laughed, and were the best of friends in the world, until the old clock of varnished wood struck ten.

"My good friends, it is growing late," said the doctor.

"If you will send the children to bed, we will talk about more serious matters."

Upon a sign from Dame Katrina, Otto, Erik, and Vanda bade them good-night and left the room.

"You wonder why I have come," said the doctor, after a moments' silence, fixing his penetrating glance upon the fisherman.

"My guests are always welcome," answered the fisherman, sententiously.

"Yes! I know that Noroe is famous for hospitality. But you must certainly have asked yourself what motive could have induced me to leave the society of my old friend Malarius and come to you. I am sure that Dame Hersebom has some suspicion of my motive."

"We shall know when you tell us," replied the good woman, diplomatically.

"Well," said the doctor, with a sigh, "since you will not help me, I must face it alone. Your son, Erik, Master Hersebom, is a most remarkable child."

"I do not complain of him," answered the fisherman.

"He is singularly intelligent, and well informed for his age," continued the doctor. "I questioned him to-day, in school, and I was very much surprised by the extraordinary ability which his answers displayed. I was also astonished, when I learned his name, to see that he bore no resemblance to you, nor indeed to any of the natives of this country."

The fisherman and his wife remained silent and motionless.

"To be brief," continued the doctor, with visible impatience, "this child not only interests me—he puzzles me. I have talked with Malarius, who told me that he was not your son, but that he had been cast on your shore by a shipwreck, and that you took him in and adopted him, bringing him up as your own, and bestowing your name upon him. This is true, is it not?"

"Yes, doctor," answered Hersebom, gravely.

"If he is not our son by birth, he is in love and affection," said Katrina, with moist eyes and trembling hands. "Between him, and Otto, and Vanda, we have made no difference—we have never thought of him only as our own child."

"These sentiments do you both honor," said the doctor, moved by the emotion of the brave woman. "But I beg of you, my friends, relate to me the history of this child. I have come to hear it, and I assure you that I wish him well."

The fisherman appeared to hesitate a moment. Then seeing that the doctor was waiting impatiently for him to speak, he concluded to gratify him.

"You have been told the truth," he said, regretfully; "the child is not our son. Twelve years ago I was fishing near the island at the entrance of the fiord, near the open sea. You know it is surrounded by a sand bank, and that cod-fish are plentiful there. After a good day's work, I drew in my lines, and was going to hoist my sail, when something white moving upon the water, about a mile off, attracted my attention. The sea was calm, and there was nothing pressing to hurry me home, so I had the curiosity to go and see what this white object was. In ten minutes I had reached it. It was a little wicker cradle, enveloped in a woolen cloth, and strongly tied to a buoy. I drew it toward me; an emotion which I could not understand seized me; I beheld a sleeping infant, about seven or eight months old, whose little fists were tightly clinched. He looked a little pale and cold, but did not appear to have suffered much from his adventurous voyage, if one might judge by his lusty screams when he awoke, as he did immediately, when he no longer felt himself rocked by the waves. Our little Otto was over two years old, and I knew how to manage such little rogues. I rolled up a bit of rag, dipped it in some *eau de vie* and water that I had with me, and gave it to him to suck. This quieted him at once, and he seemed to enjoy the cordial. But I knew that he would not be quiet long, therefore I made all haste to return to Noroe. I had untied the cradle and placed it in the boat at my feet; and while I attended to my sail, I watched the poor little one, and asked myself where it could possibly have come from. Doubtless from some shipwrecked vessel. A fierce tempest had been raging during the night, and there had been many disasters. But by what means had this infant escaped the fate of those who had had the charge of him? How had they thought of tying him to the buoy? How many hours had he been floating on the waves? Where were his father and mother, those who loved him? But all these questions had to remain unanswered, the poor baby was unable to give us any information. In half an hour I was at home, and gave my new possession to Katrina. We had a cow then, and she was immediately pressed into service as a nurse for the infant. He was so pretty, so smiling, so rosy, when he had been fed and warmed before the fire, that we fell in love with him at once; just the same as if he had been our own. And then, you see, we took care of him; we brought him up, and we have never made any difference between him and our own two children. Is it not true, wife?" added Mr. Hersebom, turning toward Katrina.

"Very true, the poor little one," answered the good dame, drying her eyes, which this recital had filled with tears. "And he is our child now, for we have adopted him. I do not know why Mr. Malarius should say anything to the contrary."

"It is true," said Hersebom, and I do not see that it concerns any one but ourselves."

"That is so," said the doctor, in a conciliatory tone, "but you must not accuse Mr. Malarius of being indiscreet. I was struck with the physiognomy of the child, and I begged my friend confidentially to relate his history. He told me that Erik believed himself to be your son, and that every one in Noroe had forgotten how he had become yours. Therefore, you see, I took care not to speak until the children had been sent to bed. You say that he was about seven or eight months old when you found him?"

"About that; he had already four teeth, the little brigand, and I assure you that it was not long before he began to use them," said Hersebom, laughing.

"Oh, he was a superb child," said Katrinn, eagerly. "He was so white, and strong, and plump; and such arms and legs. You should have seen them!"

"How was he dressed?" asked Dr. Schwaryencrona.

Hersebom did not answer, but his wife was less discreet.

"Like a little prince," she answered. "Imagine a robe of pique, trimmed all over with lace, a pelisse of quilted satin, a cloak of white velvet, and a little cap; the son of a king could not have more. Everything he had was beautiful. But you can see for yourself, for I have kept them all just as they were. You may be sure that we did not dress the baby in them. Oh, no; I put Otto's little garments on him, which I had laid away, and which also served, later on, for Vanda. But his outfit is here, and I will show it to you."

While she was speaking, the worthy woman knelt down before a large oaken chest, with an antique lock, and after lifting the lid, began searching the compartments.

She drew out, one by one, all the garments of which she had spoken, and displayed them with pride before the eyes of the doctor. She also showed the linen, which was exquisitely fine, a little quilt of silk, and a pair of white merino boots. All the articles were marked with the initials "E.D.," elegantly embroidered, as the doctor saw at a glance.

"'E.D.;' is that why you named the child Erik?" he asked.

"Precisely," answered Katrina, who it was evident enjoyed this exhibition, while her husband's face grew more gloomy. "See," she said, "this is the most beautiful of all. He wore it around his neck."

And she drew from its box a rattle of coral and gold, suspended from a little chain.

The initials "E.D." were here surrounded by a Latin motto, "Semper idem."

"We thought at first it was the baby's name, but Mr. Malarius told us it meant 'always the same,'" she continued, seeing that the doctor was trying to decipher the motto.

"Mr. Malarius told you the truth," said the doctor. "It is evident the child belonged to a rich and distinguished family," he added, while Katrina replaced the babe's outfit in the oaken chest.

"Have you any idea what country he came from?"

"How could we know anything about it, since I found him on the sea?" replied Hersebom.

"Yes, but the cradle was attached to a buoy, you said, and it is customary on all vessels to write on the buoy the name of the ship to which it belongs," answered the doctor, fixing his penetrating eyes upon those of the fisherman.

"Doubtless," said the latter, hanging his head.

"Well, this buoy, what name did it bear?"

"Doctor, I am not a *savant*. I can read my own language a little, but as for foreign tongues—and then it was so long ago."

"However, you ought to be able to remember something about it—and doubtless you showed it to Mr. Malarius, with the rest of the articles—make a little effort, Mr. Hersebom. Was not this name inscribed on the buoy, 'Cynthia'?"

"I believe it was something like that," answered the fisherman vaguely.

"It is a strange name. To what country does it belong in your judgment, Mr. Hersebom?"

"How should I know? Have I ever been beyond the shores of Noroe and Bergen, except once or twice to fish off the coast of Greenland and Iceland?" answered the good man, in a tone which grew more and more morose.

"I think it is either an English or a German name," said the doctor, taking no notice of his crossness. "It would be easy to decide on account of the shape of the letters, if I could see the buoy. Have you preserved it?"

"By my faith no. It was burnt up ages ago," answered Hersebom, triumphantly.

"As near as Mr. Malarius could remember, the letters were Roman," said the doctor, as if he were talking to himself—"and the letters on the linen certainly are. It is therefore probable that the 'Cynthia' was not a German vessel. I think it was an English one. Is not this your opinion, Mr. Hersebom?"

"Well, I have thought little about it," replied the fisherman. "Whether it was English, German, or Russian, makes no difference to me. For many years according to all appearances, they have lain beneath the sea, which alone could tell the secret."

"But you have doubtless made some effort to discover the family to whom the child belonged?" said the doctor, whose glasses seemed to shine with irony. "You doubtless wrote to the Governor of Bergen, and had him insert an advertisement in the journals?"

"I!" cried the fisherman, "I did nothing of the kind. God knows where the baby came from; why should I trouble myself about it? Can I afford to spend money to find his people, who perhaps care little for him? Put yourself in my place, doctor. I am not a millionaire, and you

22

may be sure if we had spent all we had, we should have discovered nothing. I have done the best I could; we have raised the little one as our own son, we have loved him and taken care of him."

"Even more than the two others, if it were possible," interrupted Katrina, drying her eyes on the corner of her apron. "If we have anything to reproach ourselves for, it is for bestowing upon him too large a share of our tenderness."

"Dame Hersebom, you must not do me the injustice to suppose that your kindness to the little shipwrecked child inspires me with any other feeling than the greatest admiration," said the doctor.

"No, you must not think such a thing. But if you wish me to speak frankly—I must say that this tenderness has blinded you to your duty. You should have endeavored to discover the family of the infant, as far as your means permitted."

There was perfect silence for a few minutes.

"It is possible that we have done wrong," said Mr. Hersebom, who had hung his head under this reproach. "But what is done can not be altered. Erik belongs to us now, and I do not wish any one to speak to him about these old reminiscences."

"You need have no fear, I will not betray your confidence," answered the doctor, rising.

"I must leave you, my good friends, and I wish you good-night—a night free from remorse," he added, gravely.

Then he put on his fur cloak, and shook hands cordially with his hosts, and being conducted to the door by Hersebom, he took the road toward his factory.

The fisherman stood for a moment on the threshold, watching his retreating figure in the moonlight.

"What a devil of a man!" he murmured, as at last he closed his door.

3

Mr. Hersebom's Reflections

The next morning Dr. Schwaryencrona had just finished breakfast with his overseer, after having made a thorough inspection of his factory when he saw a person enter whom he did not at first recognize as Mr. Hersebom.

He was clothed in his holiday suit: his embroidered waistcoat, his furred riding coat, and his high hat, and the fisherman looked very different to what he did in his working clothes. But what made the change more apparent, was the deep sadness and humility portrayed in his countenance. His eyes were red, and looked as if he had had no sleep all the night.

This was in fact the case. Mr. Hersebom who up to this time had never felt his conscience trouble him, had passed hours of sad remorse, on his mattress of skins.

Toward morning he had exchanged confidences with Dame Katrina, who had also been unable to close her eyes.

"Wife, I have been thinking of what the doctor said to us," he said, after several hours of wakefulness.

"I have been thinking of it also, ever since he left us," answered his worthy helpmate.

"It is my opinion that there is some truth in what he said, and that we have perhaps acted more egotistically than we should have done. Who knows but that the child may have a right to some great fortune, of which he is deprived by our negligence? Who knows if his family have not mourned for him these twelve years, and they could justly accuse us of having made no attempt to restore him to them?"

"This is precisely what I have been saying to myself," answered Katrina, sighing. "If his mother is living what frightful anguish the poor woman must have endured, in believing that her infant was drowned. I put myself in her place, and imagine that we had lost Otto in this manner. We would never have been consoled."

"It is not thoughts of his mother that trouble me, for according to all appearances, she is dead," said Hersebom, after a silence broken only by their sighs.

"How can we suppose that an infant of that age would travel without her, or that it would have been tied to a buoy and left to take its chances on the ocean, if she had been living?"

"That is true; but what do we know about it, after all. Perhaps she also has had a miraculous escape."

"Perhaps some one has taken her infant from her—this idea has often occurred to me," answered Hersebom. "Some one might be interested in his disappearance. To expose so young a child to such a hazardous proceeding is so extraordinary that such conjectures are possible, and in this case we have become accomplices of a crime—we have contributed to its success. Is it not horrible to think of?"

"And we thought we were doing such a good and charitable work in adopting the poor little one."

"Oh, it is evident that we had no malicious intentions. We nourished it, and brought it up as well as we were able, but that does not prevent me from seeing that we have acted rashly, and the little one will have a right to reproach us some of these days."

"We need not be afraid of that, I am sure. But it is too bad that we should feel at this late day that we have done anything for which we must reproach ourselves."

"How strange it is that the same action regarded from a different point of view, can be judged so differently. I never would have thought of such a thing. And yet a few words from the doctor seems to have turned my brain."

Thus these good people talked during the night.

The result of their nocturnal conversation was that Mr. Hersebom resolved to call upon the doctor, and ask him what they could do to make amends for the error of which they had been guilty.

Dr. Schwaryencrona did not revert to the conversation which had taken place the previous evening. He appeared to regard the visit of the fisherman as simply an act of politeness, and received him cordially, and began talking about the weather and the price of fish.

Mr. Hersebom tried to lead the conversation toward the subject which occupied his mind. He spoke of Mr. Malarius' school, and at last said plainly: "Doctor, my wife and I have been thinking all night about what you said to us last evening about the boy. We never thought that we were doing him a wrong in educating him as our son. But you have changed our opinion, and we want to know what you would advise us to do, in order to repair our fault. Do you think that we still ought to seek to find Erik's family?"

"It is never too late to do our duty," said the doctor, "although the task is certainly much more difficult now than it would have been at first."

"Will you interest yourself in the matter?"

"I will, with pleasure," answered the doctor; "and I promise you to use every exertion to fulfill it, upon one condition: that is, that you let me take the boy to Stockholm."

If Mr. Hersebom had been struck on the head with a club, he would not have been more astonished than he was by this proposal.

"Intrust Erik to you! Send him to Stockholm! Why should I do this, doctor?" he asked, in an altered voice.

"I will tell you. My attention was drawn to the child, not only on account of his physical appearance, which was so different to that of his companions, but by his great intelligence and his evident taste for study. Before knowing the circumstances which had brought him to Noroe, I said to myself that it was a shame to leave a boy so gifted in a village school—even under such a master as Malarius; for here there is nothing to assist in the development of his exceptionally great faculties. There are no museums, nor scientific collections, nor libraries, nor competitors who are worthy of him. I felt a strong desire to give him the advantages of a complete education. You can understand that, after the confidence which you have bestowed upon me, I am more anxious to do so than before. You can see, Mr. Hersebom, that your adopted son belongs to some rich and distinguished family. If I succeed in finding them, would you wish to restore to them a child educated in a village, and deprived of this education, without which he will feel out of place among his kindred? It is not reasonable; and you are too sensible not to understand it."

Mr. Hersebom hung his head: without his being aware of it, two large tears rolled down his cheeks.

"But then," he said, "this would be an entire separation. Before we ever know whether the child will find his relations, he must be taken from his home. It is asking too much, doctor—asking too much of my wife. The child is happy with us. Why can he not be left alone, at least until he is sure of a better one?"

"Happy. How do you know that he will be so when he grows older? How can you tell whether he may not regret having been saved? Intelligent and superior as he will be, perhaps he would be stifled with the life which you would offer him in Noroe."

"But, doctor, this life which you disdain, is good enough for us. Why is it not good enough for him?"

"I do not disdain it," said the doctor. "Nobody admires and honors those who work more than I do. Do you believe, Mr. Hersebom, that I forget my birth? My father and grandfather were fishermen like yourself, and it is just because they were so far-seeing as to educate me, that I appreciate the value of it, and I would assure it to a child who merits it. It is his interest alone which guides me, I beg of you to believe."

"Ah—what do I know about it? Erik will be almost grown up when you have made a gentleman of him, and he will not know how to use his arms. Then if you do not find his family, which is more than possible, since twelve years have passed since I found him, what a beautiful future we are preparing for him! Do you not see, doctor, that a fisherman's life is a brave one—better than any other: with a good boat under his feet and four or five dozen of cod-fish at the end of his lines, a Norwegian fisherman need have no fear, nor be indebted to any one. You say that Erik would not be happy leading such a life. Permit me to believe the contrary. I know the child well, he loves his books, but, above all, he loves the sea. It also almost seems as if he felt that he had been rocked upon it, and all the museums in the world would not console him for the loss of it."

"But we have the sea around us also at Stockholm," said the doctor, smiling—touched in spite of himself by this affectionate resistance.

"Well," said the fisherman, crossing his arms, "what do you wish to do? what do you propose, doctor?"

"There, you see, after all, the necessity of doing something. Well this is my proposition—Erik is twelve years old, nearly thirteen, and he appears to be highly gifted. We will say nothing about his origin—he is worthy of being supplied with the means of developing and utilizing his faculties; that is all we need trouble ourselves about at present. I am rich, and I have no children. I will undertake to furnish the means, and give him the best masters, and all possible facilities for profiting by their instructions. I will do this for two years. During this time I will make inquiries, insert advertisements in the newspapers; make every possible exertion, move heaven and earth to discover his parents. If I do not find them in two years, we shall never do it. If his relatives are found, they will

naturally decide his future career in life. If we do not find them, I will
send Erik back to you. He will then be fifteen years old—he will have
seen something of the world. The hour will have arrived to tell him the
truth about his birth. Then aided by our advice, and the opinions of his
teachers, he can choose what path he would prefer to follow. If he wishes
to become a fisherman, I will not oppose it. If he wishes to continue his
studies, I engage to furnish the means for him to follow any profession
that he may choose. Does this seem a reasonable proposition to you?"

"More than reasonable. It is wisdom itself issuing from your lips,
doctor," said Mr. Hersebom, overcome in spite of himself. "See what it
is to have an education!" he continued, shaking his head. "The difficulty
will be to repeat all you have said to my wife. When will you take the
child away?"

"To-morrow. I can not delay my return to Stockholm any longer."

Mr. Hersebom heaved a deep sigh, which was almost a sob.

"To-morrow! So soon!" he said. "Well, what must be, must be. I will
go and talk to my wife about it."

"Yes, do so, and consult Mr. Malarius also; you will find that he is
of my opinion."

"I do not doubt it," answered the fisherman, with a sad smile.

He shook the hand which Dr. Schwaryencrona held out to him, and
went away looking very thoughtful.

That evening before dinner the doctor again directed his steps toward the dwelling of Mr. Hersebom. He found the family assembled
round the hearth, as they were the evening before, but not wearing the
same appearance of peaceful happiness. The father was seated the fur-
thest from the fire, silent, and with idle hands. Katrina, with tears in her
eyes, held Erik's hands between her own, whose cheeks were reddened
by the hope of the new destiny which seemed opening before him, but
who looked sad at leaving all whom he loved, and who did not know
what feeling he ought to yield to.

Little Vanda's face was hidden in her father's knees, and nothing
could be seen except her long braids of golden hair. Otto, also greatly
troubled at this proposed separation, sat motionless beside his brother.

"How sad and disconsolate you look!" said the doctor, stopping on
the threshold. "If Erik were about to set out on a distant and most perilous expedition you could not show more grief. He is not going to do
anything of the kind, I assure you, my good friends. Stockholm is not at
the antipodes, and the child is not going away forever. He can write to
you, and I do not doubt that he will do so often. He is only going away

to school, like so many other boys. In two years he will return tall, and well-informed, and accomplished, I hope. Is this anything to feel sad about? Seriously, it is not reasonable."

Katrina arose with the natural dignity of the peasant of the North.

"Doctor," she said, "God is my witness that I am profoundly grateful to you for what you propose to do for Erik—but we can not help feeling sad because of his departure. Mr. Hersebom has explained to me that it is necessary, and I submit. Do not think that I shall feel no regret."

"Mother," said Erik, "I will not go, if it causes you such pain."

"No, child," answered the worthy woman, taking him in her arms. "Education is a benefit which we have no right to refuse you. Go, my son, and thank the doctor who has provided it for you, and prove to him by constant application to your studies that you appreciate his kindness."

"There, there," said the doctor, whose glasses were dimmed by a singular cloudiness, "let us rather speak of practical matters, that will be better. You know, do you not, that we must set out to-morrow very early, and that you must have everything ready. We will go by sleigh to Bergen, and thence by railroad. Erik only needs a change of linen, I will procure everything else that is necessary at Stockholm."

"Everything shall be ready," answered Dame Hersebom.

"Vanda," she added, with Norwegian hospitality, "the doctor is still standing."

The little girl hurriedly pushed a large arm-chair toward him.

"I can not stay," said the doctor. "I promised my friend Malarius to dine with him, and he is waiting for me. Little girl," he said, laying his hand gently upon Vanda's blonde head, "I hope you do not wish me any harm because I am taking your brother away from you?"

"No, doctor," she answered gravely. "Erik will be happier with you— he was not intended to live in a village."

"And you, little one, will you be very unhappy without him?"

"The shore will seem deserted," she answered; "the seagulls will look for him without finding him, the little waves will be astonished because they no longer see him, and the house will seem empty, but Erik will be contented, because he will have plenty of books, and he will become a learned man."

"And his little sister will rejoice in his happiness—is it not so, my child?" said the doctor, kissing the forehead of the little girl. "And she will be proud of him when he returns—see we have arranged the whole matter—but I must hurry away. Good-bye until to-morrow."

"Doctor," murmured Vanda, timidly, "I wish to ask a favor of you!"

"Speak, child."

"You are going in a sleigh, you said. I wish with my papa's and mamma's permission to drive you to the first relay."

"Ah, ah! but I have already arranged that. Reguild, the daughter of my overseer, should do this."

"Yes, I know it, but she is willing that I should take her place, if you will authorize me to do so."

"Well, in that case you have only to obtain the permission of your father and mother."

"I have done so."

"Then you have mine also, dear child," said the doctor, and he took his departure.

The next morning when the sleigh stopped before the door of Mr. Hersebom little Vanda held the reins according to her desire, seated upon the front seat.

She was going to drive them to the next village, where the doctor would procure another horse and sleigh, and thus procure relays until he reached Bergen. This new kind of coachman always astonishes a stranger, but it is the custom in Norway and Sweden. The men would think it a loss of time to pursue such a calling, and it is not rare to see children of ten or twelve years of age managing heavy equipages with perfect ease.

The doctor was already installed in the back of the sleigh, nearly hidden by his furs. Erik took his seat beside Vanda, after having tenderly embraced his father and brother, who contented themselves by showing by their mute sadness the sorrow which his departure caused them; but the good Katrina was more open in the expression of her feelings.

"Adieu, my son!" she said, in the midst of her tears. "Never forget what you have learned from your poor parents—be honest, and brave, and never tell a lie. Work as hard as you can—always protect those who are weaker than yourself—and if you do not find the happiness you merit come back and seek it with us."

Vanda touched the horse which set out at a trot, and made the bells ring. The air was cold, and the road as hard as glass. Just above the horizon a pale sun began to throw his golden beams upon the snowy landscape. In a few minutes Noroe was out of sight behind them.

4

At Stockholm

Doctor Schwaryencrona lived in a magnificent house in Stockholm. It was in the oldest and most aristocratic quarter of the charming capital, which is one of the most pleasant and agreeable in Europe. Strangers would visit it much more frequently if it were better known and more fashionable. But tourists, unfortunately for themselves, plan their journeys much upon the same principle as they purchase their hats. Situated between Lake Melar and the Baltic, it is built upon eight small islands, connected by innumerable bridges, and bordered by splendid quays, enlivened by numerous steam-boats, which fulfill the duties of omnibuses. The population are hardworking, gay, and contented. They are the most hospitable, the most polite, and the best educated of any nation in Europe. Stockholm, with its libraries, its museums, its scientific establishments, is in fact the Athens of the North, as well as a very important commercial center.

Erik, however, had not recovered from the sadness incident upon parting from Vanda, who had left them at the first relay. Their parting had been more sorrowful than would have been expected at their age, but they had not been able to conceal their emotion.

When the carriage stopped before a large brick house, whose double windows shone resplendently with gaslight, Erik was fairly dazzled. The copper knocker of the door appeared to him to be of fine gold. The vestibule, paved with marble and ornamented with statues, bronze torches, and large Chinese-vases, completed his amazement.

A footman in livery removed his master's furs, and inquired after his health with the affectionate cordiality which is habitual with Swedish servants. Erik looked around him with amazement.

31

The sound of voices attracted his attention toward the broad oaken staircase, covered with heavy carpet. He turned, and saw two persons whose costumes appeared to him the height of elegance.

One was a lady with gray hair, and of medium height, who wore a dress of black cloth, short enough to show her red stockings with yellow clock-work, and her buckled shoes. An enormous bunch of keys attached to a steel chain hung at her side. She carried her head high, and looked about her with piercing eyes. This was "Fru," or Madame Greta—Maria, the lady in charge of the doctor's house, and who was the undisputed autocrat of the mansion in everything that pertained to the culinary or domestic affairs. Behind her came a little girl, eleven or twelve years old, who appeared to Erik like a fairy princess. Instead of the national costume, the only one which he had ever seen worn by a child of that age, she had on a dress of deep blue velvet, over which her yellow hair was allowed to fall loosely. She wore black stockings and satin shoes; a knot of cherry-colored ribbon was poised in her hair like a butterfly, and gave a little color to her pale cheeks, while her large eyes shone with a phosphorescent light.

"How delightful, uncle, to have you back again! Have you had a pleasant journey?" she cried, clasping the doctor around the neck. She hardly deigned to cast a glance at Erik, who stood modestly aside.

The doctor returned her caresses, and shook hands with his housekeeper, then he made a sign for Erik to advance.

"Kajsa, and Dame Greta, I ask your friendship for Erik Hersebom, whom I have brought from Norway with me!" he said, "and you, my boy, do not be afraid," he said kindly. "Dame Greta is not as severe as she looks, and you and my niece Kajsa, will soon be the best of friends, is it not so, little girl?" he added, pinching gently the cheek of the little fairy.

Kajsa only responded by making a disdainful face.

As for the housekeeper, she did not appear very enthusiastic over the new recruit thus presented to her notice.

"If you please, doctor," she said, with a severe air, as they ascended the staircase, "may I ask who this child is?"

"Certainly, Dame Greta; I will tell you all about it before long. Do not be afraid; but now, if you please, give us something to eat."

In the "matsal," or dining-room, the table was beautifully laid with damask and crystal, and the "snorgas" was ready.

Poor Erik had never seen a table covered with a white cloth, for they are unknown to the peasants of Norway, who hardly use plates, as they have only recently been introduced, and many of them still eat their fish on rounds of black bread, and find it very good. Therefore the doctor had to repeat his invitation several times before the boy took his seat at the table, and the awkwardness of his movements caused "Froken," or Miss Kajsa, to cast upon him more than one ironical glance during the repast. However, his journey had sharpened his appetite, and this was of great assistance to him.

The "snorgas" was followed by a dinner that would have frightened a Frenchman by its massive solidity, and would have sufficed to appease the appetites of a battalion of infantry after a long march. Soup, fish, home-made bread, goose stuffed with chestnuts, boiled beef, flanked with a mountain of vegetables, a pyramid of potatoes, hard-boiled eggs by the dozen, and a raisin pudding; all these were gallantly attacked and dismantled.

This plentiful repast being ended, almost without a word having been spoken, they passed into the parlor, a large wainscoted room, with six windows draped with heavy curtains, large enough to have sufficed a Parisian artist with hangings for the whole apartment. The doctor seated himself in a corner by the fire, in a large leather arm-chair, Kajsa took her place at his feet upon a footstool, whilst Erik, intimidated and ill at ease, approached one of the windows, and would have gladly hidden himself in its deep embrasure.

But the doctor did not leave him alone long.

"Come and warm yourself, my boy!" he said, in his sonorous voice; "and tell us what you think of Stockholm."

"The streets are very black and very narrow, and the houses are very high," said Erik.

"Yes, a little higher than they are in Norway," answered the doctor, laughing.

"They prevent one from seeing the stars!" said the young boy.

"Because we are in the quarter where the nobility live," said Kajsa, piqued by his criticisms. "When you pass the bridges the streets are broader."

"I saw that as we rode along; but the best of them are not as wide as that which borders the fiord of Noroe," answered Erik.

"Ah, ah!" said the doctor, "are you home-sick already?"

"No," answered Erik, resolutely. "I am too much obliged to you, dear doctor, for having brought me. But you asked me what I thought of Stockholm, and I had to answer."

"Noroe must be a frightful little hole," said Kajsa.

"A frightful little hole!" repeated Erik, indignantly. "Those who say that must be without eyes. If you could only see our rocks of granite, our mountains, our glaciers, and our forests of pine, looking so black against the pale sky! And besides all this, the great sea; sometimes tumultuous and terrible, and sometimes so calm as scarcely to rock one; and then the flight of the sea-gulls, which are lost in infinitude, and then return, to fan you with their wings. Oh, it is beautiful! Yes, far more beautiful than a town."

"I was not speaking of the country but of the houses," said Kajsa, "they are only peasants' cabins—are they not, uncle?"

"In these peasants' cabins, your father and grandfather as well as myself were born, my child," answered the doctor, gravely.

Kajsa blushed and remained silent.

"They are only wooden houses, but they answer as well as any," said Erik.

"Often in the evening while my father mends his nets, and my mother is busy with her spinning-wheel, we three sit on a little bench, Otto, Vanda, and I, and we repeat together the old sagas, while we watch the shadows that play upon the ceiling; and when the wind blows outside, and all the fishermen are safe at home, it does one good to gather around the blazing fire. We are just as happy as if we were in a beautiful room like this."

"This is not the best room," said Kajsa proudly. "I must show you the grand drawing-room, it is worth seeing!"

"But there are so many books in this one," said Erik, "are there as many in the drawing-room?"

"Books—who cares for them? There are velvet armchairs, and sofas, lace curtains, a splendid French clock, and carpets from Turkey!"

Erik did not appear to be fascinated by this description, but cast envious glances toward the large oaken bookcase, which filled one side of the parlor!

"You can go and examine the books, and take any you like," said the doctor. Erik did not wait for him to repeat this permission. He chose a volume at once, and seating himself in a corner where there was a good light, he was soon completely absorbed in his reading. He hardly noticed the successive entrance of two old gentlemen, who were intimate friends of Dr. Schwaryencrona, and who came almost every evening to play a game of whist with him.

The first who arrived was Professor Hochstedt, a large man with cold and stately manners, who expressed in polished terms the pleasure which he felt at the doctor's safe return. He was scarcely seated in the arm-chair which had long borne the name of the "professor's seat," when a sharp ring was heard.

"It is Bredejord," exclaimed the two friends simultaneously.

The door soon opened to admit a thin sprightly little man, who entered like a gust of wind, seized both the doctor's hands, kissed Kajsa on the forehead affectionately, greeted the professor, and cast a glance as keen as that of a mouse around the room.

It was the Advocate Bredejord, one of the most illustrious lawyers of Stockholm.

"Ha! Who is this?" said he, suddenly, as he beheld Erik.

The doctor tried to explain in as few words as possible.

"What—a young fisherman, or rather a boy from Bergen—and who reads Gibbon in English?" he asked. For he saw at a glance what the book was which so absorbed the little peasant.

"Does that interest you, my boy?" he asked.

"Yes, sir, it is a work that I have wanted to read for a long time, the first volume of the 'Fall of the Roman Empire,'" answered Erik, simply.

"Upon my word," exclaimed the lawyer, "it appears that the peasants of Bergen are fond of serious reading. But are you from Bergen?" he asked.

"I am from Noroe, which is not far from there," answered Erik.

"Ah, have they usually eyes and hair as brown as yours at Noroe?"

"No, sir; my brother and sister, and all the others, are blondes like Miss Kajsa. But they are not dressed like her," he added, laughing; "therefore they do not look much like her."

"No; I have no doubt of it," said Mr. Bredejord. "Miss Kajsa is a product of civilization. And what are you going to do at Stockholm, my boy, if I am not too curious?"

"The doctor has been kind enough to offer to send me to school," said Erik.

"Ah, ah!" said Mr. Bredejord, tapping his snuff-box with the ends of his fingers.

His glance seemed to question the doctor about this living problem; but the latter made a sign to him, which was almost imperceptible, not to pursue his investigations, and he changed the conversation. They then talked about court affairs, the city news, and all that had taken place since the departure of the doctor. Then Dame Greta came, and opened the card-table, and laid out the cards. Soon silence reigned, while the three friends were absorbed in the mysteries of whist.

The doctor made pretension to being a great player, and had no mercy for the mistakes of his partners. He exulted loudly when their errors caused him to win, and scolded when they made him lose. After every rubber he took pleasure in showing the delinquent where he had erred; what card he should have led, and which he should have held back. It is generally the habit of whist-players, but it is not always conducive to amiability, particularly when the victims are the same every evening.

Happily for him, the doctor's two friends never lost their temper. The professor was habitually cool, and the lawyer severely skeptical.

"You are right," the first would say gravely, in answer to the most severe reproaches.

"My dear Schwaryencrona, you know very well you are only losing your time lecturing me," Mr. Bredejord would say, laughing. "All my life I have made the greatest blunders whenever I play whist, and the worst of it is, I do not improve." What could any one do with two such hardened sinners?

The doctor was compelled to discontinue his criticisms, but it was only to renew them a quarter of an hour later, for he was incorrigible.

It happened, however, that this evening he lost every game, and his consequent ill-humor made his criticisms very severe upon his two companions, and even upon the "dummy."

But the professor coolly acknowledged his faults, and the lawyer answered his most bitter reproaches by jokes.

"Why should I alter my play, when I win by playing badly, and you lose by following your correct rules?" he said to the doctor.

They played until ten o'clock. Then Kajsa made the tea in a magnificent "samovar," and served it with pretty gracefulness; then she discreetly disappeared. Soon Dame Greta appeared, and, calling Erik, she conducted him to the apartment which had been prepared for him. It was a pretty little room, clean and well furnished, on the second floor.

The three friends were now left alone.

"Now, at last, you can tell us who this young fisherman from Noroe is, who reads Gibbon in the original text?" said Mr. Bredejord, as he put some sugar into his second cup of tea. "Or is it a forbidden subject, which it is indiscreet for me to mention?"

"There is nothing mysterious about the matter, and I will willingly tell you Erik's history, for I know that I can rely upon your discretion," answered Dr. Schwaryencrona.

"Ah! I knew that he had a history," said the lawyer, seating himself comfortably in his arm-chair. "We will listen, dear doctor. I assure you that your confidence will not be misplaced. I confess this youth arouses my curiosity like a problem."

"He is, indeed, a living problem," answered the doctor, flattered by the curiosity of his friend. "A problem which I hope to be able to solve. But I must tell you all about it, and see if you think as I do."

The doctor settled himself comfortably, and began by telling them that he had been struck by Erik's appearance in the school at Noroe, and by his unusual intelligence. He had made inquiries about him, and he related all that Mr. Malarius and Mr. Hersebom had told. He omitted none of the details. He spoke of the buoy, of the name of "Cynthia," of the little garments which Dame Katrina had shown him, of the coral ornament, of the device upon it, and of the character of the letters.

"You are now in possession of all the facts as far as I have been able to learn them," he said. "And you must bear in mind that the extraordinary ability of the child is only a secondary phenomenon, and largely due to the interest with which Mr. Malarius has always regarded him, and of which he has made the best use. It was his unusual acquirements which first drew my attention to him and led me to make inquiries about him. But in reality this has little connection with the questions which now occupy me, which are: where did this child come from, and what course would it be best for me to take in order to discover his family? We have only two facts to guide us in this search. First: The physical indications of the race to which the child belongs. Second: The name 'Cynthia,' which was engraved on the buoy.

"As to the first fact, there can be no doubt; the child belongs to the Celtic race. He presents the type of a Celt in all its beauty and purity.

"Let us pass to the second fact:

"'Cynthia' is certainly the name of the vessel to which the buoy belonged. This name might have belonged to a German vessel, as well as to an English one; but it was written in the Roman characters. Therefore, the vessel was an English one—or we will say Anglo-Saxon to be more precise. Besides, everything confirms the hypothesis, for more than one English vessel going and coming from Inverness, or the Orkneys, have been driven on the coast of Norway by a tempest; and you must not forget that the little living waif could not have been floating for a long while, since he had resisted hunger, and all the dangers of his perilous journey. Well, now you know all, and what is your conclusion my dear friends?"

Neither the professor nor the lawyer thought it prudent to utter a word.

"You have not been able to arrive at any conclusion," said the doctor, in a tone which betrayed a secret triumph. "Perhaps you even think there is a contradiction between the two facts—a child of the Celtic race—an English Vessel. But this is simply because you have failed to bear in mind the existence on the coast of Great Britain of a people of the Celtic race, on her sister island, Ireland. I did not think of it at first myself, and it prevented me from solving the problem. But when it occurred to me, I said to myself: the child is Irish. Is this your opinion, Hochstedt?"

If there was anything in the world the professor disliked, it was to give a positive opinion upon any subject. It must also be confessed that to give such an opinion in this case would have been premature. He therefore contented himself with nodding his head, and saying:

"It is an incontestable fact that the Irish belong to the Celtic branch of the Arian race."

This was a sufficiently safe aphorism, but Doctor Schwaryencrona asked nothing more, and only saw in it the entire confirmation of his theory.

"You think so, yourself," he said eagerly. "The Irish were Celts, and the child has all the characteristics of the race. The 'Cynthia' having been an English vessel, it appears to me that we are in possession of the necessary links, in order to find the family of the poor child. It is in Great Britain that we must look for them. Some advertisements in the 'Times' will probably be sufficient to put us on their tracks."

The doctor continued to enlarge upon his plan of proceeding, when he remarked the obstinate silence of the lawyer and the slightly ironical expression with which he listened to his conclusions.

"If you are not of my opinion, Bredejord, I wish you would say so. You know that I do not fear to discuss the matter," he said, stopping short.

"I have nothing to say," answered Mr. Bredejord. "Hochstedt can bear witness that I have said nothing."

"No. But I see very well that you do not share my opinion; and I am curious to know why," said the doctor.

"Is Cynthia an English name?" he asked, with vehemence. "Yes! it was written in Roman characters—it could not have been German. You have heard our eminent friend, Hochstedt, affirm that the Irish are Celts. Has the child all the characteristics of the Celtic race? You can judge for yourself. You were struck by his appearance before I opened my mouth about the subject. I conclude, therefore, that it is a want of friendship for you to refuse to agree with me, and recognize the fact that the boy belongs to an Irish family."

"Want of friendship is a strong charge," answered Mr. Bredejord, "if you apply it to me. I can only say that I have not, as yet, expressed the slightest opinion."

"No; but I see that you do not spare mine."

"Have I not a right?"

"But give some facts to support your theory."

"I have not said that I have formed any."

"Then it is a systematic opposition, just for the sake of contradicting me, as you do in whist."

"Nothing is further from my thoughts, I assure you. Your reasoning appeared to me to be too peremptory, that is all."

"In what way, if you please, I am curious to know?"

"It would take too long to tell you. Eleven o'clock is striking. I will content myself with offering you a bet. Your copy of Pliny against my Quintilian, that you have not judged rightly, and that the child is not Irish."

"You know that I do not like to bet," said the doctor, softened by his unconquerable good humor. "But I shall take so much pleasure in your discomfiture that I accept your offer."

"Well, then it is a settled affair. How much time do you expect to take for your researches?"

"A few months will suffice, I hope, but I have said two years to Hersebom, in order to be sure that no efforts were wanting."

"Ah! well—I give you two years. Hochstedt shall be our witness; and there is no ill-feeling, I hope?"

"Assuredly not, but I see your Quintilian in great danger of coming to keep company with my Pliny," answered the doctor.

Then, after shaking hands with his two friends, he accompanied them to the door.

5

The Thirteen Days of Christmas

The next day Erik began his new life at school.

Dr. Schwaryencrona first took him to his tailors, and fitted him out with some new suits of clothes; then he introduced him to the principal of one of the best schools in town. It was called in Swedish "Hogre elementar larovek."

In this school were taught the ancient and modern languages, the elementary sciences, and all that it was necessary to learn before entering college. As in Germany and Italy, the students did not board in the college. They lived with their families in the town, with the professors, or wherever they could obtain comfortable accommodations. The charges are very moderate; in fact, they have been reduced almost to nothing. Large gymnasiums are attached to each of the higher classes, and physical culture is as carefully attended to as the intellectual.

Erik at once gained the head of his division. He learned everything with such extreme facility that he had a great deal of time to himself. The doctor therefore thought that it would be better for him to utilize his evenings by taking a course at the "Slodjskolan," the great industrial school of Stockholm. It was an establishment especially devoted to the practice of the sciences, particularly to making experiments in physics and chemistry, and to geometrical constructions which are only taught theoretically in the schools.

Doctor Schwaryencrona judged rightly that the teachings of this school, which was one of the wonders of Stockholm, would give a new impetus to the rapid progress which Erik was making, and he hoped for great results from this double training.

His young *protege*, proved worthy of the advantages which he procured for him. He penetrated the depths of the fundamental sciences, and instead of vague and superficial ideas, the ordinary lot of so many pupils, he stored up a provision of just, precise, and definite facts. The future development of these excellent principles could only be a question of time.

Hereafter he would be able to learn without difficulty the more elevated branches of these studies which would be required in college; in fact it would be only play to him.

The same service which Mr. Malarius had rendered him, in teaching him languages, history, and botany, the "Slodjskolan" now did for him by inculcating the A, B, C, of the industrial arts; without which the best teaching so often remains a dead letter.

Far from fatiguing Erik's brain, the multiplicity and variety of his studies strengthened it much more than a special course of instruction could have done.

Besides, the gymnasium was always open to him to recruit his body when his studies were over; and here as well as in the school Erik stood first. On holidays he never failed to pay a visit to the sea which he loved with filial tenderness. He talked with the sailors and fishermen, and often brought home a fine fish, which was well received by Dame Greta.

This good woman had conceived a great affection for this new member of the household. Erik was so gentle, and naturally so courteous and obliging, so studious and so brave, that it was impossible to know him and not to like him. In eight days he had become a favorite with Mr. Bredejord and Mr. Hochstedt, as he was already with Doctor Schwaryencrona.

The only person who treated him with coldness was Kajsa. Whether the little fairy thought that her hitherto undisputed sovereignty in the house was in danger, or whether she bore Erik a grudge, because of the sarcasms which her aristocratic air toward him inspired in the doctor, nobody knew. However, she persisted in treating him with a disdainful coldness, which no courtesy or politeness on his part could overcome. Her opportunities of displaying her disdain were fortunately rare, for Erik was always either out-of-doors, or else busy in his own little room.

Time passed in the most peaceful manner, and without any notable incidents.

We will pass with our reader without further comment over the two years which Erik spent at school and return to Noroe.

Christmas had returned for the second time since Erik's departure. It is in all Central and Northern Europe the great annual festival; because it is coincident with the dull season in nearly all industries. In

Norway especially, they prolong the festival for thirteen days.—"Tretten yule dage" (the thirteen days of Christmas), and they make it a season of great rejoicings. It is a time for family reunions, for dinners, and even for weddings.

Provisions are abundant, even in the poorest dwellings. Everywhere the greatest hospitality is the order of the day.

The "Yule ol," or Christmas beer, is drunk freely. Every visitor is offered a bumper in a wooden cup, mounted in gold, silver, or copper, which the poorest families possess, and which cups have been transmitted to them from time immemorial. The visitor must empty this cup, and exchange with his hosts the joyful wishes of the season, and for a happy New Year.

It is also at Christmas that the servants receive their new clothes; which are often the best part of their wages—that the cows, and sheep, and even the birds of the air, receive a double ration, which is exceptionally large. They say in Norway of a "poor man," that he is so poor that he can not even give the sparrows their dinner at Christmas.

Of these thirteen traditional days, Christmas-eve is the gayest. It is the custom for the young girls and boys to go around in bands on their "schnee-schuhe," or snow-shoes, and stop before the houses, and sing in chorus the old national melodies. The clear voices suddenly sounding through the fresh night air, in the lonely valleys, with their wintery surroundings, have an odd and charming effect. The doors are immediately opened, the singers are invited to enter, and they offer them cake, dried apples, and ale; and often make them dance. After this frugal supper the joyous band depart, like a flock of gulls, to perform the same ceremony further away. Distances are regarded as nothing, for on their "schnee-schuhe," which are attached to their feet by leather straps, they glide over several miles with marvelous rapidity. The peasants of Norway also use, with these show-shoes, a strong stick, to balance themselves, and help them along. This year the festival would be a joyous one for the Herseboms. They were expecting Erik.

A letter from Stockholm had announced that he would arrive that evening. Therefore Otto and Vanda could not sit still. Every moment they ran to the door, to see if he was coming. Dame Katrina, although she reproved them for their impatience, felt in the same way herself. Mr. Hersebom smoked his pipe silently, and was divided in his mind between a longing to see his adopted son, and the fear that he would not be able to keep him with them very long.

For the fiftieth time, perhaps, Otto had gone to the door, when he gave a shout and cried out:

"Mother! Vanda! I believe it is he!"

They all rushed to the door. In the distance, on the road which led from Bergen, they saw a black object. It grew larger rapidly, and soon took the shape of a young man, clothed in gray cloth, wearing a fur cap, and carrying merrily over his shoulders a knapsack of green leather. He had on snow-shoes, and would soon be near enough to recognize.

The traveler perceived those who were watching before the door, and taking off his cap, he waved it around his head.

Two minutes later Erick was in the arms of Katrina, Otto, Vanda, and even Mr. Hersebom, who had left his arm-chair and advanced to the door.

They hugged him, and almost stifled him with caresses. They went into ecstasies over his improved appearance. Dame Katrina among them all could not get accustomed to it.

"What—is this the dear babe that I nursed on my knees?" she cried. "This great boy, with such a frank and resolute air, with these strong shoulders, this elegant form, and on whose lip I can already see signs of a mustache. Is it possible?"

The brave woman was conscious of feeling a sort of respect for her former nursling. She was proud of him, above all for the tears of joy which she saw in his eyes. For he also was deeply affected.

"Mother, is it really you," he exclaimed. "I can hardly believe that I am with you all again. The two years have seemed so long to me. I have missed you all, as I know you have missed me."

"Yes," said Mr. Hersebom, gravely. "Not a day has passed without our having spoken of you. Morning and evening, and at meal times, it was your name that was constantly on our lips. But you, my boy, you have not forgotten us in the grand city? You are contented to return and see the old country and the old house?"

"I am sure that you do not doubt it," said Erik, as he embraced them all. "You were always in my thoughts. But above all when the wind blew a gale. I thought of you, father. I said to myself, Where is he? Has he returned home in safety? And in the evening I used to read the meteorological bulletin in the doctor's newspaper, to see what kind of weather you had had on the coast of Norway; if it was the same as on the coast of Sweden?—and I found that you have severe storms more often than we have in Stockholm, which come from America, and beat on our mountains. Ah! how often I have wished that I could be with you in your little boat to help you with the sail, and overcome all difficulties. And on the other hand when the weather was fine it seemed to me as if I was in prison in that great city, between the tall three-story houses. Yes! I would have given all the world to be on the sea for one hour, and to feel as formerly free, and joyfully exhilarated by the fresh air!"

A smile brightened the weather-beaten face of the fisherman.

"His books have not spoiled him," he said. "A joyful season and a happy New-Year to you, my child!" he added. "Come, let us go to the table. Dinner is only waiting for you."

When he was once more seated in his old place on the right hand of Katrina, Erik was able to look around him, and mark the changes that two years had made in the family. Otto was now a large, robust boy of sixteen years of age, and who looked twenty. As for Vanda, two years had added wonderfully to her size and beauty. Her countenance had become more refined. Her magnificent blonde hair, which lay in heavy braids upon her shoulders, formed around her forehead a light silvery cloud. Modest and sweet as usual, she busied herself, almost unconsciously, with seeing that no one wanted for anything.

"Vanda has grown to be a great girl!" said her mother, proudly. "And if you knew, Erik, how learned she has become, how hard she has worked and studied since you left us! She is the best scholar in the school now, and Mr. Malarius says she is his only consolation for no longer having you among his pupils."

"Dear Mr. Malarius! how glad I shall be to see him again," said Erik. "So our Vanda has become so learned, has she?" he replied with interest, while the young girl blushed up to the roots of her hair at these maternal praises.

"She has learned to play the organ also, and Mr. Malarius says that she has the sweetest voice of all the choir?"

"Oh, decidedly, it is a very accomplished young person whom I find on my return," Erik said, laughing, to relieve the embarrassment of his sister. "We must make her display all her talents to-morrow."

And without affectation he began to talk about all the good people of Noroe, asking questions about each one; inquiring for his old schoolmates, and about all that had happened since he went away. He asked about their fishing adventures, and all the details of their daily life. Then on his part, he satisfied the curiosity of his family, by giving an account of his mode of life in Stockholm; he told them about Dame Greta, about Kajsa, and the doctor.

"That reminds me that I have a letter for you, father," he said, drawing it out of the inside pocket of his vest. "I do not know what it contains, but the doctor told me to take good care of it, for it was about me."

Mr. Hersebom took the letter, and laid it on the table by his side.

"Well!" said Erik, "are you not going to read it?"

"No," answered the fisherman, laconically.

"But, since it concerns me?" persisted the young man.

"It is addressed to me," said Mr. Hersebom, holding the letter before his eyes. "Yes, I will read it at my leisure." Filial obedience is the basis of family government in Norway.

Erik bowed his head in acquiescence.

When they rose from the table, the three children seated themselves on their little bench in the chimney-corner, as they had so often done before, and began one of those confidential conversations, where each one relates what the other is curious to know, and where they tell the same things a hundred times.

Katrina busied herself about the room, putting everything in order; insisting that Vanda should for once "play the lady," as she said, and not trouble herself about household matters.

As for Mr. Hersebom, he had seated himself in his favorite arm-chair, and was smoking his pipe in silence. It was only after he had finished this important operation that he decided to open the doctor's letter.

He read it through without saying a single word; then he folded it up, put it in his pocket, and smoked a second pipe, like the first, without uttering a sound. He seemed to be absorbed in his own reflections.

Although he was never a talkative man, his silence appeared singular to Dame Katrina. After she had finished her work, she went and seated herself beside him, and made two or three attempts to draw him into conversation, but she only received the most brief replies. Being thus repulsed, she became melancholy, and the children themselves, after talking breathlessly for some time, began to be affected by the evident sadness of their parents.

Twenty youthful voices singing in chorus before the door suddenly greeted their ears, and made a happy diversion. It was a merry band of Erik's old classmates, who had conceived the pleasant idea of coming to give him a cordial welcome home.

They hastened to invite them into the house, and offered them the customary feast, whilst they eagerly pressed around their old friend to express the great pleasure which they felt in seeing him again. Erik was touched by the unexpected visit of the friends of his childhood, and was anxious to go with them on their Christmas journey, and Vanda and Otto also were, naturally, eager to be of the party. Dame Katrina charged them not to go too far, but to bring their brother back early, as he needed rest after his journey.

The door was hardly closed upon them, when she resumed her seat beside her husband.

"Well, has the doctor discovered anything?" she asked, anxiously.

Instead of answering, Mr. Hersebom took the letter from his pocket, and read it aloud, but not without hesitating over some words which were strange to him:

"MY DEAR HERSEBOM," (*wrote the Doctor,*)

"it is now two years since you intrusted your dear child to my care, and every day I have had renewed pleasure in watching his progress in all the studies that he has undertaken. His intelligence is as remarkable as his heart is generous. Erik is truly one of nature's nobleman, and the parents who have lost such a son, if they knew the extent of their misfortune, would be objects of pity. But it is very doubtful whether his parents are still living. As we agreed, I have spared no efforts to discover them. I have written to several persons in England who have an agency for making special researches. I have had advertisements inserted in twenty different newspapers, English, Irish, and Scotch. Not the least ray of light has been thrown upon this mystery, and I have to confess that all the information which I have succeeded in procuring has rather tended to deepen the mystery.

"The name 'Cynthia,' I find in very common use in the English navy. From Lloyd's office, they inform me, that there are seventeen ships, of different tonnage, bearing this name. Some of these ships belong to English ports, and some to Scotland and Ireland. My supposition concerning the nationality of the child is therefore confirmed, and it becomes more and more evident to me that Erik is of Irish parentage. I do not know whether you agree with me on this point, but I have already mentioned it to two of my most intimate friends in Stockholm, and everything seems to confirm it.

"Whether this Irish family are all dead, or whether they have some interest in remaining unknown, I have not been able to discover any trace of them.

"Another singular circumstance, and which I also think looks still more suspicious, is the fact that no shipwreck registered at Lloyd's, or at any of the marine insurance companies, corresponds with the date of the infant's arrival on your coast. Two vessels named 'Cynthia' have been lost, it is true, during this century; but one was in the Indian Ocean, thirty-two years ago, and the other was in sight of Portsmouth eighteen years ago.

"We are therefore obliged to conclude that the infant was not the victim of a shipwreck.

"Doubtless he was intentionally exposed to the mercy of the waves. This would explain why all my inquiries have been fruitless.

"Be this as it may, after having questioned successively all the proprietors of the vessels bearing the name of 'Cynthia,' without obtaining any information, and after exhausting all known means of pursuing my investigations, I have been compelled to conclude that there is no hope of discovering Erik's family.

"The question that arises for us to decide, my dear Hersebom, and particularly for you, is what we ought to say to the boy, and what we ought to do for him.

"If I were in your place, I should now tell him all the facts about himself which affect him so nearly, and leave him free to choose his own path in life. You know we agreed to adopt this course if my efforts should prove unsuccessful. The time has come for you to keep your word. I have wished to leave it to you to relate all this to Erik. He is returning to Noroe still ignorant that he is not your son, and he does not know whether he is to return to Stockholm or remain with you. It is for you to tell him.

"Remember, if you refuse to fulfill this duty, Erik would have the right some day, perhaps, to be astonished at you. Recall to mind also that he is a boy of too remarkable abilities to be condemned to an obscure and illiterate life. Such a sentence would have been unmerited two years ago, and now, after his brilliant career at Stockholm, it would be positively unjustifiable.

"I therefore renew my offer: let him return to me and finish his studies, and take at Upsal the degree of Doctor of Medicine. I will continue to provide for him as if he were my own son, and he has only to go on and win honors and a fortune.

"I know that, in addressing you and the excellent adopted mother of Erik, I leave his future in good hands. No personal consideration, I am sure, will prevent you from accepting my offer. Take Mr. Malarius' advice in this matter.

"While awaiting your reply, Mr. Hersebom, I greet you affectionately, and I beg you to remember me most kindly to your worthy wife and children.

"R.W. SCHWARYENCRONA, M.D."

47

JULES VERNE & ANDRE LAURIE

When the fisherman had finished reading this letter, Dame Katrina, who had been silently weeping while she listened to it, asked him what he intended to do.

"My duty is very clear," he said. "I shall tell the boy everything."

"That is my opinion also; it must be done, or we should never have another peaceful moment," she murmured, as she dried her eyes.

Then they both relapsed into silence.

It was past midnight when the three children returned from their expedition. Their cheeks were rosy, and their eyes shone with pleasure from their walk in the fresh air. They seated themselves around the fire to finish gayly their Christmas-eve by eating a last cake before the enormous log which looked like a burning cavern.

6

Erik's Decision

The next day the fisherman called Erik to him, and in the presence of Katrina, Otto, and Vanda, spoke to him as follows:

"Erik, the letter of Doctor Schwaryencrona was about you. He writes that you have given entire satisfaction to your teachers, and the doctor offers to pay all the expenses of your education, if you wish to continue your studies. But this letter also requires you to decide for yourself, whether you will accept this offer, or remain with us at Noroe, which we would like so much to have you do, as you no doubt know. But before you make up your mind, I must tell you a great secret, a secret that my wife and I would have preferred to keep to ourselves."

At this moment Dame Katrina could not restrain her tears, and, sobbing, she took the hand of Erik and pressed it to her heart, as if protesting against the information which the young man was now to hear.

"This secret," continued Mr. Hersebom, in a strangely altered voice, "is that you are our son only by adoption. I found you on the sea, my child, and brought you home when you were only eight or nine months old. God is my witness that we never intended to tell you this, and neither my wife nor myself have ever made the least difference between you, and Otto, and Vanda. But Doctor Schwaryencrona requires us to do so. Therefore, I wish you to read what he has written to me."

Erik had suddenly become deadly pale. Otto and Vanda, surprised at what they had heard, both uttered a cry of astonishment. Then they put their arms around Erik, and clung closely to him, one on the right, and the other on the left.

Then Erik took the doctor's letter, and without trying to conceal his emotion, he read what he had written to Mr. Hersebom.

The fisherman then told him all the facts about himself. He explained how Dr. Schwaryencrona had undertaken to try and discover the family to which he belonged; and, also, that he had been unsuccessful. How, that but for his advice and suggestions, they would never have thought of doing so. Then Dame Katrina arose, and going to the oaken chest, brought out the garments that the baby had worn, and showed him also the coral which had been fastened around his neck. The story was naturally so full of dramatic interest to the children, that they forgot for a time, at least, how sad it was. They looked with wonder at the lace, and velvet, the golden setting of the coral, and the inscription. It almost seemed to them as if they were taking part in some fairy tale. The impossibility of obtaining any information, as reported by the doctor, only made them regard these articles as almost sacred.

Erik looked at them as if he were in a dream, and his thoughts flew to the unknown mother, who, without doubt, had herself dressed him in these little garments, and more than once shook the coral before the eyes of the baby to make him smile. It seemed to him when he touched them as if he held direct communion with her through time and space.

But where was this mother? Was she still living, or had she perished? Was she weeping for her lost son, or must the son, on the contrary, think of her as forever lost to him?

He remained for some minutes absorbed in these reflections, with his head bent, but a word from Dame Katrina recalled him to himself.

"Erik, you are always our child," she cried, disturbed by his silence.

The eyes of the young man as he looked around him fell on all their loving countenances—the maternal look of the loving wife, the honest face of Mr. Hersebom, that of Otto even more affectionate than usual, and that of Vanda, serious and troubled. As he read the tenderness and disquietude displayed on all their faces, Erik felt as if his heart was melting within him. In a moment he realized his situation, and saw vividly the scene which his father had described. The cradle abandoned to the mercy of the waves, rescued by the hardy fisherman, and carried to his wife; and these people, humble and poor as they were, had not hesitated to take care of the little stranger, to adopt and cherish him as their own son. They had not spoken of the matter for fourteen years, and now they were hanging on his words as if they were a matter of life and death to them.

All this touched him so deeply that suddenly his tears came. An irresistible feeling of love and gratitude overwhelmed him. He felt eager on his part to repay by some devotion the tenderness which they had shown to him. He resolved to stay with them at Noroe forever, and content himself with their humble lot, while he endeavored to do everything in his power to repay them.

"Mother," said he, throwing himself into Katrina's arms, "do you think that I can hesitate, now that I know all? We will write to the doctor, and thank him for his kind offer, and tell him that I have chosen to remain with you. I will be a fisherman, like you, father, and like Otto. Since you have given me a place at your fireside, I would prefer to retain it. Since you have nourished me by the labor of your hands, I ask to be allowed to repay you in your old age for your generosity toward me when I was a helpless infant."

"God be praised!" cried Dame Katrina, pressing Erik to her heart in a transport of joy and tenderness.

"I knew that the child would prefer the sea to all their books," said Mr. Hersebom, not understanding the sacrifice that Erik's decision would be to him.

"Come, the matter is settled. We will not talk about it any more, but only try to enjoy this good festival of Christmas!"

They all embraced each other, with eyes humid with happiness, and vowed they would never be separated.

When Erik was alone he could not help a stifled sigh, as he thought about all his former dreams of work, and of the career which he had renounced. But still he experienced at the same time a joy which he believed would repay him for the sacrifice.

"Since it is the wish of my adopted parents," he said to himself, "the rest does not signify. I ought to be willing to work for them in the sphere and condition where their devotion has placed me. If I have sometimes felt ambitious to take a higher position in the world, was it not that I might be able to assist them? Since it makes them happy to have me with them, and as they desire nothing better than their present life, I must try to be contented, and endeavor by good conduct and hard work to give them satisfaction. Adieu, then, to my books."

Thus he mused, and soon his thoughts returned to the time when the fisherman had found him floating in his little cradle on the waves. What country did he belong to? Who were his parents? Were they still alive? Had he in some foreign country brothers and sisters whom he would never know?

Christmas had also been in Dr. Schwaryencrona's house in Stockholm a season of great festivity. It was at this time, as the reader doubtless remembers, that they had agreed to decide the bet between him and Mr. Bredejord, and that Professor Hochstedt was to be the umpire.

For two years not a word had been said by either of them about this bet. The doctor had been patiently pursuing his researches in England, writing to the maritime agencies, and multiplying his advertisements in the newspapers; but he had taken care not to confess that his efforts had been fruitless.

As for Mr. Bredejord, he had had the good taste to avoid all allusion to the subject, and contented himself with occasionally admiring the beautiful binding of the Pliny which was displayed in the doctor's book-case.

But when he struck his snuff-box sharply with the ends of his fingers, while he looked at the book, the doctor correctly interpreted the pantomime, which was a shock to his nerves, and said to himself:

"Oh, yes; he is thinking how well the Pliny will look beside his elegant editions of Quintilian and Horace."

On these evenings he was more merciless than ever, if his unfortunate partner made any mistakes at whist.

But time had taken its flight, and he was now obliged to submit the question to the impartial arbitration of Professor Hochstedt.

Dr. Schwaryencrona approached the subject frankly. Kajsa had hardly left him alone with his two friends when he confessed to them, as he had confessed in his letter to Mr. Hersebom, that his investigations had been without result. Nothing had occurred to throw any light on the mystery which surrounded Erik's origin, and the doctor in all sincerity declared that the problem was thought by him to be insolvable.

"But," he continued, "I should be doing myself an injustice if I did not declare with equal sincerity that I do not believe that I have lost my bet. I have not discovered Erik's family, it is true, but all the information that I have been able to obtain corroborates the conclusion which I had arrived at. The 'Cynthia' was, no doubt, an English vessel, for there are at least seventeen ships bearing this name registered at Lloyd's. As for ethnographical characteristics, they are clearly Celtic. My hypothesis, therefore, as to the nationality of Erik is victoriously confirmed. I am more than ever certain that he is of Irish extraction as I at first surmised. But I can not compel his family to come forward and acknowledge him, if they have any reasons of their own for wishing him to continue lost to them. This is all I have to say, my dear Hochstedt; and now you must be the judge as to whether the Quintilian of our friend Bredejord should not legitimately be transferred to my book-case!"

At these words, which seemed to occasion a strong inclination to laugh, the lawyer fell back in his arm-chair, raised his hands as if in protestation, then he fixed his brilliant eyes upon Professor Hochstedt to see how he would regard the matter. The professor did not betray the embarrassment which might have been expected. He would have certainly felt miserable if the doctor had urged any incontrovertible argument, which would have compelled him to decide in favor of one or the other. His prudent character led him to speak in indefinite terms. He excelled in presenting, one after the other, both sides of a question, and he reveled in his vagaries, like a fish in water. Therefore, this evening he felt quite equal to the situation.

"The fact is incontestable," he said, shaking his head, "that there are seventeen English vessels bearing the name of 'Cynthia,' and this seems to favor the conclusion arrived at by our eminent friend. The characteristic traits also have assuredly great weight, and I do not hesitate to say that they appear to me to be quite conclusive. I do not hesitate to confess that if I were called upon to give an opinion as to Erik's nationality, I should say that he was Irish. But to decide the bet in question we require something more than probabilities; we must have facts to guide us. The chances so far greatly favor the opinion of Dr. Schwaryencrona, but Bredejord can allege that nothing has actually been proved. I see, therefore, no sufficient reason for declaring that the Quintilian has been won by the doctor; neither can I say that the professor has lost his Pliny. In my opinion, as the question remains undecided, it ought to be annulled, which is the best thing to do in such a case."

The doctor's face clearly betrayed his dissatisfaction. As for Mr. Bredejord he leaped to his feet, saying:

"Your argument is a beautiful one, my dear Hochstedt, but I think you are hasty in your conclusions. Schwaryencrona, you say, has not verified his opinions sufficiently for you to say positively that he has won the bet, although you think that all the probabilities are in his favor. What will you say then, if I prove to you immediately that the 'Cynthia' was not an English vessel at all?"

"What would I say?" said the professor, somewhat troubled by this sudden attack. "Upon my word I do not know. I would have to consider the question in a different aspect."

"Examine it then at your leisure," answered the advocate, thrusting his hand into the inner pocket of his coat, and taking out a case from which he selected a letter inclosed in one of those yellow envelopes, which betray at the first glance their American origin.

"This is a document which you can not controvert," he added, placing the letter before the doctor's eyes, who read aloud:

"*To*

MR. BREDEJORD, STOCKHOLM.
"*New York, October 27th.*

"SIR,

In reply to your letter of the 5th instant, I hasten to write you the following facts:—

"1st.— A vessel named 'Cynthia,' commanded by Captain Barton, and the property of the Canadian General Transportation Company, was lost, with her cargo and all on board, just fourteen years ago, in the neighborhood of the Faroe Islands.

"2d.— This vessel was insured in the General Steam Navigation Company of New York for the sum of eight hundred thousand dollars.

"3d.— The disappearance of the 'Cynthia' having remained unexplained, and the causes of the sad accident never having been clearly proved to the satisfaction of the insurance company, a lawsuit ensued, which was lost by the proprietors of the said vessel.

"4th.— The loss of this lawsuit occasioned the dissolution of the Canadian General Transportation Company, which has ceased to exist for the last eleven years, having gone into liquidation. While waiting to hear from you again, I beg of you, sir, to accept our sincere salutations.

"JEREMIAH SMITH, WALKER & CO.,
"MARITIME AGENTS."

"Well, what do you say to that?" asked Mr. Bredejord, when the doctor had finished reading the letter. "It is a document of some value, I think. Do you agree with me?"

"I quite agree with you," answered the doctor. "How did you procure it?"

"In the simplest way in the world. That evening when you spoke to me about the 'Cynthia' being necessarily an English vessel, I thought that you were taking too limited a field for your researches, and that the vessel might be an American one. When time passed, and you received no intelligence, for you would have told us if you had, the idea occurred to me of writing to New York. The third letter brought the result which you have before you. The affair is no longer a complicated one. Do you not think that it assures to me beyond contest the possession of your Pliny?"

"It appears to me to be rather a forced conclusion," replied the doctor, taking the letter and reading it over again, to see if he could find any new arguments to support his theory.

"How forced?" cried the advocate.

"I have proved to you that the vessel was an American one, and that she was lost off the Faroe Islands, that is to say, near the coast of Norway, precisely at the time which corresponds to the arrival of the infant, and still you are not convinced of your error."

"Not in the least, my dear friend. I do not dispute the value or your document. You have discovered what I have found it impossible to do— the true 'Cynthia,' which was lost at a little distance from our coast, and at a specified epoch; but permit me to say, that this only confirms precisely my theory, for the vessel was a Canadian one, or in other words, English, and the Irish element is very strong in some parts of Canada, and I have therefore more reason than ever for being sure that the child is of Irish origin."

"Ah, is that what you find in my letter?" said Mr. Bredejord, more vexed than he was willing to appear to be. "Then without doubt you persist in believing that you have not lost your Pliny?"

"Assuredly!"

"Perhaps you think you have a right to my Quintilian?"

"I hope in any case to be able to prove my right, thanks to your discovery, if you will only give me time by renewing the bet."

"I am willing. I ask nothing better. How much time do you want?"

"Let us take two more years, and wait until the second Christmas after this one."

"It is agreed," answered Mr. Bredejord. "But be assured, doctor, that you will finally see me in possession of your Pliny!"

"By my faith no. It will make a fine appearance in my book-case beside your Quintilian."

7

Vanda's Opinion

In the beginning, Erik burning with zeal at the sacrifice which he had made, devoted all his energies to a fisherman's life, and tried to forget that he had ever known any other. He was always the first to rise and prepare the boat for his adopted father, who found every morning all the arrangements completed, and he had only to step on board. If the wind failed, then Erik took the heavy oars, and rowed with all his strength, seeming to choose the hardest and most fatiguing duties. Nothing discouraged him, neither the long waiting for the fish to seize the bait, nor the various preparations to which the captive was subjected—first, the removal of the tongue, which is a most delicate morsel; then the head, then the bones, before placing them in the reservoir, where they receive their first salting. Whatever their work was, Erik did his part not only conscientiously, but eagerly. He astonished the placid Otto by his extreme application to the smallest details of their business.

"How you must have suffered, when you were shut up in the town," said the lad to him, naively. "You only seem to be in your element when you are on the borders of the fiord or on the open sea."

When their conversation took this turn, Erik always remained silent. Sometimes, however, he would revert to the subject himself, and try to prove to Otto, or rather to himself, that there was no better state of existence than their own.

"It is what I have always heard," the other would answer with his calm smile.

And poor Erik would turn away and stifle a sigh.

The truth is that he suffered cruelly after renouncing his studies and seeing himself condemned to a life of manual labor. When these thoughts came to him he fought against them with all his might. He did

56

not wish any one to suspect that he felt in this way, and in hiding them within his own breast he suffered all the more.

A catastrophe which occurred at the beginning of the spring, only served to increase his discouragement.

One day, as there was a great deal of work to do at home in piling together the salted fish, Mr. Hersebom had intrusted it to Erik and to Otto, and had gone out to fish alone. The weather was stormy, and the sky very cloudy for the time of the year. The two young men, although they worked actively, could not help noticing that it was exceptionally dull, and they felt the atmosphere very heavy.

"It is singular!" said Erik, "but I feel a roaring in my ears as if I were some distance above the earth in a balloon."

Almost immediately his nose began to bleed. Otto had a similar sensation, although not quite so severe.

"I think the barometer must be very low," said Erik. "If I had time I would run to Mr. Malarius' and see."

"You have plenty of time," said Otto. "Our work is nearly done, and even if you were delayed I could easily finish it alone."

"Then I will go," replied Erik. "I do not know why the state of the atmosphere should trouble me so much. I wish father was home."

As he walked toward the school, he met Mr. Malarius on the road.

"Is it you, Erik?" said the teacher. "I am glad to see you, and make sure that you are not on the sea. I was just going to inquire. The barometer has fallen with such rapidity during the last half hour. I have never seen anything like it. We are surely going to have a change of weather."

Mr. Malarius had hardly finished speaking, when a distant grumbling, followed by a lugubrious roaring, fell upon their ears. The sky became covered with a cloud as black as ink, which spread rapidly in all directions, and obscured every object with great swiftness. Then suddenly, after an interval of complete silence, the leaves of the trees, the bits of straw, the sand, and even the stones, were swept away by a sudden gust of wind.

The hurricane had begun.

It raged with unheard-of violence. The chimneys, the window shutters, and in some places even the roofs of the houses were blown down; and the boat-houses without exception were carried away and destroyed by the wind. In the fiord, which was usually as calm as a well in a courtyard, the most terrible tempest raged; the waves were enormous and came and went, breaking against the shore with a deafening noise.

The cyclone raged for an hour, then arrested in its course by the heights of Norway, it moved toward the south, and swept over continental Europe. It is noted in meteorological annals as one of the most extraordinary and disastrous that ever was known upon the Atlantic coast. These great changes of the atmosphere are now generally announced beforehand by the telegraph. Most of the European sea-ports forewarned of the danger have time to warn vessels and seamen of the threatened tempest, and they seek a safe anchorage. By this means many disasters are averted.

But on the distant and less frequented coasts, in the fishing-hamlets, the number of shipwrecks was beyond computation.

In one office, that of "Veritas" in France, there were registered not less than 730.

The first thought of all the members of the Hersebom family, as well as of all the other families of fishermen, was naturally for those who were on the sea on this disastrous day. Mr. Hersebom went most often to the western coast of a large island which was about two miles distant, beyond the entrance to the fiord. It was the spot where he had first seen Erik. They hoped that during the tempest he had been able to find shelter by running his boat upon the low and sandy shore. But Erik and Otto felt so anxious that they could not wait until evening to see if this hope was well founded.

The fiord had hardly resumed its ordinary placidity, after the passage of the hurricane, when they borrowed a boat of one of their neighbors, in order to go in search of him. Mr. Malarius insisted upon accompanying the young men upon their expedition, and they all three set out, anxiously watched by Katrina and her daughter.

On the fiord the wind had nearly gone down, but it blew from the west, and to reach the entrance to the harbor they were obliged to use their oars. This took them more than an hour.

When they reached the entrance an unexpected obstacle presented itself. The tempest was still raging on the ocean, and the waves dashed against the island which, formed the entrance to the fiord of Noroe, forming two currents, which came and went with such violence in the narrow pass that it was impossible to gain the open sea. A steamboat could not have ventured through it, and a weak boat could not have resisted it for a moment.

The only thing they could do, therefore, was to return to Noroe, and wait as patiently as they could.

The hour when he habitually came home passed without bringing Mr. Hersebom, but none of the other fishermen returned; so they hoped that they were all detained by the impassable state of the entrance to the fiord, and would not believe that he had personally met with any disaster. That evening was a very sad one at all the firesides where a member was missing. As the night passed without any of the absent men making their appearance, the anxieties of their families increased. In Mr. Hersebom's house nobody went to bed. They passed the long hours of waiting seated in a circle around the fire, silent and anxious.

Dawn is late in these high latitudes in March, but when at last it grew light it was bright and clear. The wind was calm, and they hoped they would be able to get through the pass. A regular fleet of boats, composed of every one who could get away from Noroe, was ready to go in search of the absent men. Just at this moment several vessels hove in sight, and soon reached the village. They were the fishermen who had gone out the day before, not expecting such a cyclone; but Mr. Hersebom was not among them.

Nobody could give any account of him, and the fact of his not returning with the others increased their anxiety as all the men had been in great peril. Some had been surprised by the cyclone and dashed upon the shore, others had time to shelter themselves in a secure place of anchorage. A few had reached the land just in time to save themselves.

It was decided that the flotilla should go in search of those who were missing. Mr. Malarius who still wished to take part in the expedition accompanied Erik and Otto. A large yellow dog begged so earnestly to go with them, that at length they yielded. It was Kaas, the Greenland dog that Mr. Hersebom had brought back with him, after a voyage to Cape Farewell.

After issuing from the pass the boats separated, some going to the right, and others to the left, to explore the shores of the innumerable islands which lie scattered near the entrance to the fiord of Noroe, as well as all along the coast of Norway.

When they met at midday at a given point, which had been agreed upon before separating, no trace of Mr. Hersebom had been discovered. As the search had apparently been well conducted, everyone was of the opinion that they had nothing more to do but to go home.

But Erik was not willing to own himself defeated, and give up all hope so easily. He declared that having visited all the islands which lay toward the south, he now wished to explore those which were in the north. Mr. Malarius and Otto supported him; and seeing this they granted his desire.

This persistence deserved some recompense. Toward two o'clock as they approached a large island, Kaas began suddenly to bark furiously; then before they could prevent him he threw himself into the water, and swam to the shore.

Erik and Otto rowed with all their strength in the same direction. Soon they saw the dog reach the island, and bound, while he uttered loud howls, toward what appeared to be a human form lying extended upon the sand. They made all possible haste, and soon saw beyond a doubt that it was a man who was lying there, and this man was Mr. Hersebom; bloody, pale, cold, inanimate—dead, perhaps. Kaas was licking his hands, and uttering mournful cries.

Erik's first action was to drop on his knees beside the cold body, and apply his ear to his heart.

"He is alive, I feel it beat," he cried.

Mr. Malarias had taken one of Mr. Hersebom's hand's, and was feeling his pulse and he shook his head, sadly and doubtfully; but he would not neglect any of the means which are usually tried in such cases. After taking off a large woolen girdle which he wore around his waist, he tore it in three pieces, and giving one to each of the young men, they rubbed vigorously the body, the arms, and the legs of the fisherman.

It was soon manifest that this simple treatment had produced the effect of restoring the circulation. The beating of the heart grew stronger, the chest rose, and a feeble respiration escaped through the lips. In a little while Mr. Hersebom was partially restored to consciousness, for he distinctly moaned.

Mr. Malarias, and the two young men lifted him from the ground, and carried him to the boat, where they hastily arranged a bed for him of sails. As they laid him in the bottom of the boat he opened his eyes.

"A drink!" he said in a weak voice.

Erik held a flask of brandy to his lips. He swallowed a mouthful and appeared to be conscious of their arrival, for he tried to give them an affectionate and grateful smile. But fatigue overcame him almost immediately, and he fell into a heavy sleep which resembled a complete lethargy. Thinking justly that the best thing they could do was to get him home as speedily as possible, they took their oars and rowed vigorously; and in a very short time they reached Noroe.

Mr. Hersebom was carried to his bed, and his wounds were dressed with arnica. He was fed with broth, and given a glass of beer, and in a short time he recovered consciousness. His injuries were not of a very grave nature. One of his arms was fractured, and his body was covered with wound and bruises. But Mr. Malarius insisted that he should remain quiet and rest, and not fatigue himself by attempting to talk. He was soon sleeping peacefully.

It was not until the next day that they permitted him to speak and explain in a few words what had happened to him.

He had been overtaken by the cyclone just as he had hoisted his sail to return to Noroe. He had been dashed against the rocks of the island and his boat had been broken into a thousand pieces and carried away by the waves. He had thrown himself into the sea to escape the frightful shock, when she struck, but in spite of all his efforts, he had been dashed by the waves upon the rocks and terribly wounded; he had only been able to drag himself beyond the reach of the waves.

Exhausted by fatigue, one arm broken, and his whole body covered with wounds, he had lain in an unconscious state, unable to move. He could give no account of the manner in which he had passed the twenty hours; doubtless he had either been delirious or unconscious.

Now that he was saved, he began to lament for the loss of his boat, and because of his broken arm, which was now in splints. What would become of him, even admitting that he might be able to use his arm again after eight or ten weeks? The boat was the only capital possessed by the family, and the boat had been broken to pieces by the wind.

It would be very hard for a man of his age to be compelled to work for others. Besides, could he find work? It was very doubtful, for nobody in Noroe employed any assistant, and the factory even had lately reduced its hands.

Such were the bitter reflections of Mr. Hersebom, while he lay upon his bed of pain; and he felt still worse when he was able to get up, and occupy his accustomed seat in his arm-chair.

While waiting for his complete recovery, the family lived upon such provisions as they had in the house, and by the sale of the salt cod-fish which still remained. But the future looked very dark, and nobody could see how it was to be lightened.

This imminent distress had given a new turn to Erik's thoughts. For two or three days he reflected that it was by his good fortune that Mr. Hersebom had been discovered. How could he help feeling proud, when he saw Dame Katrina and Vanda look at him with intense gratitude, as they said: "Dear Erik, our father saved you from the waves, and now, in your turn, you have snatched him from death."

Certainly it was the highest recompense that he could desire for the self-abnegation of which he had given such a noble proof, in condemning himself to a fisherman's life. To feel that he had been able to render his adopted family such an inestimable benefit was to him a thought full of sweetness and strength. This family, who had so generously shared with him all that they possessed, were now in trouble, and in want of food. But, could he remain to be a burden to them? Was it not rather his duty to try and do something to assist them?

Erik did not doubt his obligation to do this. He only hesitated as to the best way for him to do it. Should he go to Bergen and become a sailor? or was there some better occupation open to him, where he could be immediately useful to them. He resolved to consult Mr. Malarius, who listened to his reasons, and approved of them, but did not think well of his project of becoming a sailor.

"I understood, but I deplored your decision when you were resigned to remain here and share the life of your adopted parents; but I can not understand why you should condemn yourself to the life of a sailor, which would take you far away from them, when Doctor Schwaryencrona offers you every advantage to pursue a more congenial career," said Mr. Malarius. "Reflect, my dear child, before you make such a decision."

Mr. Malarius did not tell him that he had already written to Stockholm to inform the doctor of the sad state of their affairs, and the change which the cyclone of the 3d of March had made in the circumstances of Erik's family. He was not surprised, when three days after his conversation with Erik, he received the following letter, which he lost no time in carrying to the house of Mr. Hersebom.

The letter read as follows:

"STOCKHOLM, *March 17th.*

"MY DEAR MR. MALARIUS,

I thank you cordially for informing me of the disastrous consequences of the cyclone of the 3d of March to the worthy Mr. Hersebom. I am proud and happy to learn that Erik acted in these circumstances, as always before, like a brave boy and a devoted son. You will find a check in this letter for 500 kroners; and I beg you to give them to him from me. Tell him if it is not enough to buy at Bergen a first-class boat, he must let me know without delay. He must name this boat 'Cynthia,' and then present it to Mr. Hersebom as a souvenir of filial love. That done, if Erik wishes to please me he will return to Stockholm and resume his studies. His place is always ready for him at my fireside, and if he needs a motive to assist in this decision, I add that I have at length obtained some information, and hope yet to be able to solve the mystery enshrouding his birth.

"Believe me, my dear Malarius, your sincere and devoted friend,

"R.W. SCHWARYENCRONA, M.D."

You may imagine with what joy this letter was received. The doctor, by sending this gift to Erik, showed that he understood the character of the old fisherman. If he had offered it directly to him, it is hardly probable that Mr. Hersebom would have accepted it. But he could not refuse the boat from Erik's hand, and bearing the name of "Cynthia," which recalled how Erik had become a member of the family. Their only grief now, which already began to sadden all their countenances, was the thought that he must soon leave them again. Nobody dared to speak about it, although it was constantly in their thoughts. Erik himself, with his head bowed, was divided between the desire of satisfying the doctor, and realizing the secret wishes of his own heart, and the no less natural wish of giving no offense to his adopted parents.

It was Vanda who first broke the reserve, and spoke upon the subject.

"Erik," she said, in her sweet grave voice, "you can not say 'No' to the doctor after receiving such a letter. You can not do it, because it would be treating him most ungratefully, and sinning against yourself. Your place is among scholars, and not among fishermen. I have thought so for a long time. Nobody has dared to tell you, therefore I tell you."

"Vanda is right," said Mr. Malarius, with a smile.

"Vanda is right," repeated Dame Katrina, drying her eyes.

And in this manner, for the second time, Erik's departure was decided.

8

Patrick O'Donoghan

The information which Dr. Schwaryencrona had received was not very important, but it sufficed to start his inquiries in a new direction.

He had learned the name of the ex-director of the Canadian Transportation Company, it was Mr. Joshua Churchill. But they did not know what had become of this gentleman since the dissolution of the company. If they could succeed in finding him, he might be able to give them some information about the old records of the company; perhaps there might have been a list of the passengers by the "Cynthia," and the baby might have been registered with his family or with the persons who had charge of him. But their investigations proved very unsatisfactory. The solicitor who had formerly had the books in his possession as the receiver of the company about ten years before; did not know what had become of Mr. Churchill. For a moment Dr. Schwaryencrona consoled himself with a false hope. He remembered that the American newspapers usually published a list of the passengers embarking for Europe, and he sent for a number of old gazettes to see if he could find the "Cynthia's" list; but he was soon convinced that this was a fruitless effort. He discovered that the practice of publishing the names of passengers on European steamships was of comparatively recent date. But the old gazettes were of one use to him, they gave the exact date of sailing of the "Cynthia," which had left on the 3d of November, not from a Canadian port as they had at first supposed, but from New York, to go to Hamburg.

It was therefore in New York that the doctor must first make his investigations, and, if unsuccessful, then in other parts of the United States.

At Hamburg all his inquiries proved to be useless. The consignee of the Canadian Transportation Company knew nothing about the passengers of the "Cynthia," and could only give them information about the freight, which they had already obtained.

Erik had been in Stockholm six months when they learned that the ex-director, Mr. Joshua Churchill, had died several years before, in an hospital, without leaving any known heirs, or probably any money. As for the registers of the company, they had probably been sold long before as waste paper.

These long researches led to nothing, except to provoke the sarcasms of Mr. Bredejord, which were wounding, to the doctor's self-love, who, however, did not as yet give way to despair.

Erik's history was now well known in the doctor's household. They no longer forbore to speak openly about it, and the results of their researches were talked of both in the dining-room and the parlor.

Perhaps the doctor had acted more discreetly during the first two years of Erik's sojourn with him, when he had kept his affairs a secret. Now they furnished food for the gossiping of Kajsa and Dame Greta, and even occupied the thoughts of Erik himself; and his reflections were often very melancholy.

Not to know whether his parents were still living, to reflect that he might never be able to discover the secret of his birth, was in itself a sad thought to him; but it was still more sad to be ignorant of the land of his birth.

"The poorest child in the streets, the most miserable peasant, knew at least what his country was, and to what branch of the great human family he belonged," he would sometimes say to himself, as he thought of those things. "But I am ignorant of all this. I am cast on the globe like a waif, like a grain of dust tossed by the winds, and nobody knows where I came from. I have no tradition—no past. The spot where my mother was born, and where her ashes now rest, is perhaps profaned and trodden under foot, and I am powerless to defend and protect it."

These thoughts saddened Erik. Sometimes he would tell himself that he had a mother in Dame Katrina, and a home at Mr. Hersebom's, and that Noroe was his country. He vowed that he would repay their kindness to him fourfold, and would always be a devoted son to Norway, but still he felt himself in an exceptional position.

Sometimes when he caught a glimpse of himself in a mirror, he could observe the physical difference between himself and those surrounding him. The color of his eyes and his skin often occasioned him gloomy reflections. Sometimes he would ask himself which country he would prefer to be a native of if he had a choice, and he studied history and geography that he might become better acquainted with the civilization of different countries, and with the habits of their inhabitants. It was a sort of consolation to him to believe that he belonged to the Celtic race, and he sought in books a confirmation of the theory of the doctor.

But when the learned man repeated that in his opinion he was certainly Irish, Erik felt depressed. Why among all the Celtic race should he belong to the people who were the most oppressed? If he had felt absolutely sure of this, he would have loved this unfortunate country. But all proof being wanting, why might he not rather believe that he was French? There were certainly Celts in France, and it was a country that he would have been proud to claim as his own, with her glorious traditions, her dramatic history, and her fruitful principles, which she had disseminated all over the world. Oh! he could have passionately loved, and served with devotion, such a country. He would have felt a filial interest in studying her glorious annals, in reading the works of her great authors, and in studying her poets. But alas! all these delicate emotions were denied him, and he felt that the problem of his origin would never be solved, since after so many years spent in making inquiries they had learned nothing.

However, it seemed to Erik that if he could pursue these inquiries himself, and follow up the information already obtained, that he might discover something which might lead to some result, and his activity and zeal might succeed where money had failed. Would he not work with an ardor which must overcome all difficulties?

This idea took possession of his mind, and insensibly had a marked effect in his studies, giving them a special direction; although he was not aware of this fact himself. As he had made up his mind to travel, he commenced to study cosmography and nautical matters; in fact, everything that was taught in the school for marines.

"Some day," he said to himself, "I will pass my examination as a captain, and then I shall go to New York in my own vessel, and pursue my inquiries with regard to the 'Cynthia.'"

As a natural consequence, this project of personally investigating the matter of his birth soon became known, for he was candor itself.

Dr. Schwaryencrona, Mr. Bredejord and Professor Hochstedt ended by becoming interested, and finally adopted his views as their own. The question of Erik's birth, which had at first only been an interesting problem in their eyes, engrossed them more and more. They saw how much Erik took it to heart, and as they were sincerely attached to him, they realized how important it was to him, and they were disposed to do everything in their power to cast some light upon the mystery.

One fine evening, just as the vacation was approaching, it occurred to them that it would be a good idea to make an excursion to New York together, and see if they could, obtain any further news about the matter.

Who first conceived this idea was a disputed point among them, and gave rise to many discussions between the doctor and Mr. Bredejord, each claiming a priority. Doubtless it occurred to them both simultaneously; but be this as it may, the proposal was adopted unanimously, and in the month of September the three friends, accompanied by Erik, embarked at Christiana for New York. Ten days later they had reached that city, and opened communication with the house of Jeremiah Smith, Walker & Company, from whom they had received the first intelligence.

And now a new agent appeared on the scene, whose assistance they had had little suspicion of, and this was Erik himself. In New York he only saw what would assist him in his search. He was up at daybreak visiting the wharves, accosting the sailors, whom he might chance to meet, working with indefatigable activity to collect the most minute intelligence.

"Do you know anything about the Canadian Transportation Company? Could you tell me of any officer, or passenger, or sailor, who had sailed on the 'Cynthia'?" he asked everywhere.

Thanks to his perfect knowledge of the English language, his sweet and serious countenance, and his familiarity with everything pertaining to the sea, he was well received everywhere. They mentioned to him successively several old officers, sailors, and employs, of the Canadian Transportation Company. Sometimes he was able to find them. Sometimes all traces of them were lost. But none of them could give him any useful information about the last voyage of the "Cynthia." It took fifteen days of walking, and searching incessantly, to obtain one little bit of information which might prove valuable, among all the confused and contradictory accounts which were poured into poor Erik's willing ears.

This one little truth however seemed to be worth its weight in gold.

They assured him that a sailor named Patrick O'Donoghan, had survived the shipwreck of the "Cynthia," and had even returned to New York several times since that eventful voyage. This Patrick O'Donoghan had been on the "Cynthia," on her last voyage, and had been a special attendant of the captain. In all probability he would know the first-class passengers, who always eat at the captain's table. They judged by the fineness of the infant's clothing that he belonged to this class. It was now a matter of the greatest importance to find this sailor.

This was the conclusion of Dr. Schwaryencrona and Mr. Bredejord, when Erik informed them of his discovery, when he returned to the Fifth Avenue Hotel to dinner.

As usual it led to a discussion, since the doctor tried to draw from this discovery a confirmation of his favorite theory.

"If ever there was an Irish name," he cried, "Patrick O'Donoghan is one. Did I not always say that I was sure that Erik was of Irish birth?"

"Does this discovery prove it?" asked Mr. Bredejord laughing. "An Irish cabin-boy does not prove much. It would be difficult, I fancy, to find an American vessel without one or two natives of Erin among her crew."

They discussed the matter for two or three hours, neither of them willing to give way to the other.

From that day Erik devoted all his energies to the task of finding Patrick O'Donoghan.

He was not successful it is true, but by force of seeking, and questioning, he discovered a sailor who had known this man, and who was able to give him some information. Patrick O'Donoghan was a native of the County Cork. He was between thirty-three and thirty-four years old, of medium height, with red hair, black eyes, and a nose which had been broken by some accident.

"A boy one would remember among a thousand," said the sailor. "I recollect him very well, although I have not seen him for seven or eight years."

"Is it in New York you usually meet him?" asked Erik.

"Yes, in New York, and in other places; but the last time was in New York."

"Do you know any one who could give me any information about him, so that I could find out what has become of him?"

"No, unless it is the proprietor of the hotel called the Red Anchor, in Brooklyn. Patrick O'Donoghan lodges there when he is in New York. The name of the hotel-keeper is Mr. Bowles, and he is an old sailor. If he does not know, I do not know of any one else who can tell you anything about him."

Erik hurried on board one of the ferry-boats that cross the East River, and ten minutes later he was in Brooklyn.

At the door-way of the Red Anchor he saw an old woman, who was neatly dressed, and busily occupied in peeling potatoes.

"Is Mr. Bowles at home?" he said, saluting her politely, after the custom of his adopted country.

"He is at home, but he is taking a nap," answered the good woman, looking with curiosity at her questioner. "If you have any message for him, you can give it to me. I am Mrs. Bowles."

"Oh, madam, you can no doubt give me the information I desire as well as Mr. Bowles," answered Erik. "I wish to know whether you are acquainted with a sailor named Patrick O'Donoghan, and whether he is now with you, or if you can tell me where I can find him?"

"Patrick O'Donoghan: yes, I know him, but it is five or six years since he has been here, and I am unable to say where he is now."

Erik's countenance displayed such great disappointment that the old woman was touched.

"Are you so anxious to find Patrick O'Donoghan that you are disappointed in not finding him here?" she asked.

"Yes, indeed," he answered. "He alone can solve a mystery that I shall seek all my life to make clear."

During the three weeks that Erik had been running everywhere in search of information, he gained a certain amount of experience in human nature. He saw that the curiosity of Mrs. Bowles was aroused by his questions, he therefore entered the hotel and asked for a glass of soda-water.

The low room in which he found himself was furnished with green tables, and wooden chairs, but it was empty. This circumstance emboldened Erik to enter into conversation with Mrs. Bowles, when she handed him the bottle of soda-water which he had ordered.

"You are doubtless wondering, madam, what I can want with Patrick O'Donoghan, and I will tell you," said he, with a smile.

"An American vessel called the 'Cynthia' was lost about seventeen years ago on the coast of Norway; Patrick O'Donoghan was employed on board. I was picked up by a Norwegian fisherman when I was about nine months old. I was floating in a cradle attached to a buoy of the 'Cynthia.' I am seeking O'Donoghan to see if he can give me any information about my family, or at least about my country."

Mrs. Bowles uttered a cry that put a stop to Erik's explanation.

"To a buoy, do you say? You were tied to a buoy?"

But without waiting for any reply she ran to the stairway. "Bowles! Bowles! come down quickly," she cried, in a piercing voice.

"On a buoy! you are the child who was tied to the buoy! Who ever would have expected such a thing to happen?" she said, as she returned to Erik, who had turned pale from surprise.

Was he going to learn the secret which he was so anxious to make out.

A heavy footstep was heard on the stairs, and soon an old man, fat and rosy, clothed in a complete suit of blue cloth, and with gold rings in his ears, appeared on the threshold.

"What is the matter?" he asked, rubbing his eyes.

"Here is somebody who wants you," said Mrs. Bowles; "sit down and listen to the gentleman, who will repeat what he has told me."

Mr. Bowles obeyed without any protestation; Erik did the same. He repeated in as few words as he could what he had told the old woman.

As he listened, the countenance of Mr. Bowles dilated like a full moon, his lips parted in a broad smile, and he looked at his wife, and rubbed his hands. She on her side appeared equally well pleased.

"Must I suppose that you are already acquainted with my story?" asked Erik, with a beating heart.

Mr. Bowles made an affirmative sign, and scratching his ear, made up his mind to speak:

"I know it without your telling me," he said, at length, "and my wife knows it as well as I do. We have often talked about it without understanding it."

Erik, pale and with tightly compressed lips, hung upon his words, expecting some revelation, but this he had to wait for. Mr. Bowles had not the gift of either eloquence or clearness, and perhaps his ideas were still clouded with sleep, and in order to recover his faculties he took two or three glasses of a liquor called "pick me up," which greatly resembled gin.

After his wife had placed the bottle and two glasses before him, and he had sufficiently fortified himself, he began to speak.

His story was so confused, and mingled with so many useless details, that it was impossible to draw any conclusions from it, but Erik listened attentively to all he said, and by questioning and insisting, and aided by Mrs. Bowles, he ended by gathering some facts about himself.

9

In Which a Reward of Five Hundred Pounds Sterling is Offered.

Patrick O'Donoghan, as far as Erik could make out through Mr. Bowles' rambling account of him, was not a model of virtue. The proprietor of the Red Anchor had known him as a cabin-boy and sailor, both before and after the loss of the "Cynthia." Up to that time Patrick O'Donoghan had been poor, as all sailors are. After the shipwreck he had returned from Europe with a large bundle of bank-notes, pretending to have inherited some money in Ireland, which seemed likely enough.

Mr. Bowles, however, had never believed in this inheritance. He thought that this sudden accession of wealth was connected in some way with the loss of the "Cynthia," and that Patrick O'Donoghan was afraid to say so; for it was evident that contrary to the usual habit of seamen in such cases, he carefully avoided speaking about the sad occurrence. He would always turn the conversation if any one alluded to it before him, and he was very anxious to start on a long voyage before the lawsuit brought by the company to recover the insurance due on the "Cynthia" should take place. He did not wish to be summoned as a witness. This conduct appeared very suspicious, as he was the sole known survivor from the shipwreck. Mr. Bowles and his wife had always suspected him, but they had kept their own counsel.

What looked still more suspicious was the fact that when Patrick O'Donoghan was in New York he was never short of money. He brought back very little with him after a voyage, but a few days after his return he always had gold and bank-notes; and when he was tipsy, which frequently happened, he would boast of being in possession of a secret which was worth a fortune to him. The words which most frequently escaped from his lips were, "the baby tied to the buoy!"

"The baby tied to the buoy," he would say, striking the table with his fist, "The baby tied to the buoy is worth its weight in gold."

Then he would laugh, as if well satisfied with himself. But they could never draw out of him any explanation of these words, and for many years the Bowles household were lost in conjectures as to what they could possibly mean.

This accounted for Mrs. Bowles' excitement, when Erik suddenly announced to her that he was the famous baby who had been tied to a buoy.

Patrick O'Donoghan, who had been in the habit of lodging at the Red Anchor, whenever he was in New York, for more than fifteen years, had not been seen there now for more than four years. There had also been something mysterious about his last departure. He had received a visit from a man who had been closeted with him for more than an hour. After this visit Patrick O'Donoghan, who had seemed worried and troubled, had paid his board bill, taken his carpet bag, and left in a hurry.

They had never seen him since that day.

Mr. and Mrs. Bowles were naturally ignorant of the cause of his sudden departure, but they had always thought that it had some connection with the loss of the "Cynthia." In their opinion the visitor had come to warn Patrick O'Donoghan of some danger which threatened him, and the Irishman had thought it prudent to leave New York immediately. Mrs. Bowles did not think he had ever returned. If he had done so, they would have been sure to hear of him through other seamen who frequented their house, and who would have been astonished if Patrick O'Donoghan had boarded anywhere else, and would have been sure to ask questions as to the reasons for his doing so.

This was the substance of the story related to Erik, and he hastened to communicate it to his friends.

His report was naturally received with all the interest which it merited. For the first time, after so many years, they were on the track of a man who had made reiterated allusions to the baby tied to a buoy. It was true they did not know where this man was, but they hoped to find him some day. It was the most important piece of news which they had as yet obtained. They resolved to telegraph to Mrs. Bowles, and beg her to prepare a dinner for six persons. Mr. Bredejord had suggested this idea, as a good means of drawing the worthy couple out; for while they talked during the dinner, they might be able to glean some new facts.

Erik had little hopes of obtaining any further information. He thought that he already knew Mr. and Mrs. Bowles well enough to be convinced that they had told him all that they knew. But he did not take into account Mr. Bredejord's skill in questioning witnesses, and in drawing from them information which they themselves were scarcely aware of.

Mrs. Bowles had surpassed herself in preparing the dinner. She had laid the table in the best room on the first floor. She felt very much flattered at being invited to partake of it, in the society of such distinguished guests, and answered willingly all of Mr. Bredejord's questions.

They gathered from this conversation a certain number of facts which were not unimportant.

One was that Patrick O'Donoghan had said at the time, of the lawsuit against the insurance company, that he was going away to avoid being summoned as a witness. This was evident proof that he did not wish to explain the circumstances under which the shipwreck had occurred, and his subsequent conduct confirmed this theory. It was also evident that in New York or its environs he received the suspicious revenue which seemed to be connected with his secret. For when he arrived he was always without money, but after he had been about for a short time he always returned with his pockets full of gold. They could not doubt that his secret was connected with the infant tied to the buoy, for he had frequently affirmed that such was the case.

The evening before his sudden departure Patrick O'Donoghan had said that he was tired of a sea-faring life, and that he thought he should give up making voyages, and settle in New York for the remainder of his life.

Lastly, the individual who had called to see Patrick O'Donoghan was interested in his departure, for he had called the next day and asked for the Irishman who was boarding at the Red Anchor, and had seemed pleased to hear that he was no longer there. Mr. Bowles felt sure that he would recognize this man if he saw him again. By his conversation and actions he had believed him to be a detective, or some agent of the police.

Mr. Bredejord concluded from these facts that Patrick O'Donoghan had been systematically frightened by the person from whom he drew the money, and that this man had been sent to make him fear that criminal proceedings were about to be taken against him. This would explain his precipitate flight, and why he had never returned to New York.

It was important to find this detective, as well as Patrick O'Donoghan.

Mr. and Mrs. Bowles, by referring to their books, were able to give the exact date of the Irishman's departure, which was four years, lacking three months; although they had previously believed that it was four or five years ago.

Dr. Schwaryencrona was immediately struck by the fact that the date of his departure, and consequently of the visit of the detective, corresponded precisely with the date of the first advertisements which he had caused to be made in Great Britain for the survivors of the "Cynthia." This coincidence was so striking that it was impossible not to believe that there was some connection between them.

They began to understand the mystery a little better. The abandonment of Erik on the buoy had been the result of some crime—a crime of which the cabin-boy O'Donoghan had been a witness or an accomplice. He knew the authors of this crime, who lived in New York or its environs, and he had for a long time enjoyed the reward of his secrecy. Then a day had come when the excessive demands of the Irishman had become burdensome, and the announcement in the newspapers by advertisement had been made use of to frighten Patrick, and cause his hurried departure.

In any case, even if these deductions were not correct in every point, they had obtained sufficient information to entitle them to demand a judicial investigation.

Erik and his friends therefore left the Red Anchor full of hope that they would soon obtain some favorable intelligence.

The next day Mr. Bredejord was introduced by the Swedish consul to the chief of police of New York, and he made him acquainted with the facts which had become known to him. At the same time he entered into conversation with the officers of the insurance company who had refused to pay the claims due on the "Cynthia," and read the old documents relative to this matter, which had lain undisturbed so many years. But the examination of these papers did not afford him any important intelligence. The matter had been decided upon technical points, relating to an excess of insurance far above the value of the vessel and cargo. Neither side had been able to produce any person who had been a witness of the shipwreck. The owners of the "Cynthia" had not been able to prove their good faith, or to explain how the shipwreck had taken place, and the Court had decided in favor of their adversaries. Their defense had been weak, and their opponents had triumphed.

The insurance company, however, had been compelled to pay several claims on the lives of the passengers to their heirs. But, in all these law proceedings, there was no trace of any infant nine months old.

These examinations had occupied several days. Finally, the chief of police informed Mr. Bredejord that he had been unable to obtain any intelligence about the matter. Nobody in New York knew any detective who answered to Mr. Bowles' description. Nobody could tell who the individual was who was interested in the departure of Patrick O'Donoghan. As for this sailor, he did not appear to have set his foot in the United States for at least four years. All they could do was to keep the address of the place where he was born, which might prove useful some time. But the chief of police told Mr. Bredejord, without any dissimulation, that the affair had happened so long ago—now nearly twenty years—that even if Patrick O'Donoghan ever returned to New York, it was at least doubtful if the authorities would be willing to investigate the matter.

At the moment when Erik believed that he was about to obtain a solution of the mystery which clouded his life, all their investigations came to a sudden end, and without producing the slightest result. The only thing that remained to be done was to pass through Ireland as they returned to Sweden, to see if perchance Patrick O'Donoghan had returned there to pass the remainder of his days planting cabbages.

Dr. Schwaryencrona and his friends, after taking leave of Mr. and Mrs. Bowles, resolved to pursue this route. The steamers between New York and Liverpool touch at Cork, and this was only a few miles from Innishannon, the place where Patrick was born. There they learned that Patrick O'Donoghan had never returned to his native place since he left it at the age of twelve years, and that they had never heard from him.

"Where shall we look for him now?" asked Dr. Schwaryencrona, as they embarked for England, on the way to Stockholm.

"At the seaport towns evidently, and clearly at those which are not American," answered Mr. Bredejord. "For note this point, a sailor, a sea-faring man, does not renounce his profession at the age of thirty-five. It is the only one he knows. Patrick is doubtless still on the sea. And all vessels have some port or other for their destination, and it is only there that we can hope to find this man. What do you think, Hochstedt?"

"Your reasoning seems to be just, although not altogether indisputable," answered the professor, with his customary prudence.

"Admit that it is right," continued Mr. Bredejord. "We know that Patrick O'Donoghan was frightened away and would be in dread of pursuit, perhaps of being extradited. In that case, he would avoid his old companions, and seek in preference ports where he was not likely to meet any of them. I know that my ideas can be contradicted, but let us suppose they are well founded. The number of ports which are not frequented by American vessels is not very large. I think we might begin by seeking in these places news of Patrick O'Donoghan."

"Why not have recourse to advertisements?" asked Dr. Schwaryencrona.

"Because Patrick O'Donoghan would not answer them if he is trying to hide himself; even supposing that a sailor would be likely to see your advertisement."

"But you could word your advertisement so as to assure him that you intended to do him no injury, but rather that it would be greatly to his advantage to communicate with you."

"You are right, but still I am afraid that an ordinary seaman would not be likely to see such an advertisement."

"Well, you might try offering a reward to Patrick O'Donoghan, or to any one who would give you information as to where he might be found. What do you think about it, Erik?"

"It seems to me that such an advertisement to produce any result would have to be continued for a long time, and in a great many different papers. That would cost a great deal, and might only frighten Patrick O'Donoghan, no matter how well worded the advertisement might be, provided it is to his interest to remain concealed. Would it not be better to employ some one to visit personally those seaports which this man would be likely to frequent?"

"But where could we find a trusty man who would be willing to undertake such a task?"

"I can furnish one, if you wish it," answered Erik. "I would go myself."

"You, my dear child—and what would become of your studies?"

"My studies need not suffer. There is nothing to prevent me from pursuing them, even during my travels. And another thing, doctor, I must confess to you, that I have already secured the means of doing so without costing me anything."

"How is that possible," asked Dr. Schwaryencrona, Mr. Bredejord, and Professor Hochstedt, simultaneously.

"I have simply been preparing myself for a sea-faring life. I can pass the examination to-day if necessary. Once in possession of my diploma, it would be easy for me to obtain a position as a lieutenant in any sea-port.

"And you have done all this without saying a word to me?" said the doctor, half grieved, while the lawyer and the professor both laughed heartily.

"Well," said Erik, "I do not think that I have committed any great crime. I have only made inquiries as to the requisite amount of knowledge, and I have mastered it. I should not have made any use of it without asking your permission, and I now solicit it."

"And I shall grant it, wicked boy," said the doctor, "But to let you set out all alone now is another matter—we will wait until you have attained your majority."

Erik submitted to this decision willingly and gratefully.

However, the doctor was not willing to give up his own ideas. To search the sea-ports personally he regarded as a last expedient. An advertisement on the other hand would go everywhere. If Patrick O'Donoghan was not hiding away, they might possibly find him by this means. If he was hiding, some one might see it and betray him. He therefore had this advertisement written in seven or eight different languages, and dispatched to the four quarters of the globe in a hundred of the most widely circulated newspapers.

"Patrick O'Donoghan, a sailor, has been absent from New York for four years. A reward of one hundred pounds sterling will be paid to any one who can give me news of him. Five hundred pounds sterling will be given to the said Patrick O'Donoghan if he will communicate with the advertiser. He need fear nothing, as no advantage will be taken of him.

"DOCTOR SCHWARYENCRONA.
"STOCKHOLM."

By the 20th of October, the doctor and his companions had returned to their homes.

The next day the advertisement was sent to the advertising agency in Stockholm, and three days afterward it had made its appearance in several newspapers. Erik could not repress a sigh and a presentiment that it would be unsuccessful as he read it.

As for Mr. Bredejord, he declared openly that it was the greatest folly in the world, and that for the future he considered the affair a failure.

But Erik and Mr. Bredejord were deceived, as events afterward proved.

10

Tudor Brown, Esquire

One morning in May the doctor was in his office, when his servant brought him a visitor's card. This card, which was small as is usual in America, had the name of "Mr. Tudor Brown, on board the 'Albatross'" printed upon it.

"Mr. Tudor Brown," said the doctor, trying to remember whom he had ever known who bore this name.

"This gentleman asked to see the doctor," said the servant.

"Can he not come at my office-hour?" asked the doctor.

"He said his business was about a personal matter."

"Show him in, then," said the doctor, with a sigh.

He lifted his head as the door opened again, and was surprised when he beheld the singular person who answered to the feudal name of Tudor, and the plebeian name of Brown.

He was a man about fifty years of age, his forehead was covered with a profusion of little ringlets, of a carroty color, while the most superficial examination betrayed that they were made of curled silk; his nose was hooked, and surmounted with an enormous pair of gold spectacles; his teeth were as long as those of a horse, his cheeks were smooth, but under his chin he wore a little red beard. This odd head, covered by a high hat which he did not pretend to remove, surmounted a thin angular body, clothed from head to foot in a woolen suit. In his cravat he wore a pin, containing a diamond as large as a walnut; also a large gold chain, and his vest buttons were amethysts. He had a dozen rings on his fingers, which were as knotty as those of a chimpanzee. Altogether he was the most pretentious and grotesque-looking man that it was possible to behold. This person entered the doctor's office as if he had been entering a railway station, without even bowing. He stopped to say, in a voice that resembled that of Punch, its tone was so nasal and guttural:

"Are you Doctor Schwaryencrona?"

"I am," answered the doctor, very much astonished at his manners.

He was debating in his mind whether he should ring for his servant to conduct this offensive person to the door, when a word put a stop to his intention.

"I saw your advertisement about Patrick O'Donoghan," said the stranger, "and I thought you would like to know that I can tell you something about him."

"Take a seat, sir," answered the doctor.

But he perceived that the stranger had not waited to be asked.

After selecting the most comfortable arm-chair, he drew it toward the doctor, then he seated himself with his hands in his pockets, lifted his feet and placed his heels on the window-sill, and looked at the doctor with the most self-satisfied air in the world.

"I thought," he said, "that you would listen to these details with pleasure, since you offer five hundred pounds for them. That is why I have called upon you."

The doctor bowed without saying a word.

"Doubtless," continued the other, in his nasal voice, "you are wondering who I am. I am going to tell you. My card has informed you as to my name, and I am a British subject."

"Irish perhaps?" asked the doctor with interest.

The Granger, evidently surprised, hesitated a moment, and then said:

"No, Scotch. Oh, I know I do not look like a Scotchman, they take me very often for a Yankee—but that is nothing—I am Scotch."

As he gave this piece of information, he looked at Dr. Schwaryencrona as much as to say:

"You can believe what you please, it is a matter of indifference to me."

"From Inverness, perhaps?" suggested the doctor, still clinging to his favorite theory.

The stranger again hesitated for a moment.

"No, from Edinburgh," he answered. "But that is of no importance after all, and has nothing to do with the matter in hand. I have an independent fortune and owe nothing to anybody. If I tell you who I am, it is because it gives me pleasure to do so, for I am not obliged to do it."

"Permit me to observe that I did not ask you," said the doctor, smiling.

"No, but do not interrupt me, or we shall never reach the end of this matter. You published an advertisement to find out what became of

Patrick O'Donoghan, did you not?—you therefore have some interest in knowing. I know what has become of him."

"You know?" asked the doctor, drawing his seat closer to that of the stranger.

"I know, but before I tell you, I want to ask you what interest you have in finding him?"

"That is only just," answered the doctor.

In as few words as possible, he related Erik's history, to which his visitor listened with profound attention.

"And this boy is still living?" asked Tudor Brown.

"Assuredly he is living. He is in good health, and in October next he will begin his studies in the Medical University at Upsal."

"Ah! ah!" answered the stranger, who seemed lost in reflection. "Tell me," he said at length, "have you no other means of solving this mystery of his birth except by finding Patrick O'Donoghan?"

"I know of no other," replied the doctor. "After years of searching I only found out that this O'Donoghan was in possession of the secret, that he alone could reveal it to me, and that is why I have advertised for him in the papers. I must confess that I had no great hopes of finding him by this means."

"How is that?"

"Because I had reasons for believing that this O'Donoghan has grave motives for remaining unknown, consequently it was not likely that he would respond to my advertisement. I had the intention of resorting to other means. I have a description of him. I know what ports he would be likely to frequent, and I propose to employ special agents to be on the lookout for him."

Dr. Schwaryencrona did not say this lightly. He spoke with the intention of seeing what effect these words would produce on the man before him. And as he watched him intently, he saw that in spite of the affected coolness of the stranger his eyelids fell and the muscles of his mouth contracted. But almost immediately Tudor Brown recovered his self-possession, and said:

"Well, doctor, if you have no other means of solving this mystery, except by discovering Patrick O'Donoghan, I am afraid that you will never find it out. Patrick O'Donoghan is dead."

The doctor was too much taken aback by this disappointing announcement to say a word, and only looked at his visitor, who continued:

"Dead and buried, three hundred fathoms beneath the sea. This man, whose past life always appeared to me to have been mysterious, was employed three years on board my yacht, the 'Albatross.' I must tell you that my yacht is a stanch vessel, in which I often cruise for seven or eight months at a time. Nearly three years ago we were passing through the Straits of Madeira, when Patrick O'Donoghan fell overboard. I had the vessel stopped, and some boats lowered, and after a diligent search we recovered him; but though we spared no pains to restore him to life, our efforts were in vain. Patrick O'Donoghan was dead. We were compelled to return to the sea the prey which we had snatched from it. The accident was put down on the ship's log, and recorded in the notary's office at the nearest place we reached. Thinking that this act might be useful to you, I have brought you a certified copy of it."

As he said this, Mr. Tudor Brown took out his pocket-book and presented the doctor with a paper stamped with a notarial seal.

The latter read it quickly. It was a record of the death of Patrick O'Donoghan, while passing through the Straits of Madeira, duly signed and sworn to, before two witnesses, as being an exact copy of the original—it was also registered in London, at Somerset House, by the commissioners of her Britannic Majesty.

This instrument was evidently authentic. But the manner in which he had received it was so strange that the doctor could not conceal his astonishment. He took it, however, with his habitual courtesy.

"Permit me to ask one question, sir," he said to his visitor.

"Speak, doctor."

"How is it that you have this document in your pocket duly prepared and certified? And why have you brought it to me?"

"If I can count, you have asked two questions," said Tudor Brown. "I will answer them, however—I had this paper in my pocket, because I read your advertisement two months ago, and wishing to furnish you with the information which you asked for, I thought it better to give it to you, in the most complete and definite form that lay in my power. I have brought it to you personally, because I happened to be cruising in these waters; and I wished at the same time to gratify your curiosity and my own."

There was nothing to answer to this reasoning—this was the only conclusion the doctor could draw.

"Yon are here, then, with the 'Albatross'?" he asked, eagerly.

"Without doubt."

"And you have still on board some sailors who have known Patrick O'Donoghan?"

"Yes, several."

"Would you permit me to see them?"

"As many as you please. Will you accompany me on board now?"

"If you have no objection."

"I have none," said the stranger, as he arose.

Dr. Schwaryencrona touched his bell, and they brought him his fur pelisse, his hat, and his cane, and he departed with Mr. Tudor Brown.

Fifteen minutes later they were on board the "Albatross."

They were received by an old gray-headed seaman, with a rubicund face, whose open countenance betrayed only truth and loyalty.

"Mr. Ward, this gentleman wishes to make some inquiries about the fate of Patrick O'Donoghan," said Mr. Tudor Brown.

"Patrick O'Donoghan," answered the old sailor, "God rest his soul. He gave us trouble enough to pick him up the day he was drowned in the Straits of Madeira. What is the use of inquiries now that he has gone to feed the fishes?"

"Had you known him for a long time?" asked the doctor.

"The rascal—no—for a year or two perhaps. I believe that it was at Zanzibar that we took him on board—am I right, Tommy Duff?"

"Is any one hailing me?" asked a young sailor, who was busily employed in polishing a copper bowl.

"Come here," said the other—"Was it at Zanzibar that we recruited Patrick O'Donoghan?"

"Patrick O'Donoghan," repeated the young sailor, as if his remembrance of the man was not very good. "Oh yes, I remember him. The man who fell overboard in the Straits of Maderia. Yes, Mr. Ward, it was at Zanzibar that he came on board."

Dr. Schwaryencrona made him describe Patrick O'Donoghan, and was convinced that it was the same man whom he was seeking. Both these men seemed honest and sincere. They had honest and open countenances. The uniformity of their answers seemed a little strange, and almost preconcerted; but after all it might be only the natural consequence of relating facts. Having known Patrick O'Donoghan only a year at the most, they would have but little to say about him, except the fact of his death.

Besides the "Albatross" was a yacht of such large proportions, that if she had been furnished with some cannon she might easily have passed for a man-of-war. The most rigorous cleanliness was observed on board. The sailors were in good condition, well clothed, and under perfect discipline. The general appearance of the vessel insensiby acted upon the doctor, and carried conviction of the truth of the statement which he had just heard. He therefore declared himself perfectly satisfied, and could not leave without inviting Mr. Tudor Brown to dine with him. But Mr. Tudor Brown did not think it best to accept this invitation. He declined it in these courteous terms:

"No—I can not—I never dine in town."

It now only remained for Dr. Schwaryencrona to retire. This he did without having obtained even the slightest bow from this strange individual.

The doctor's first thought was to go and relate his adventure to Mr. Bredejord, who listened to him without saying a word, only promising himself to institute counter inquiries.

But he, with Erik, who had been told the whole story upon his return from school, repaired to the vessel to see if they could elicit any further information, but the "Albatross" had left Stockholm, without leaving word where she was going, and they could not, therefore, obtain even the address of Mr. Tudor Brown.

All that resulted from this affair was the possession of the document, which legally proved the death of Patrick O'Donoghan.

Was this paper of any value? This was the question that Mr. Bredejord could not help doubting, in spite of the evidence of the British consul at Stockholm, whom he questioned, and who declared that the signatures and stamp were perfectly authentic. He also caused inquiries to be made at Edinburgh, but nobody knew Mr. Tudor Brown, which he thought looked suspicious.

But it was an undeniable fact that they obtained no further intelligence of Patrick O'Donoghan, and all their advertisements were ineffectual.

If Patrick O'Donoghan had disappeared for good, they had no hope of penetrating the mystery that surrounded Erik's birth. He himself saw this, and was obliged to recognize the fact that, for the future, the inquiries would have to be based upon some other theory. He therefore made no opposition about commencing his medical studies the following autumn at the university at Upsal, according to the doctor's wishes. He only desired, first, to pass his examination as a captain, but this sufficed to show that he had not renounced his project of traveling.

Besides, he had another trouble which lay heavy at his heart, and for which he saw no other remedy but absence.

Erik wished to find some pretext for leaving the doctor's house as soon as his studies were completed; but he wished to do this without exciting any suspicion. The only pretext which he could think of was this plan of traveling. He desired to do this because of the aversion of

Kajsa, the doctor's niece. She lost no occasion of showing her dislike; but he would not at any price have had the excellent man suspect this state of affairs between them. His relations toward the young girl had always been most singular. In the eyes of Erik during these seven years as well as on the first day of his arrival at Stockholm, the pretty little fairy had always been a model of elegance and all earthly perfections. He had bestowed on her his unreserved admiration, and had made heroic efforts to overcome her dislike, and become her friend.

But Kajsa could not make up her mind calmly to see this "intruder," as she called Erik, take his place in the doctor's home, be treated as an adopted son, and become a favorite of her uncle and his friends. The scholastic success of Erik, his goodness and his gentleness, far from making him pleasing in her eyes, were only new motives of jealousy.

In her heart Kajsa could not pardon the young man for being only a fisherman and a peasant. It seemed to her that he brought discredit upon the doctor's household and on herself, who, she liked to believe, occupied a very high position in the social scale.

But it was worse when she learned that Erik was even less than a peasant, only a child that had been picked up. That appeared to her monstrous and dishonorable. She thought that such a child had a lower place in society than a cat or a dog; she manifested these sentiments by the most disdainful looks, the most mortifying silence, and the most cruel insults. If Erik was invited with her to any little social gathering at the house of a friend, she would positively refuse to dance with him. At the table she would not answer anything he said, nor pay any attention to him. She tried on all occasions, and in every possible way, to humiliate him.

Poor Erik had divined the cause of this uncharitable conduct, but he could not understand how ignorance of his family, and of the land of his birth, could be regarded by her as such a heinous crime. He tried one day to reason with Kajsa, and to make her understand the injustice and cruelty of such a prejudice, but she would not even deign to listen to him. Then as they both grew older, the abyss which separated them seemed to widen. At eighteen Kajsa made her *debut* in society. She was flattered and noticed as the rich heiress, and this homage only confirmed her in the opinion that she was superior to common mortals.

Erik, who was at first greatly afflicted by her disdain, ended by becoming indignant, and vowing to triumph over it. This feeling of humiliation had a great share in producing the passionate ardor with which he pursued his studies. He dreamed of raising himself so high in public esteem, by the force of his own industry, that every one would bow before him. But he also vowed that he would go away on the first opportunity, and that he would not remain under a roof where every day he was exposed to some secret humiliation.

Only the good doctor must be kept in ignorance of the cause of his departure. He must attribute it solely to a passion for traveling. And Erik therefore frequently spoke of his desire, when his studies were completed, of engaging in some scientific expedition. While pursuing his studies at Upsal, he prepared himself by work, and the most severe exercise, for the life of fatigue and danger which is the lot of great travelers.

11

The "Vega."

In the month of December, 1878, Erik had attained the age of twenty, and passed his first examination for his doctor's degree. The learned men of Sweden were greatly excited about the proposed arctic expedition of the navigator Nordenskiold, and their enthusiasm was shared by a large proportion of the population. After preparing himself for the undertaking by several voyages to the polar regions, and after studying the problem in all its aspects, Nordenskiold intended to attempt once more to discover the north-east passage from the Atlantic to the Pacific, which for three centuries had defied the efforts of all the maritime nations.

The programme for the expedition had been defined by the Swedish navigator, and he announced the reasons which led him to believe that the north-east passage was practicable in summer, and the means by which he hoped to realize this geographical desideratum. The intelligent liberality of two Scandinavian gentlemen, and the assistance of the Swedish government, enabled him to organize his expedition upon a plan which he believed would insure its success.

It was on the 21st of July, 1878, that Nordenskiold quitted Fromsae, on board of the "Vega," to attempt to reach Behring's Strait by passing to the north of Russia and Siberia. Lieutenant Palanders, of the Swedish navy, was in command of the vessel, with the instigator of the voyage, and they had also a staff of botanists, geologists, and astronomical doctors.

The "Vega," which had been especially prepared for the expedition under the surveillance of Nordenskiold, was a vessel of five hundred tons, which had been recently built at Bremen, and carried an engine of sixty-horse power. Three ships were to accompany her to successive points on the Siberian coast, which had been previously determined upon. They were all provisioned for a cruise of two years, in case it might be necessary for them to winter in those arctic regions. But Nordenskiold did not conceal his hope of being able to reach Behring's Strait before autumn, on account of his careful arrangements, and all Sweden shared this hope.

They started from the most northerly point of Norway, and the "Vega" reached Nova Zembla on the 29th of July, on the 1st of August the Sea of Kara, and on the 6th of August the mouth of the Gulf Yenisei. On the 9th of August she doubled Cape Schelynshin, or Cape North-East, the extreme point of the continent, which no vessel had hitherto been able to reach. On the 7th of September she cast anchor at the mouth of the Lena, and separated from the third of the vessels which had accompanied her thus far. On the 16th of October a telegraphic dispatch from Irkutsk announced to the world that the expedition had been successful up to this point.

We can imagine the impatience with which the friends of the Swedish navigator waited for the details of the expedition. These details did not reach them until the 1st of December. For if electricity flies over space with the rapidity of thought, it is not the same with the Siberian post. The letters from the "Vega," although deposited in the post-office at Irkutsk, at the same time that the telegraphic message was dispatched, did not reach Sweden until six weeks afterward. But they arrived at last; and on the 5th of December one of the principal newspapers of Sweden published an account of the first part of the expedition, which had been written by a young medical doctor attached to the "Vega."

That same day, at breakfast, Mr. Bredejord was occupied in reading with great interest the details of the voyage, given in four columns, when his eyes fell upon a paragraph which almost upset him. He re-read it attentively, and then read it again; then he arose, and seizing his hat and coat, he rushed to the house of Dr. Schwaryencrona.

"Have you read the correspondence of the 'Vega'?" he cried, as he rushed like a hurricane into the dining-room where the doctor and Kajsa were taking their breakfast.

"I have just commenced it," replied the doctor, "and was intending to finish reading it after breakfast, while I smoked my pipe."

"Then you have not seen!" exclaimed Mr. Bredejord, out of breath. "You do not know what this correspondence contains?"

"No," replied Doctor Schwaryencrona, with perfect calmness.

"Well, listen to this," continued Mr. Bredejord, approaching the window. "It is the journal of one of your brethren, the aid of the naturalist of the 'Vega.'"

"'30th and 31st of July, we entered the strait of Jugor, and cast anchor before a Samoyede village called Chabarova. We landed, and I questioned some of the natives to discover, by Holmgren's method, the extent of their perception of colors. I found that this sense was normally developed among them. Bought of a Samoyede fisherman two magnificent salmon.'"

"Pardon me," interrupted the doctor; "but is this a charade you are reading to me. I confess I do not see how these details can interest me."

"Ah! they do not interest you?" said Mr. Bredejord, in a triumphant tone. "Well, wait a moment and you will see:

"'Bought of a Samoyede fisherman two magnificent salmon, which I have preserved in alcohol, notwithstanding the protestations of our cook. This fisherman fell into the water as he was quitting the ship. They pulled him out half suffocated and stiffened by the cold, so that he resembled a bar of iron, and he, also, had a serious cut on his head. We were just under way, and they carried him to the infirmary of the "Vega," while still unconscious, undressed him, and put him to bed. They then discovered that this fisherman was an European. He had red hair; his nose had been broken by some accident, and on his chest, on a level with his heart, these words were tattooed: "Patrick O'Donoghan—Cynthia."'"

Here Dr. Schwaryencrona uttered a cry of surprise.

"Wait! listen to the rest of it," said Mr. Bredejord; and he continued his reading:

"'Being subjected to an energetic massage treatment, he was soon restored to life. But as it was impossible for him to leave us in that condition, we were compelled to take care of him. A fever set in and he became delirious. Our experiment of the appreciation of colors among the Samoyedes, therefore, was frustrated.—3d of August. The fisherman of Chabarova has recovered from the effects of his bath. He appeared to be surprised to find himself on board the "Vega," and *en route* for Cape Tahelyuskin, but soon became reconciled to his fate. His knowledge of the Ganwyede language may be useful to, us, and we have determined to take him with us on the coast of Siberia. He speaks English with a nasal accent like a Yankee, but pretends to be Scotch, and calls himself Tommy Bowles. He came from Nova Zembla with some fishermen, and he has lived on these shores for the last twelve years. The name tattooed upon his chest he says, 'is that of one of the friends of his infancy who has been dead for a long time.'"

"It is evidently our man," cried the doctor, with great emotion.

"Yes, there can be no doubt of it," answered the lawyer. "The name, the vessel, the description, all prove it; even this choice of a pseudonym Johnny Bowles, and his declaring that Patrick O'Donoghan was dead, these are superabundant proofs!"

They were both silent, reflecting upon the possible consequences of this discovery."

"How can we go so far in search of him?" said the doctor, at length.

"It will be very difficult, evidently," replied Mr. Bredejord. "But it is something to know that he is alive, and the part of the world where he can be found. And, besides, who can tell what the future may have in store? He may even return to Stockholm in the 'Vega,' and explain all that we wish to find out. If he does not do this, perhaps we may, sooner or later, find an opportunity to communicate with him. Voyages to Nova Zembla will become more frequent, on account of this expedition of the 'Vega.' Ship-owners are already talking about sending every year some vessels to the mouth of the Yenisei."

The discussion of this topic was inexhaustible, and the two friends were still talking about the matter, when Erik arrived from Upsal, at two o'clock. He also had read this great piece of news, and had taken the train for home without losing a moment. But it was a singular fact that he was not joyful, but rather disturbed by this new intelligence.

"Do you know what I am afraid of?" said he to the doctor and Mr. Bredejord. "I fear that some misfortune has happened to the 'Vega.' You know it is now the 5th of December, and you know the leaders of the expedition counted upon arriving at Behring's Strait before October. If this expectation had been realized, we should have heard from her by this time; for she would have reached Japan, or at least Petropaulosk, in the Aleutian Islands, or some station in the Pacific, from which we should have received news of her. The dispatches and letters here came by the way of Irkutsk, and are dated the 7th of September, so that for three entire months we have heard nothing from the 'Vega.' So we must conclude that they did not reach Behring's Strait as soon as they expected, and that she has succumbed to the common fate of all expeditious which for the last three centuries have attempted to discover the north-east passage. This is the deplorable conclusion which I have been compelled to arrive at."

"The 'Vega' might have been obliged to encounter in the Polar regions a great deal which was unforeseen, and she might have been unprovided for such a contingency," replied Dr. Schwaryencrona.

"Evidently; but this is the most favorable hypothesis; and a winter in that region is surrounded by so many dangers that it is equivalent to a shipwreck. In any case, it is an indisputable fact that if we ever have any news of the 'Vega' it will not be possible to do so before next summer."

"Why, how is that?"

"Because, if the 'Vega' has not perished she is inclosed in the ice, and she will not be able, at the best, to extricate herself before June or July."

"That is true," answered Mr. Bredejord.

"What conclusion do you draw from this reasoning?" asked the doctor, disturbed by the sad tone of Erik's voice as he made the announcement.

"The conclusion that it is impossible to wait so long before solving a question which is of such great importance to me."

"What do you want to do? We must submit to what is inevitable."

"Perhaps it only appears to be so," answered Erik. "The letters which have reached us have come across the Arctic Ocean by the way of Irkutsk. Why could I not follow the same route? I would keep close to the coast of Siberia. I would endeavor to communicate with the people of that country, and find out whether any foreign vessel had been shipwrecked, or was held prisoner among the icebergs. Perhaps I might succeed in finding Nordenskiold, and Patrick O'Donoghan. It is an enterprise worth undertaking."

"In the middle of winter?"

"Why not? It is the most favorable season for traveling in sleighs in that latitude."

"Yes; but you forget that you are not there yet, and that it will be spring before you could get there."

"That is true," said Erik, who was compelled to recognize the force of this argument. He sat with his eyes fixed on the floor, absorbed in thought.

"No, matter," said he suddenly; "Nordenskiold must be found, and with him Patrick O'Donoghan. They shall be, or it will not be my fault."

Erik's plan was a very simple one. He proposed to write an anonymous letter to the leading newspapers of Stockholm, and thus proclaim his fears as to the fate of the "Vega." Had she been shipwrecked, or was she held a prisoner by icebergs, and he concluded his communication by representing how important it was that some vessel should be sent to her assistance in the latter case.

The truth of his reasoning was so apparent, and the interest in the expedition so general, that the young student of Upsal was certain that the question would be warmly discussed in scientific circles.

But the effect of his letter was beyond his highest expectations. All the newspapers without exception expressed their approval of his proposition while commenting upon his communication.

Public opinion was unanimously in favor of fitting out a relief expedition. Commercial men, manufacturers, the members of schools and colleges, the judicial corps—in fact, all classes voluntarily contributed to the enterprise. A rich ship-owner offered to equip a vessel at his own expense, to go to the relief of the "Vega;" and he named it the "Nordenskiold."

The enthusiasm increased as days passed without bringing any intelligence of the "Vega." By the end of December, the subscription had reached a considerable sum. Dr. Sehwaryencrona and Mr. Bredejord had headed the list with a subscription of ten thousand kroners each. They were members of the committee who had chosen Erik for their secretary.

The latter was in fact the soul of the undertaking. His ardor, his modesty, his evident ability with regard to all questions relative to the expedition, which he studied untiringly, soon acquired for him a most decided influence. From the first he did not conceal the fact that it was his dream to take part in the enterprise, if only as a simple sailor, and that he had a supreme and personal interest in the matter. This only gave the greater weight to the excellent suggestions which he made to the originators of the expedition, and he personally directed all the preparatory labors.

It was agreed that a second vessel should accompany the "Nordenskiold," and that it should be like the "Vega," a steamship. Nordenskiold himself had demonstrated that the principal cause of the failure of previous attempts had been the employment of sailing vessels. Arctic navigators, especially when on an exploring expedition, must not be dependent upon the wind, but must be able to force their way speedily through a difficult or perilous pass—and above all, always be able to take the open sea, which it was often impossible to do with a sailing vessel.

This fundamental point having been established, it was decided also to cover the vessel with a lining of green oak, six inches thick, and to divide it into compartments, so that it would be better able to resist a blow from the ice. They were also desirous that she should not draw too much water, and that all her arrangements should be so made as to enable her to carry a full supply of coal. Among the offers which were made to the committee, was a vessel of one hundred and forty tons, which had been recently built at Bremen, and which had a crew of eighteen men, who could easily maneuver her. She was a schooner, but while she carried her masts, she also was furnished with an engine of eighty horse-power. One of her boilers was so arranged that it could burn oil or fat, which was easily procurable in the arctic regions, in case their coal should fail. The schooner protected by its lining of oak, was further strengthened by transverse beams, so as to offer the greatest possible resistance to the pressure of the ice. Lastly, the front of it was armed with a spur of steel, to enable it to break its way through a thick field of ice. The vessel when placed on the stocks, was named the "Alaska," on account of the direction which she was destined to take. It had been decided that while the "Nordenskiold" should pursue the same route which the "Vega" had followed, that the second vessel should take an opposite direction around the world, and gain the Siberian Ocean, by the island of Alaska and Behring's Straits. The chances of meeting the Swedish expedition, or of discovering traces of her if she had perished would thus, they thought, be double, for while one vessel followed on her track, the other would, as it were, precede her.

Erik, who had been the originator of this plan, had often asked himself which of the vessels he had better join, and he had finally concluded to attach himself to the second.

The "Nordenskiold," he said to himself, would follow the same course as the "Vega." It was therefore necessary that she should be equally successful in making the first part of the voyage, and double Cape Tchelynskin, but they might not be able to do this, since it had only been accomplished once. Besides, the last news which they had received from the "Vega," she was only two or three hundred leagues from Behring's Straits; therefore they would have a better chance of meeting her. The "Nordenskiold" might follow her for many months without overtaking her. But the other vessel could hardly fail to meet her, if she was still in existence.

The principal thing in Erik's eyes was to reach the "Vega" as quickly as possible, in order to meet Patrick O'Donoghan without delay.

The doctor and Mr. Bredejord warmly approved of his motives when he explained them to them.

The work of preparing the "Alaska" was pushed on as rapidly as possible. Her provisions, equipments, and the clothing, were all carefully chosen, for they profited by the experience of former Arctic explorers. Her crew were all experienced seamen, who had been inured to cold by frequent fishing voyages to Iceland and Greenland. Lastly, the captain chosen by the committee, was an officer of the Swedish marines, then in the employment of a maritime company, and well known on account of his voyages to the Arctic Ocean; his name was Lieutenant Marsilas. He chose for his first lieutenant Erik himself, who seemed designed for the position by the energy he had displayed in the service of the expedition, and who was also qualified by his diploma. The second and third officers were tried seamen, Mr. Bosewitz and Mr. Kjellguist.

The "Alaska" carried some explosive material in order to break the ice, if it should be necessary, and abundant provisions of an anti-scorbutic character, in order to preserve the officers and crew from the common Arctic maladies. The vessel was furnished with a heater, in order to preserve an even temperature, and also with a portable observatory called a "raven's nest," which they could hoist to the top of the highest mast, in those regions where they meet with floating ice, to signal the approach of icebergs.

By Erik's proposal this observatory contained a powerful electric light, which at night could illuminate the route of the "Alaska." Seven small boats, of which two were whale-boats, a steam-cutter, six sledges, snow-shoes for each of the crew, four Gatling cannons and thirty guns, with the necessary ammunition, were stored away on board. These preparations were approaching an end, when Mr. Hersebom and his son Otto arrived from Noroe with their large dog Kaas, and solicited the favor of being employed as seamen on board of the "Alaska." They knew from a letter of Erik's the strong personal interest which he had in this voyage, and they wished to share its dangers with him.

Mr. Hersebom spoke of the value of his experience as a fisherman on the coast of Greenland, and of the usefulness of his dog Kaas, who could be used as a leader of the dogs which would be necessary to draw the sledges. Otto had only his good health, his herculean strength, and his devotion to the cause to recommend him. Thanks to the influence of the doctor and Mr. Bredejord, they were all three engaged by the committee.

By the beginning of February, 1879, all was ready. The "Alaska" had therefore five months before the first of June to reach Behring's Straits, which was accounted the most favorable season for the exploration. They intended also to take the most direct route, that is to say, through the Mediterranean, the Suez Canal, the Indian Ocean, and the China Seas, stopping successively to take in coal at Gibraltar, Aden, Colombo in Ceylon, Singapore, Hong Kong, Yokohama, and Petropaulosk.

From all these stations the "Alaska" was to telegraph to Stockholm, and it was also agreed that, if in the meantime any news was received of the "Vega," they should not fail to send information.

The voyage of the "Alaska," although intended primarily for an arctic exploration, would begin by a voyage through tropical seas, and along the continents most favored by the sun. The programme had not, however, been arranged to give them pleasure; it was the result of an imperative necessity, since they must reach Behring's Straits by the shortest route and remain in telegraphic communication with Stockholm up to the last moment. But a serious difficulty threatened to retard the expedition. They had spent so much in equipping the vessel that the funds which were indispensable for the success of the enterprise, began to run short. They would require considerable to purchase coal, and for other incidental expenses.

A new appeal for money became necessary. As soon as it was issued the committee received two letters simultaneously.

One was from Mr. Malarius, the public teacher of Noroe, and laureate of the Botanical Society. It contained a check for one hundred kroners, and begged that he might be attached to the expedition as the assistant naturalist of the "Alaska."

The other contained a check for twenty-five thousand kroners, with this laconic note:

> "For the voyage of the 'Alaska,' from Mr. Tudor Brown, on condition that he is received as a passenger."

12

Unexpected Passengers

The request of Mr. Malarius could only be received with gratitude by the committee. It was therefore passed enthusiastically, and the worthy teacher, whose reputation as a botanist was greater than he himself suspected, was appointed assistant naturalist of the expedition.

As for the condition upon which Tudor Brown bestowed his donation of twenty-five thousand kroners, both Dr. Schwaryencrona and Mr. Bredejord were strongly inclined to refuse to grant it. But if called upon to give some motive for their repugnance, they had to confess that they would not know what to say. What sufficient reason could they give the committee if they asked them to refuse such a large subscription? They really had no valid one. Tudor Brown had called upon Dr. Schwaryencrona, and brought him a certified account of the death of Patrick O'Donoghan; and now Patrick O'Donoghan appeared to be living. But they could not prove that Tudor Brown had willfully deceived them in this matter, and the committee would require some sufficient cause before rejecting so large a sum. Tudor Brown could easily declare that he had been truthful. His present attitude seemed to prove it. Perhaps he intended to go himself, only to find out how Patrick O'Donoghan, whom he believed to have been drowned in the Straits of Madeira, could now be living on the shores of Siberia. But even supposing that Tudor Brown had other projects, it would be to their interest to find them out, and keep him in their hands. For, one of two facts was certain: either Tudor Brown had no interest in the search which had occupied Erik's friends for so long a time, and in that case it would be useless to treat him as an enemy; or he had some slight personal interest in the matter, and then it would be better to watch his plans, and overthrow them.

The doctor and Mr. Bredejord therefore concluded that they would not oppose his becoming a passenger. Then they gradually were filled with a desire to study this singular man, and find out why he wished to take passage on the "Alaska." But how could they do this without sailing with him. It would not be such an absurd thing to do after all. The course which the "Alaska" was to take was a very attractive one, at least the first part of it. To be brief, Dr. Schwaryencrona, who was a great traveler, asked to be taken as a passenger, to accompany the expedition as far as the China seas, by paying such a price as the committee might judge proper.

This example immediately acted with irresistible force upon Mr. Bredejord, who had dreamed for a long time about an excursion to the land of the Sun. He also solicited a cabin under the same conditions.

Every one in Stockholm now believed that Mr. Hochstedt would do the same, partly out of scientific curiosity, and partly from terror at the thought of passing so many months without the society of his friends. But all Stockholm was deceived. The professor was strongly tempted to go, and he reviewed all the arguments for and against it, and found it almost impossible to arrive at any decision, but fate ordained that he should stay at home.

The time of their departure was irrevocably fixed for the 10th of February. On the 9th Erik went to meet Mr. Malarius, and was agreeably surprised to see Dame Hersebom, and Vanda, who had come to bid him farewell. They were modestly intending to go to a hotel in the town, but the doctor insisted that they should come and stay with him, to the great displeasure of Kajsa, who did not think that they were sufficiently distinguished.

Vanda was now a tall girl, whose beauty fulfilled its early promise. She had passed successfully a very difficult examination at Bergen which entitled her to take a professor's chair, in a superior school. But she preferred to remain at Noroe with her mother, and she was going to fill Mr. Malarius' place during his absence: always serious and gentle, she found in teaching a strange and inexplicable charm, but it had not changed the simplicity of her home life. This beautiful girl, in her quaint Norwegian costume, was able to give tranquilly her opinion on the deepest scientific subjects, or seat herself at the piano, and play with consummate skill a sonata of Beethoven. But her greatest charm was the absence of all pretension, and her perfectly natural manners. She no more thought of being vain of her talents, or of making any display of them, than she did of blushing on account of her rural costume. She bloomed like some wild flower, that, growing beside the fiord, had been transplanted by her old master, and cultivated and cherished in his little garden behind the school.

In the evening all Erik's adopted family were assembled in the parlor of Dr. Schwaryencrona; Mr. Bredejord and the doctor were about to play a last game of whist with Mr. Hochstedt. They discovered that Mr. Malarius was also an authority in this noble game, which would enable them to while away many leisure hours on board the "Alaska." Unfortunately the worthy instructor also told them, at the same time, that he was always a victim of sea-sickness, and nearly always confined to his bed as soon as he set foot upon a vessel. Only his affection for Erik had induced him to join the expedition, added to the ambition, long fondly cherished, of being able to add some more varieties to his catalogue of botanical families.

After which they had a little music: Kajsa, with a disdainful air, played a fashionable waltz; Vanda sung an old Scandinavian melody with a sweetness that surprised them all. The tea was served, and a large bowl of punch, which they drunk to the success of the expedition, followed. Erik noticed that Kajsa avoided touching his glass.

"Will you not wish me a happy voyage?" he said to her, in a low tone.

"What is the use of wishing for what we do not expect to see granted?" she answered.

The next morning, at day-break, every one went on board, except Tudor Brown.

Since the receipt of his letter containing the check they had not heard a word from him.

The time of departure had been fixed for ten o'clock. At the first stroke, the commander, Mr. Marsilas, had the anchor hoisted, and rang the bell to warn all visitors to leave the ship.

"Adieu, Erik!" cried Vanda, throwing her arms around his neck.

"Adieu, my son!" said Katrina, pressing the young lieutenant to her heart.

"And you, Kajsa, have you nothing to say to me?" he asked, as he walked toward her as if to embrace her also.

"I hope that you will not get your nose frozen, and that you will discover that you are a prince in disguise!" said she, laughing impertinently.

"If that should happen, then at least I might hope to win a little of your affection?" he said, trying to smile, to hide his feelings, for her sarcasm had cut him to the heart.

"Do you doubt it?" answered Kajsa, as she turned toward her uncle, to show that her adieu to him was finished.

The time of departure had indeed come. The warning bell rang imperiously.

The crowd of visitors descended the stairs to the boats which were waiting for them.

In the midst of this confusion every one noticed the arrival of a tardy passenger, who mounted to the deck with his valise in his hand.

The tardy one was Tudor Brown. He presented himself to the captain, and claimed his cabin, to which he was immediately shown.

A moment later, after two or three prolonged whistles, the engine began to work, and a sea of foam whitening the waters behind her, the "Alaska" glided majestically over the green waters of the Baltic, and soon left Stockholm behind her, followed by the acclamations of the crowd who were waving their hats and handkerchiefs.

Erik, on the bridge, directed the maneuvers of the vessel, while Mr. Bredejord and the doctor waved a last farewell to Vanda from the deck.

Mr. Malarius, already frightfully seasick, had retired to his bed. They were all so occupied with saying farewell that not one of them had noticed the arrival of Tudor Brown.

Therefore the doctor could not repress a start of surprise when as he turned around, he saw him ascending from the depths of the vessel, and marching straight toward him, with his hands in his pockets, clothed as he had been at their first interview, and with his hat always seemingly glued to his head.

"Fine weather!" said Tudor Brown, by way of salutation and introduction.

The doctor was stupefied by his effrontery. He waited for some moments to see if this strange man would make any excuse, or give any explanation of his conduct.

Seeing that he did not intend to say anything, he opened the subject himself.

"Well, sir, it appears that Patrick O'Donoghan is not dead, as we supposed!" he said, with his customary vivacity.

"That is precisely what I want to find out, and it is on that account I have undertaken this voyage."

After saying this, Tudor Brown turned away, and began to walk up and down the deck, whistling his favorite air, appearing to think that his explanation was perfectly satisfactory.

Erik and Mr. Bredejord listened to this conversation with a natural curiosity. They had never seen Tudor Brown before, and they studied him attentively, even more so than Dr. Schwaryencrona. It seemed to them that the man, although he affected indifference, cast a furtive glance at them from time to time, to see what impression he made upon them. Perceiving this, they also immediately feigned to take no notice of him, and did not address a word to him. But as soon as they descended to the saloon, upon which their cabins opened, they took counsel together.

"What could have been Tudor Brown's motive in trying to make them believe that Patrick O'Donoghan was dead? And what was his purpose in taking this voyage upon the 'Alaska'? It was impossible for them to say. But it was difficult not to believe that it had some connection with the shipwreck of the 'Cynthia,' and the infant tied to the buoy. The only interest which Patrick O'Donoghan had for Erik and his friends, was the fact of his supposed knowledge of the affair, and this was their only reason for seeking for him. Now they had before them a man who was uninvited, and who had come to them, and declared that Patrick O'Donoghan was dead. And this man had forced his society upon the members of the expedition, as soon as his assertion in the most unexpected manner had been proved to be false. They were therefore obliged to conclude that he had some personal interest in the matter, and the fact of his seeking out Doctor Schwaryencrona indicated the connection between his interests, and the inquiries instituted by the doctor."

All these facts therefore seemed to indicate that Tudor Brown was in this problem a factor quite as important as Patrick O'Donoghan himself. Who could tell whether he was not already in possession of the secret which they were trying to elucidate? If this was the case, was it a happy thing for them that they had him on board, or should they rather be disturbed by his presence?

Mr. Bredejord inclined to the latter opinion, and did not consider his appearance among them as at all reassuring. The doctor, on the other side, argued that Tudor Brown might have acted in good faith, and also that he might be honest at heart, notwithstanding his unattractive exterior.

"If he knows anything," said he, "we can hope that the familiarity which a long voyage necessarily produces may induce him to speak out; in that case it would be a stroke of good luck to have had him with us. At least we shall see what he can have to do with O'Donoghan, if we ever find the Irishman."

As for Erik, he did not even dare to express the sentiments which the sight of this man awakened in him. It was more than repulsion, it was positive hatred, and an instinctive desire to rush upon him and throw him into the sea. He was convinced that this man had had some share in the misfortune of his life, but he would have blushed to abandon himself to such a conviction, or even to speak of it. He contented himself with saying that he would never have allowed Tudor Brown to come on board if he had had any voice in the matter.

How should they treat him?

On this point also they were divided. The doctor declared that it would be politic to treat Tudor Brown with at least outward courtesy, in the hope of inducing him to speak out. Mr. Bredejord, as well as Erik, felt a great repugnance to act out such a comedy, and it was by no means certain that Dr. Schwaryencrona himself would be able to conform to his own programme. They determined to leave the matter to be decided by circumstances, and the behavior of Tudor Brown himself.

They did not have to wait long. Precisely at midday the bell rang for dinner. Mr. Bredejord and the doctor, went to the table of the commander. There they found Tudor Brown already seated, with his hat on his head, and he did not manifest the least inclination to enter into any relations with his neighbors. The man proved to be so rude and coarse that he disarmed indignation. He seemed to be ignorant of the simplest rules of politeness. He helped himself first, chose the best portions, and ate and drank like an ogre. Two or three times the commander, and Dr. Schwaryencrona addressed a few words to him. He did not even deign to speak, but answered them by gestures.

That did not prevent him however, when he had finished his repast, and armed himself with an enormous tooth-pick, from throwing himself back in his seat, and saying to Mr. Marsilas:

"What day shall we reach Gibraltar?"

"About the nineteenth or twentieth I think," answered the captain.

Tudor Brown drew a book from his pocket, and examined his calendar.

"That will bring us to Malta on the twenty-second, to Alexandria on the twenty-fifth, and to Aden at the end of the month," said he, as if speaking to himself.

Then he got up, and going on deck again, began to pace up and down.

"A pleasant traveling companion truly," Mr. Marsilas could not help saying.

Mr. Bredejord was about to answer, when a frightful noise at the head of the staircase prevented him. They heard cries, and barking, and a confusion of voices. Everybody arose and ran on deck.

The tumult had been caused by Kaas, Mr. Hersebom's Greenland dog. It seemed that he did not approve of Mr. Tudor Brown, for after evincing his displeasure by low growls every time he passed and repassed him, he finished by seizing him by the legs. Tudor Brown had drawn his revolver from his pocket, and was about to use it when Otto appeared on the scene and prevented him from doing so, and then sent Kaas away to his kennel. A stormy discussion then took place. Tudor Brown, white with rage and terror, insisted that the dog's brains should be blown out. Mr. Hersebom, who had come to the rescue, protested warmly against such a project.

The commander arriving at this moment, settled the matter by desiring Tudor Brown to put away his revolver, and decreeing that henceforth Kaas must be kept chained.

This ridiculous incident was the only one that varied the monotony of their first days of voyaging. Every one became accustomed to the silence and strange manners of Tudor Brown. At the captain's table they at length took no more notice of him than if he had not been in existence. Everybody pursued their own avocations.

Mr. Malarius, after passing two days in bed, was able to crawl upon deck, he commenced to eat, and was soon able to take his place at the innumerable whist parties of the doctor and Mr. Bredejord.

Erik, very much occupied with his business as lieutenant, spent every spare moment in reading.

On the eleventh they passed the island of Oland, on the thirteenth they reached Shayer Rock, passed through the sound, signaled Heligoland on the fourteenth, and on the sixteenth they doubled Cape Hogue.

On the following night Erik was sleeping in his cabin when he was awakened by a sudden silence, and perceived that he no longer felt the vibrations of the engine. He was not however alarmed, for he knew that Mr. Kjellguist was in charge of the vessel; but out of curiosity he arose and went on deck to see what had happened.

He was told by the chief engineer that the engine had broken down, and that they would be compelled to extinguish the fires. They could proceed, however, under sail, with a light breeze from the south-west.

A careful inspection threw no light on the cause of the damage, and the engineer asked permission to repair to the nearest port to repair the injury.

Commander Marsilas, after a personal examination, was of the same opinion. They found that they were thirty miles from Brest, and the order was given to steer for the great French port.

13

The Shipwreck

The next day the "Alaska" entered the harbor of Brest. The damage which she had sustained was fortunately not important. An engineer who was applied to immediately promised that her injuries should be repaired in three days. It was therefore not a very serious delay, and they could make up for it in a measure by taking in coal. They would therefore not be obliged to stop at Gibraltar for this purpose, as they had at first intended. Their next stopping-place was to be at Malta, which they hoped to reach twenty-four hours earlier than they had at first expected, and thus would reduce the time of their delay in reality to two days. They therefore had nothing to worry themselves about, and everyone felt disposed to view the accident in the most philosophical manner.

It soon became evident that their mischance was going to be turned into a festival. In a few hours the arrival of the "Alaska" became known through the town, and as the newspapers made known the object of the expedition, the commander of the Swedish vessel soon found himself the recipient of the most flattering attentions. The admiral and Mayor of Brest, the commander of the port, and the captains of the vessels which were lying at anchor, all came to pay an official visit to Captain Marsilas. A dinner and a ball were tendered to the hardy explorers, who were to take part in the search for the "Nordenskiold." Although the doctor and Mr. Malarius cared little for such gatherings, they were obliged to take their places at the table which was prepared for them. As for Mr. Bredejord, he was in his true element.

Among the friends invited by the admiral, was a grand-looking old man with a refined but sad countenance. He soon attracted Erik's attention, who felt a sympathy for him which he could hardly explain. It was Mr. Durrien, Honorary Consul-general, and an active member of the Geographical Society, who was well known on account of his travels and researches in Asia Minor and the Soudan.

Erik had read his works with very great interest, and he mentioned that he had done so, when he had been presented to the French *savant*, who experienced a feeling of satisfaction as he listened to the enthusiastic young man.

It is often the fate of travelers, when their adventures make a stir in the world, to receive the loud admiration of the crowd; but to find that their labors are appreciated, by those who are well informed and capable of judging, does not occur so frequently. Therefore the respectful curiosity of Erik went straight to the heart of the old geographer, and brought a smile to his pale lips.

"I have never attached any great merit to my discoveries," he said, in reply to a few words from Erik, regarding the fortunate excavations which had recently been made. "I went ahead seeking, to forget my own cruel misfortunes, and not caring so much for the results as I did for prosecuting a work which was in entire accordance with my tastes. Chance has done the rest."

Seeing Erik and Mr. Durrien so friendly, the admiral took care to seat them together at table, so that they could continue their conversation during dinner.

As they were taking their coffee, the young lieutenant of the "Alaska" was accosted by a little bald-headed man, who had been introduced to him as Dr. Kergaridec, who asked him without any preamble to what country he belonged. A little surprised at first by the question, Erik answered that he was from Sweden, or, to be more exact, from Norway, and that his family lived in the province of Bergen. Then he inquired his motive for asking the question.

"My motive is a very simple one," answered his interlocutor. "For an hour I have been studying your face across the table, while we were at dinner, and I have never seen anywhere such a perfect type of the Celt as I behold in you! I must tell you that I am devoted to Celtic studies, and it is the first time that I have met with this type among the Scandinavians. Perhaps this is a precious indication for science, and we may be able to place Norway among the regions visited by our Gaelic ancestors?"

Erik was about to explain to the worthy *savant* the reasons which would invalidate this hypothesis, when Dr. Kergaridec turned away to pay his respects to a lady who had just entered the room, and their conversation was not resumed.

The young lieutenant of the "Alaska" would probably never have thought of this incident again, but the next day as they were passing through a street near the market, Dr. Schwaryencrona said suddenly to him:

"My dear child, if I have ever had a doubt as to your Celtic origin, I should have lost it here. See how you resemble these Bretons. They have the same brown eyes, black hair, bony neck, colored skin and general appearance. Bredejord may say what he likes, but you are a pure-blooded Celt—you may depend upon it." Erik then told him what old Dr. Kergaridec had said to him, and Dr. Schwaryencrona was so delighted that he could not talk of anything else all the day.

With the other passengers of the "Alaska," Tudor Brown had received and accepted an invitation from the prefect. They thought up to the last moment that he would go in his accustomed dress, for he had made his appearance in it just as they were all going ashore to the dinner. But doubtless the necessity of removing his precious hat appeared too hard to him, for they saw him no more that evening.

When he returned after the ball, Erik learned from Mr. Hersebom that Tudor Brown had returned at seven o'clock and dined alone. After that, he had entered the captain's room to consult a marine chart; then he had returned to the town in the same small boat which had brought him on board.

This was the last news which they received of him.

The next evening at five o'clock Tudor Brown had not made his appearance. He knew, however, that the machinery of the "Alaska" would be repaired by that time, and her fires kindled, after which it would be impossible to defer her departure. The captain had been careful to notify every one. He gave the order to hoist the anchor.

The vessel had been loosened from her moorings when a small boat was signaled making all speed toward them. Every one believed that it carried Tudor Brown, but they soon saw that it was only a letter which had been sent on board. It occasion general surprise when it was discovered that this letter was directed to Erik.

When he opened it, Erik found that it simply contained the card of Mr. Durrien, the Honorary Consul-general, and member of the Geographical Society, with these words written in pencil:

"A good voyage—a speedy return."

We can not explain Erik's feelings.

This attention from an amiable and distinguished *savant* brought tears to his eyes. In leaving this hospitable shore where he had remained three days, it seemed to him as if he was leaving his own country. He placed Mr. Durrien's card in his memorandum book, and said to himself that this adieu from an old man could not fail to bring him good luck.

It was now the 20th of February. The weather was fine. The sun had sunk below the horizon, leaving a sky as cloudless as that of summer.

Erik had the watch during the first quarter, and he walked the quarter-deck with a light step. It seemed to him that, with the departure of Tudor Brown, the evil genius of the expedition had disappeared.

"Provided that he does not intend to rejoin us at Malta or Suez," he said to himself.

It was possible—indeed, even probable—if Tudor Brown wished to spare himself the long voyage which the "Alaska" would make before reaching Egypt. While the vessel was going around the coasts of France and Spain, he could, if it so pleased him, stay for a week in Paris, or at any other place, and then take the mail packet either to Alexandria or Suez, and rejoin the "Alaska" at either of those places; or he could even defer doing so until they reached Singapore or Yokohama.

But this was only a possibility. The fact was that he was no longer on board, and that he could not cast a damper upon the spirits of the company.

Their dinner, also, which they took at six o'clock, as usual, was the gayest which they had yet sat down to. At dessert they drank to the success of the expedition, and every one, in his heart, associated it, more or less, with the absence of Tudor Brown. Then they went on deck and smoked their cigars.

It was a dark night, but in the distance toward the north they could see the light of Cape Saint Matthew. They soon signaled, also, the little light on the shore at Bec-du-Raze, which proved that they were in their right course. A good breeze from the north-east accelerated the speed of the vessel, which rolled very little, although the sea was quite rough.

As the dinner-party reached the deck, one of the sailors approached the captain, and said: "Six knots and a quarter."

"In that case we shall not want any more coal until we arrive at Behring's Straits," answered the captain. After saying these words, he left the doctor and went down to his room. There he selected a large chart, which he spread out before him under a brilliant light, which was suspended from the ceiling. It was a map of the British Admiralty, and indicated all the details of the course which the "Alaska" intended to take. The shores, the islands, the sand-banks, the light-houses, revolving lights, and the most minute details were all clearly marked out. With such a chart and a compass it seemed as if even a child might be able to guide the largest ship through these perilous passes; and yet, a distinguished officer of the French Navy, Lieutenant Mage, who had explored the Niger, had been lost in these waters, with all his companions, and his vessel, the "Magician."

It had happened that Captain Marsilas had never before navigated in these waters. In fact, it was only the necessity of stopping at Brest which had brought him here now, otherwise he would have passed a long distance from shore. Therefore he was careful to study his chart attentively, in order to keep his proper course. It seemed a very easy matter, keeping on his left the Pointe-du-Van, the Bec-du-Raze, and the Island of Sein, the legendary abode of the nine Druidesses, and which was nearly always veiled by the spray of the roaring waters; he had only to run straight to the west and to the south to reach the open sea. The light on the island indicated clearly his position, and according to the chart, the island ended in rocky heights, bordered by the open sea, whose depth reached one hundred meters. The light on the island was a useful guide on a dark night, and he resolved to keep closer to it than he would have done in broad daylight. He therefore ascended to the deck, and told Erik to sail twenty-five degrees toward the southwest.

This order appeared to surprise the young lieutenant.

"To the south-west, did you say?" he asked in a respectful manner, believing that he had been mistaken.

"Yes, I said to the south-west!" repeated the commander, dryly: "Do you not like this route?"

"Since you ask me the question, captain, I must confess that I do not. I should have preferred running west for some time."

"To what purpose? we should only lose another night."

The commander spoke in a tone that did not permit of any contradiction, and Erik gave the order which he had received. After all the captain was an experienced seaman in whom they might have perfect confidence.

Slight as was the change in her course, it sufficed to modify sensibly the sailing of the vessel. The "Alaska" commenced to roll a great deal, and to dip her prow in the waves. The log indicated fourteen knots, and as the wind was increasing, Erik thought it prudent to take a couple of reefs.

The doctor and Mr. Bredejord both became a prey to seasickness, and descended to their cabins. The captain, who had for some time been pacing up and down the deck, soon followed their example.

He had hardly entered his own apartment when Erik stood before him.

"Captain," said the young man, "I have heard suspicious noises, like waves breaking over rocks. I feel conscientiously bound to tell you that in my opinion we are following a dangerous route."

"Certainly, sir, you are gifted with tenaciousness," cried the captain. "What danger can you fear when we have this light at least three good miles, if not four, distant from us?"

And he impatiently with his finger pointed out their position upon the chart, which he had kept spread out upon his table.

Erik followed the direction of his finger, and he saw clearly that the island was surrounded by very deep waters. Nothing could be more decisive and reassuring, in the eyes of a mariner. But still he felt sure that it was not an illusion, those noises which he had heard, and which certainly were made by waves breaking upon a rocky shore very close to them.

It was a strange case, and Erik hardly liked to acknowledge it to himself, but it did not seem to him that he could recognize in this profile of the coast which lay spread out before his eyes the dangerous spot which he remembered in the same geographical studies which he had pursued. But could he venture to oppose his dim impressions and vague remembrances against a chart of the British Admiralty? Erik dared not do it. These charts are made expressly to guard navigators against errors or any illusions of their memory. He therefore bowed respectfully to his chief and returned to his position on deck.

He had scarcely reached it when he heard this cry resounding through the vessel, "Breakers on the starboard!" followed almost immediately by a second shout of "Breakers on the larboard!"

There was a loud whistle and a clattering of many feet followed by a series of effective maneuvers. The "Alaska" slackened her course, and tried to back out. The captain made a rush up the stairs.

At this moment he heard a grating noise, then suddenly a terrible shock which shook the vessel from prow to stern. Then all was silent, and the "Alaska" remained motionless.

She was wedged in between two submarine rocks.

Commander Marsilas, his head bleeding from a fall, mounted the deck, where the greatest confusion reigned. The dismayed sailors made a rush for the boats. The waves dashed furiously over the rocks upon which the vessel had been shipwrecked. The distant light-houses, with their fixed lights, seemed to reproach the "Alaska" for having thrown herself into the dangers which it was their duty to point out. Erik tried vainly to penetrate through the gloom and discover the extent of the damage which the vessel had sustained.

"What is the matter?" cried the captain, still half-stunned by his fall.

"By sailing south-west, sir, according to your orders, we have run upon breakers," replied Erik.

Commander Marsilas did not say a word. What could he answer? He turned on his heel, and walked toward the staircase again.

Their situation was a tragical one, although they did not appear to be in any immediate peril. The vessel remained motionless between the rocks which seemed to hold her firmly, and their adventure appeared to be more sad than frightful. Erik had only one thought—the expedition was brought to a full stop—his hope of finding Patrick O'Donoghan was lost.

He had scarcely made his somewhat hasty reply to the captain, which had been dictated by this bitter disappointment, than he regretted having done so. He therefore left the deck to go in search of his superior officer with the generous intention of comforting him, if it were possible to do so. But the captain had disappeared, and three minutes had not elapsed when a detonation was heard.

Erik ran to his room. The door was fastened on the inside. He forced it open with a blow of his fist.

Commander Marsilas lay stretched out upon the carpet, with a revolver in his right hand, and a bullet wound in his forehead.

Seeing that the vessel was shipwrecked by his fault, he had blown his brains out. Death had been instantaneous. The doctor and Mr. Bredejord, who had run in after the young lieutenant, could only verify the sad fact.

But there was no time for vain regrets. Erik left to his two friends the care of lifting the body and laying it upon the couch. His duty compelled him to return to the deck, and attend to the safety of the crew and passengers.

As he passed the door of Mr. Malarius, the excellent man, who had been awakened by the stopping of the vessel, and also by the report of the pistol, opened his door and put out his white head, covered by his black silk night-cap. He had been sleeping ever since they left Brest, and was therefore ignorant of all that had occurred.

"Ah, well, what is it? Has anything happened?" he asked quietly.

"What has happened?" replied Erik. "My dear master, the 'Alaska' has been cast upon breakers, and the captain has killed himself!"

"Oh!" said Mr. Malarius, overcome with surprise. "Then, my dear child, adieu to our expedition!"

"That is another affair," said Erik. "I am not dead, and as long as a spark of life remains in me, I shall say, 'Go forward!'"

14

On the Rocks

The "Alaska" had been thrown upon the rocks with such violence that she remained perfectly motionless, and the situation did not appear to be immediately dangerous for her crew and passengers. The waves, encountering this unusual obstacle, beat over the deck, and covered everything with their spray; but the sea was not rough enough to make this state of affairs dangerous. If the weather did not change, day would break without any further disaster. Erik saw this at a glance. He had naturally taken command of the vessel, as he was the first officer. Having given orders to close the port-holes and scuttles carefully, and to throw tarred cloths over all openings, in case the sea should become rougher, he descended to the bottom of the hold, in company with the master carpenter. There he saw with great satisfaction that no water had entered. The exterior covering of the "Alaska" had protected her, and the precaution which they had taken against polar icebergs had proved very efficacious against the rocky coast; in fact the engine had stopped at once, being disarranged by the frightful shock, but it had produced no explosion, and they had, therefore, no vital damage to deplore. Erik resolved to wait for daybreak, and then disembark his passengers if it should prove necessary.

He, therefore, contented himself with firing a cannon to ask aid from the inhabitants of the Island of Sein, and with dispatching his small steam launch to L'Orient.

He said to himself, that at no place would they find the means of repairing their damages so promptly and well as at this great maritime arsenal of Western France.

Thus in this glooming hour when every one on board believed that their chances were irretrievably lost, he already began to feel hopeful, or rather he was one of those courageous souls who know no discouragement and never confess themselves vanquished.

"If we can only get the 'Alaska' off these rocks, everything may yet go well with us," he said.

But he was careful not to express this hope to the others, who would doubtless have considered it chimerical. He only told them when he returned from his visit to the hold that they were in no danger at present, and that there was plenty of time for them to receive aid.

Then he ordered a distribution of tea and rum to all the crew.

This sufficed to put these children of a larger growth in a good humor, and their little steam-boat was speedily launched.

Some rockets from the light-house of Sein soon announced that aid was coming to the assistance of the shipwrecked vessel. Red lights now became visible, and voices hailed them. They answered that they had been shipwrecked upon the rocks surrounding Sein.

It was a full hour before the boat could reach them. The breakers were so strong that the attempt was perilous. But at length six men succeeded in seizing a small cable, and hoisting themselves on board of the "Alaska."

They were six rude fishermen of Sein—strong, intrepid fellows—and it was not the first time they had gone to the assistance of shipwrecked mariners. They fully approved of the idea of sending to L'Orient for assistance, for their little port could not offer the necessary resources. It was agreed that two of them should depart in the little steamer with Mr. Hersebom and Otto, as soon as the moon arose above the horizon. While they were waiting for it to do so, they gave some account of the place where they were shipwrecked.

The rocks extend in a westerly direction for nine miles beyond the Island of Sein. They are divided into two parts, which are called the Pont du Sein and the Basse Froid.

The Pont du Sein is about four miles long, and a mile and a half wide. It is composed of a succession of high rocks, which form a chain above the waters. The Basse Froid extends beyond the Pont du Sein for five miles, and is two thirds of a mile wide; it consist of a great number of rocks of about an equal height, which can be seen at a great distance. The principal rocks are the Cornengen, Schomeur, Cornoc-ar-Goulet-Bas-ven, Madiou and Ar-men. These are the least dangerous, because they can be seen. The number and irregularity of their points under the water are not fully known, for the sea beats over them with extreme violence, the force of the current is very strong, and they are the scene of many shipwrecks. Light-houses have been erected on the Island of

Sein and at Bec-du-Raze, so that these rocks can be seen and avoided by vessels coming from the west, but they are very dangerous for vessels coming from the south. Unfortunately there is no rock or small island at the extreme end where a signal could be placed, and the turbulence of the waters will not permit a floating one to be placed there. Therefore it was resolved to build a light-house on the rock Ar-men, which is three miles from the extreme point. This work is so extremely difficult that although it was commenced in 1867, twelve years later, in 1879, it was only half built. They say that during the latter year it was only possible to work for eight hours, although the workmen were always ready to seize a favorable moment. The light-house therefore was not yet completed at the time when the "Alaska" met with her disaster. But this did not suffice to explain how, after leaving Brest, they had been run into such peril. Erik promised himself that he would solve this difficulty as soon as the little steam-boat had been dispatched for aid. This departure was easily effected, the moon having soon made its appearance. The young captain then appointed the night watch, and sent the rest of the crew to bed, then he descended to the captain's room.

Mr. Bredejord, Mr. Malarius, and the doctor were keeping watch beside the corpse. They arose as soon as they saw Erik.

"My poor child, what is the cause of this sad state of things? How did it happen?" asked the doctor.

"It is inexplicable," answered the young man, looking at the chart which lay open upon the table. "I felt instinctively that we were out of our route, and I said so; but in my estimation we are at least three miles from the light-house; and all the seamen agree with me," he added, designating a spot with his finger on the map—and you see no danger is indicated—no sand-banks or rocks. This coloring indicates deep water. It is inconceivable how the mistake can have occurred. We can not suppose that a chart of the British Admiralty can be at fault, for it is a region well known to mariners, as it has been minutely explored for centuries!"

"Is it not possible to make a mistake as to our position? Could not one light be mistaken for another?" asked Mr. Bredejord.

"That is scarcely possible in a voyage as short as ours has been since we left Brest," said Erik. "Remember that we have not lost, sight of land for a moment, and that we have been passing from one point to another. We can only suppose that one of the lights indicated on the chart has not been lighted or that some supplementary light has been added—in a word, we must imagine what is highly improbable. Our course has been so regular, the soundings have been so carefully made, that it seems impossible that we could have mistaken our route, and yet the fact remains that we are on the rocks, when we ought to have been some distance out to sea."

"But how is it going to end? That is what I want to know," cried the doctor.

"We shall soon see," answered Erik, "if the maritime authorities show any eagerness to come to our assistance. For the present the best thing that every one can do is to go quietly to bed, since we are as secure as if we were at anchor in some quiet bay."

The young commander did not add that it was his intention to keep watch while his friends slept.

Nevertheless this is what he did for the remainder of the night, sometimes promenading the deck and encouraging the men, sometimes descending for a few minutes to the saloon.

As day commenced to dawn he had the satisfaction of perceiving that the waves visibly receded, and if they continued to do so the "Alaska" would be left almost on dry rocks. This gave him hope of being able speedily to determine the extent of the damage which the vessel had received, and, in fact, toward seven o'clock they were able to proceed with this examination.

They found that three points of the rocks had pierced the "Alaska," and held her firmly on her rocky bed. The direction in which she lay, slightly inclined to the north, which was contrary to her course, showed that the commands given by Erik to back the vessel had saved her, and also rendered the shock, when she struck, less severe. The engine had been reversed some seconds before she touched, and she had been carried on the reef by the remainder of her previous speed, and by the force of the current. Doubtless but for this she would have gone to pieces. Besides, the waves having continued to break against her all night in the same direction, had helped to keep her in her place instead of fixing her more firmly on the rocks, which would have happened if the wind had changed. So, after all, there was a favorable view to take of the disaster. The question now was how to get the vessel off before the wind should change, and reverse these favorable conditions.

Erik resolved not to lose a moment. Immediately after breakfast he set all his men to work. He hoped that when the tow-boat should arrive, which he had sent for from L'Orient, it might be possible at high tide to disengage the "Alaska."

We can therefore imagine that the young captain waited impatiently for the first trace of smoke upon the horizon.

All turned out as he desired. The water remained calm and peaceful. Toward noon the boat arrived.

Erik, with his staff, received the mariners with due honors.

"But explain to me," said the captain of the tow-boat, "how you came to cast your vessel on these rocks after leaving Brest?"

"This chart will explain it," said Erik. "It does not point out any such danger."

The French officer examined the chart with curiosity at first, and then he looked stupefied.

"In fact the Basse-Froide is not marked down, nor the point of Sein," he cried. "What unparalleled negligence. Why, even the position of the light-house is not correctly marked. I am more and more surprised. This is a chart of the British Admiralty. I should say that some one has taken pleasure in making it as deceitful and perfidious as possible. Navigators of olden times frequently played such tricks upon their rivals. I should never have believed such traditions would be imitated in England."

"Are you sure that this is an English chart?" asked Mr. Bredejord. "For myself I suspect that the chart is the work of a rascal, and has been placed with criminal intentions among the charts of the 'Alaska.'"

"By Tudor Brown!" cried Erik, impetuously. "That evening when we dined with the authorities at Brest he entered the captain's room upon the pretense of examining the charts. Oh, the infamous wretch! This then is the reason that he did not come on board again!"

"It appears to be only too evident that he is the culprit," said Dr. Schwaryencrona. "But such a dastardly action betrays such an abyss of iniquity. What motive could he have for committing such a crime?"

"What was his motive in coming to Stockholm, expressly to tell you that Patrick O'Donoghan was dead?" answered Mr. Bredejord. "For what purpose did he subscribe twenty thousand kroners for the voyage of the 'Alaska,' when it was doubtful if she would ever make the journey? Why did he embark with us to leave us at Brest? I think we must be blind indeed if we do not see in these facts a chain of evidence as logical as it is frightful. What interest has Tudor Brown in all this? I do not know. But this interest must be very strong, very powerful, to induce him to have recourse to such means to prevent our journey; for I am convinced now that it was he who caused the accident which detained us at Brest, and it was he who led us upon these rocks, where he expected we would all lose our lives."

"It seems difficult, however, to believe that he could have foreseen the route that Captain Marsilas would choose!" objected Mr. Malarias.

"Why did he not indicate this route by altering the chart? After delaying us for three days, he felt certain that the captain would take the shortest way. The latter, believing that the waters were safe around Sein, was thrown upon the rocks."

"It is true," said Erik; "but the proof that the result of his maneuvers was uncertain lies in the fact that I insisted, before Captain Marsilas, that we ought still to keep to the west."

"But who knows whether he has not prepared other charts to lead us astray, in case this one failed to do so?" said Mr. Bredejord.

"That is easily determined," answered Erik, who went and brought all the charts and maps that were in the case.

The first one which they opened was that of Corunna, and at a glance the French officer pointed out two or three grave errors. The second was that of Cape Vincent. It was the same.

The third was that of Gibraltar. Here the errors were apparent to every eye. A more thorough examination would have been superfluous, as it was impossible to doubt any longer. If the "Alaska" had not been shipwrecked on the Island of Sein, this fate would surely have awaited her before she could have reached Malta.

A careful examination of the charts revealed the means which had been employed to effect these changes. They were undoubtedly English charts, but they had been partly effaced by some chemical process, and then retouched so as to indicate false routes among the true ones. They had been recolored so skillfully that only a very slight difference in the tints could be perceived after the most careful scrutiny.

But there was one circumstance which betrayed the criminal intentions with which they had been placed on board the "Alaska." All the charts belonging to the vessel bore the seal of the secretary of the Swedish navy. The forger had foreseen that they would not be examined too minutely, and had hoped that by following them they would all come to a watery grave.

These successive discoveries had produced consternation in the breasts of all who were present.

Erik was the first to break the silence which had succeeded the conversation.

"Poor Captain Marsilas!" he said, in a trembling voice, "he has suffered for us all. But since we have escaped almost by a miracle the fate which was prepared for us, let us run no more risks. The tide is rising, and it may be possible to draw the 'Alaska' off the rocks. If you are willing, gentlemen, we will go and commence operations without delay."

He spoke with simple authority and a modest dignity, with which the feeling of responsibility had already inspired him.

To see a young man of his age invested with the command of a ship under such circumstances, and for such a hazardous expedition, was certainly an unforeseen occurrence. But he felt that he was equal to the performance of all his duties. He knew that he could rely upon himself and upon his crew, and these thoughts transfigured him. The youth of yesterday was a man to-day. The spirit of a hero burned in his eyes. He rose superior to the calamity which had befallen them. His ability impressed all who approached him. Even the doctor and Mr. Bredejord submitted to him like the others.

The operation of preparing for their morning's work proved easier than they had hoped.

Lifted by the rising waters, the vessel only required a slight force to take her off the rocks. A few hours of hard work were sufficient to accomplish this, and the "Alaska" was once more afloat, strained indeed, and weighed down by the water which made its way into some of her compartments, and with her engine silent, but manageable.

All the crew, who were assembled on the deck, watched anxiously the result of these efforts, and a loud hurrah greeted the deliverance of the "Alaska."

The Frenchmen replied to this joyful cry with similar acclamations. It was now three o'clock in the afternoon. Above the horizon the beautiful February sun inundated the calm sparkling sea with floods of sunshine, which fell also on the rocks of the Basse-Froide, as if to efface all remembrance of the drama which had been enacted there the previous night.

That same evening the "Alaska" had been safely towed into the harbor of L'Orient.

The next day the French maritime authorities, with the utmost courtesy, authorized the necessary repairs to be made without delay. The damage which the vessel had sustained was not serious, but that of the machinery was more complicated, although not irremediable. Necessarily it would take some time to render her seaworthy, but nowhere in the world, as Erik had foreseen, could this be accomplished so speedily as at this port, which possessed such immense resources for naval construction. The house of Gainard, Norris & Co., undertook to make the repairs in three weeks. It was now the 23d of February; on the 16th of March they would be able to resume their voyage, and this time with good charts.

That would leave three months and a half for them to reach Behring's Strait by the end of June. It was not impossible to do this, although the time was very limited. Erik would not hear of abandoning the enterprise. He feared only one thing, and that was being compelled to do so. Therefore he refused to send to Stockholm a report of the shipwreck, and he would not make a formal complaint against the presumed author of the attempt to shipwreck them for fear of being delayed by legal proceedings, yet he had his fears that this might encourage Tudor Brown to throw some new obstacle in the way of the "Alaska." This is what Dr. Schwaryencrona and Mr. Bredejord asked each other as they were playing at whist with Mr. Malarius, in the little sitting-room of the hotel to which they had gone after arriving at L'Orient.

As for Mr. Bredejord, he had no doubts about the matter.

A rascal like Tudor Brown, if he knew of the failure of his scheme—and how could any one doubt that he was acquainted with this fact?—would not hesitate to renew the attempt.

To believe that they would ever succeed in reaching Behring's Strait was therefore more than self-delusion—it was foolishness. Mr. Bredejord did not know what steps Tudor Brown would take to prevent this, but he felt certain that he would find some means of doing so. Dr. Schwaryencrona was inclined to the same opinion, and even Mr. Malarius could not think of anything very reassuring to say. The games of whist were therefore not very lively, and the long strolls that the three friends took were not very gay.

Their principal occupation was to watch the erection of the mausoleum which they were building for poor Captain Marsilas, whose funeral obsequies had been attended by the entire population of L'Orient.

The sight of this funeral monument was not calculated to raise the spirits of the survivors of the "Alaska."

But when they joined Erik again their hopes revived. His resolution was unshakable, his activity untiring, he was so bent upon overcoming all obstacles, so certain of success, that it was impossible for them to express, or even to preserve, less heroic sentiments.

They had a new proof of the malignity of Tudor Brown, and that he still was pursuing them.

On the 14th of March, Erik saw that the work upon the machinery was almost finished. They only had to adjust the pumps, and that was to be done the next day.

But in the night, between the 14th and 15th, the body of the pump disappeared from the workshop of the Messrs. Gainard, Norris & Co.

It was impossible to find it.

How had it been taken away—who had done it?

After investigation they were unable to discover.

However, it would take ten days more to replace it, and that would make it the 25th of March before the "Alaska" could leave L'Orient.

It was a singular fact, but this incident affected Erik's spirits more than the shipwreck had done. He saw in it a sure sign of a persistent desire to prevent the voyage of the "Alaska."

But these efforts only redoubled his ardor, and he determined that nothing should be wanting on his part to bring the expedition to a successful termination.

These ten days of delay were almost exclusively occupied by him in considering the question in all its aspects. The more he studied, the more he became convinced that he could not reach Behring's Straits in three months, for they had suffered a detention of forty days since they had left Stockholm, and to persist would only be to court failure and perhaps some irremediable disaster.

This conclusion did not stop him, but it only led him to think that some modification of their original plans was indispensable.

He took care, however, to say nothing, rightly judging that secrecy was the first condition of victory. He contented himself with watching more closely than ever the work of repairing the vessel.

But his companions thought that they perceived that he was less eager to set out.

They therefore concluded that he saw that the enterprise was impracticable, which they had also believed for some time.

But they were mistaken.

On the 25th of March, at midday, the repairs of the "Alaska" were completed, and she was once more afloat in the harbor of L'Orient.

15

The Shortest Route

Night was closing in when Erik summoned his three friends and counselors to hold a serious consultation.

"I have reflected a great deal," he said to them, "upon the circumstances which have made our voyage memorable since we left Stockholm. I have been forced to arrive at one conclusion, which is that we must expect to meet with obstacles or accidents during our voyage. Perhaps they may befall us at Gibraltar or at Malta. If we are not destroyed, it appears to me certain that we shall be delayed. In that case we can not reach Behring's Straits during the summer, which is the only season when it is practicable to navigate the polar sea!"

"That is also the conclusion which I formed some time ago," declared Mr. Bredejord: "but I kept it to myself, as I did not wish to dampen your hopes, my dear boy. But I am sure that we must give up the idea of reaching Behring's Strait in three months!"

"That is also my opinion," said the doctor.

Mr. Malarius on his part indicated by a motion of his head that he agreed with them all.

"Well!" said Erik, "having settled that point, what line of conduct now remains for us to adopt?"

"There is one right course which it is our duty to take," answered Mr. Bredejord, "it is to renounce an enterprise which we see clearly is impracticable and return to Stockholm. You understand this fact, my child, and I congratulate you upon being able to look the situation calmly in the face!"

"You pay me a compliment which I can not accept," said Erik smiling, "for I do not merit it. No—I have no thoughts of abandoning the expedition, for I am far from regarding it as impracticable. I only think that it is best for us all to baffle the machinations of that scoundrel who is lying in wait for us, and the first thing to do is to change our route."

"Such a change would only complicate our difficulties," replied the doctor, "since we have adopted the shortest one. If it would be difficult to reach Behring's Straits by the Mediterranean and the Suez Canal, it would be impossible by the Cape of Good Hope, or Cape Horn, for either of these routes would necessarily take five or six months."

"There is another way which would shorten our voyage, instead of lengthening it, and where we would be sure not to meet Tudor Brown," said Erik.

"Another way?" answered Dr. Schwaryencrona; "upon my word I do not know of any unless you are thinking of the way of Panama. But it is not yet practicable for vessels, and it will not be yet for several years."

"I am not thinking of Panama, nor of Cape Horn, nor of the Cape of Good Hope," answered the young captain of the "Alaska." "The route I propose is the only one by which we can reach Behring's Strait in three months: it is to go by way of the Arctic Ocean, the north-west passage."

Then seeing that his friends were stupefied by this unexpected announcement, Erik proceeded to develop his plans.

"The north-west passage now is no longer what it was formerly, frightful to navigators—it is intermittent, since it is only open for eight or ten weeks every year, but it is now well known, marked out upon excellent charts, and frequented by hundreds of whaling-vessels. It is rarely taken by any vessel going from the Atlantic to the Pacific Ocean, I must admit. Most of them who enter it from either side only traverse it partially. It might even happen, if circumstances were not favorable, that we might find the passage closed, or that it might not be open at the precise time when we desired to enter it. It is a risk that one must take. But I think there are many reasons to make us hopeful of success if we take this route, whilst as far as I can see there is none, if we take any of the others. This being the state of affairs, I think it is our duty—a duty which we owe to those who have fitted out the expedition—to take the shortest way of reaching Behring's Strait. An ordinary vessel equipped for navigating tropical waters might hesitate before deciding upon such a course, but with a vessel like the 'Alaska' fitted out especially for polar navigation, we need not hesitate. For my part I declare that I will not return to Stockholm before having attempted to find Nordenskiold."

Erik's reasoning was so sound that nobody tried to contradict it.

What objections could the doctor, Mr. Bredejord, and Mr. Malarius raise?

They saw the difficulties which beset the new plan. But it was possible that these difficulties might not prove insurmountable, whilst, if they pursued any other course, they must abandon all hopes of success. Besides, they did not hesitate to agree with Erik that it would be more glorious, in any case, to make the attempt, than to return to Stockholm and acknowledge themselves conquered.

"I see but one serious objection, for my part," said Dr. Schwaryencrona, after he had remained for a few moments lost in reflection. "It is the difficulty of procuring coal in the arctic regions. For without coal, adieu to the possibility of making the north-west passage, and of profiting by the time, often very short, during which it is practicable."

"I have foreseen this difficulty, which is in fact the only one," answered Erik, "and I do not think it is insurmountable. In place of going to Malta or Gibraltar, where we might doubtless expect new machinations on the part of Tudor Brown, I propose that we go to London; from there I can send, by transatlantic cable, a dispatch to a house in Montreal, to send without delay a boat loaded with coal to wait for us in Baffin's Bay, and to a house in San Francisco to send to Behring's Strait. We have the necessary funds at our disposal, and, besides, we will not require as much as we would have done if we had gone by the way of Asia, for our new route is a much shorter one. It is useless for us to reach Baffin's Bay before the end of May, and we can not hope to reach Behring's Strait before the end of June. Our correspondents in Montreal and San Francisco will therefore have plenty of time to execute our orders, which will be covered by funds deposited with bankers in London. This accomplished, we shall only have to find out whether the north-west passage is practicable, and that evidently depends upon ourselves. But, if we find the passage closed, at least we shall have the consolation of knowing that we have neglected nothing that could have insured our success."

"It is evident!" said Mr. Malarius, "that your arguments are unanswerable!"

"Gently, gently," said Mr. Bredejord. "Do not let us go too fast. I have another objection. Do you think, my dear Erik, that the 'Alaska' can pass unnoticed through these waters? No, it is not possible. The newspapers would mention our arrival. The telegraph companies would make it known. Tudor Brown would know it. He would know that we had changed our plans. What would prevent him from altering his? Do you think, for example, that it would be very difficult to prevent our boat with coals from reaching us?—and without it we could do nothing!"

"That is true," answered Erik, "and it proves that we must think of everything. We must not go to London. We must put into Lisbon as if we were *en route* to Gibraltar and Suez. Then one of us must go *incognito* to Madrid, and without explaining why, or for whom it is intended, must open telegraphic communications with Montreal and San Francisco, to order the supply of coal. The crews of these boats must not know for whom the coal is destined, but remain at designated points at the disposition of a captain who will carry an order to them previously agreed upon!"

"A perfect arrangement. It will be almost impossible for Tudor Brown to track us."

"You mean to track me, for I hope that you do not think of accompanying me to these arctic regions," said Erik.

"Indeed that is my intention!" answered the doctor. "It shall not be said that that rascal, Tudor Brown, made me turn back!"

"Nor me either," cried Mr. Bredejord and Mr. Malarius together.

The young captain tried to combat this resolution, and explained to his friends the dangers and monotony of the voyage which they proposed to take with him. But he could not alter their decision. The perils which they had already encountered, made them feel it a duty to keep together; for the only way of rendering such a voyage acceptable to them all was not to separate. Every precaution had been taken to protect the persons on board the "Alaska" from suffering unduly from cold; and neither Swedes nor Norwegians fear frost.

Erik was obliged to yield to their wishes, only stipulating that their change of route should not be made known to the crew of the vessel.

The first part of their voyage was quickly accomplished.

On the 2d of April the "Alaska" reached Lisbon. Before the newspapers had given notice of their arrival, Mr. Bredejord had gone to Madrid, and by means of a banking-house opened communications with two large firms, one in Montreal and one in San Francisco.

He had arranged to have two boat-loads of coal sent to two designated points, and had given the sign by which Erik was to make himself known.

This sign was the words found upon him when he was discovered floating, tied to the buoy of the "Cynthia," "Semper idem."

Finally these arrangements having all been happily concluded, on the 9th of April Mr. Bredejord returned to Lisbon, and the "Alaska" resumed her voyage.

On the twenty-fifth of the same month, having crossed the Atlantic and reached Montreal, where they took in coal, and Erik was assured that his orders had been punctually fulfilled, they left the waters of the St. Lawrence and Straits of Belle Isle, which separate Labrador from Newfoundland. On the 10th of May they reached the coast of Greenland and found the vessel with their coal, it having arrived before them.

Erik knew very well that at this early date it would be useless to attempt to force his way through the Arctic Ocean, which was still firmly frozen over the largest part of his route. But he counted upon obtaining on these shores, which were much frequented by whaling-vessels, precise information as to the best charts, and he was not mistaken. He was also able to buy, although at a high price, a dozen dogs, who with Kaas could draw their sledges if necessary.

Among the Danish stations on the coast of Greenland, he found Godhaven, which is only a poor village, and is used as a depot by dealers in oil and the furs of the country. At this time of the year the cold is not more severe than at Stockholm or Noroe. But Erik and his friends beheld with surprise the great difference between the two countries, both situated at the same distance from the pole. Godhaven is in precisely the same latitude as Bergen. But whilst the southern port of Norway is in April covered with green forests and fruit trees, and even cultivated vines trained upon trellises above green meadows, Greenland is still in May covered with ice and snow, without a tree to enliven the monotony. The shape of the Norwegian coast, deeply indented by forests and sheltered by chains of islands, which contribute almost as much as the warmth of the Gulf Stream to raise the temperature of the country. Greenland, on the contrary, has a low regular coast and receives the full shock of the cold blasts from the pole, consequently she is enveloped almost to the middle of the island by fields of ice several feet in thickness.

They spent fifteen days in the harbor and then the "Alaska" mounted Davis' Straits, and keeping along the coast of Greenland, gained the polar sea.

On the 28th of May for the first time they encountered floating ice in 70 15' of north latitude, with a temperature two degrees below zero. These first icebergs, it is true, were in a crumbling condition, rapidly breaking up into small fragments. But soon they became more dense, and frequently they had to break their way through them. Navigation, although difficult, was not as yet dangerous. By a thousand signs they perceived, however, that they were in a new world. All objects at a little distance appeared to be colorless, and almost without form; the eye could find no place to repose in this perpetually changing horizon, which every minute assumed a new aspect.

"Who can describe," says an eye-witness, "these melancholy surroundings, the roaring of the waves beating beneath the floating ice, the singular noise made by the snow as it falls suddenly into the abyss of waters? Who can imagine the beauty of the cascades which gush out on all sides, the sea of foam produced by their fall, the fright of the sea-birds who, having fallen asleep on a pyramid of ice, suddenly find their resting-place overturned and themselves obliged to fly to some other spot? And in the morning, when the sun bursts through the fog, at first only a little of the blue sky is visible, but it gradually widens, until the view is only limited by the horizon."

These spectacles, presented by the polar sea, Erik and his friends were able to contemplate at their leisure as they left the coast of Greenland, to which they had kept close until they had reached Uppernavik. Then they sailed westward across Baffin's Bay. Here navigation became more difficult, for this sea is the ordinary course of the polar icebergs which are drawn in by the innumerable currents which traverse it. Sometimes they found their course checked by insurmountable barriers of ice, which it was impossible to break, and therefore they were compelled to turn aside. The "Alaska" was obliged continually to break her way through immense fields of ice. Sometimes a tempest of snow assailed them which covered the deck and the masts with a thick coat. Sometimes they were assailed by ice dashed over them by the wind, which threatened to sink the vessel by its weight. Sometimes they found themselves in a sort of lake, surrounded on all sides by fields of ice apparently firm and impassable, and from which they had great difficulty to extricate themselves and gain the open sea. Then they had to exercise great vigilance to escape some enormous iceberg sailing down from the north with incredible swiftness, a frightful mass, which could have crushed the "Alaska" like a walnut. But a greater danger still was the submarine ice, which could injure her and act like a battering-ram.

The "Alaska" lost her two large boats. One must experience the dangers which polar navigation presents at every moment to have any just appreciation of them.

After one or two weeks of such experience the most intrepid crew become exhausted, and repose is necessary for them.

Sometimes, although surrounded by all these dangers, they made rapid progress; at others they made scarcely any; but at length, on the 11th of June, they came in sight of land again, and cast anchor at the entrance to Lancaster Sound.

Erik had expected to be obliged to wait some days before being able to enter the sound; but, to his surprise and joy, he found it open, at least at the entrance. He entered resolutely, but only to find the next day his passage impeded by ice, which held them prisoners for three days; but, thanks to the violent currents which sweep through this Arctic canal, he at last was able to free his vessel and continue his route as the whalers of Godhaven had told him he would be able to do.

On the seventeenth he arrived at Barrow's Straits, and made all the speed he could; but on the nineteenth, as he was about to enter Melville Sound, he was again blocked in by the ice.

At first he patiently accepted the situation, waiting for it to break up; but day succeeded to day and still this did not happen.

There were, however, many sources of amusement open to the voyagers. They were near the coast and supplied with everything that could render their life comfortable in that latitude. They could take sleigh-rides and see in the distance the whales enjoying their diversions. The summer solstice was approaching. Since the fifteenth the occupants of the "Alaska" had beheld a new and astonishing spectacle, even for Norwegians and the natives of southern Sweden; it was the sun at midnight touching the horizon without disappearing and then mounting again in the sky. In these high latitudes and desolate coasts the star of day describes in twenty-four hours a complete circle in space. The light, it is true, is pale and languishing, objects lose their perfect shape, and all nature has a shadowy appearance. One realizes profoundly how far he is removed from the world, and how near he is to the pole. The cold, however, was not extreme. The temperature did not fall more than four or five degrees below zero, and the air was sometimes so mild that they could hardly believe that they were in the center of the arctic zone.

But those novel surrounding were not sufficient to satisfy Erik, or make him lose sight of the supreme object which had brought them there. He had not come to herbalize like Mr. Malarius, who returned every evening more and more delighted with his explorations, both of the country and of its unknown plants, which he added to his collection; nor to enjoy with Dr. Schwaryencrona and Mr. Bredejord the novelty of the sights which nature offered to them in these polar regions. He wanted to find Nordenskiold and Patrick O'Donoghan—to fulfill a sacred duty while he discovered, perhaps, the secret of his birth. This was why he sought untiringly to break the circle of ice which hemmed them in. He made excursions with his sleigh and on his snow-shoes, reconnoitered in every direction for ten days, but it was all in vain. At the west, as well as the north and east, the banks of ice remained firm.

It was the 20th of June, and they were still far from the Siberian Sea.

Must he confess himself vanquished? Erik could not make up his mind to do this. Repeated soundings had revealed that under the ice there was a swift current running toward Franklin's Strait, that is to say toward the south; he told himself that some effort might suffice to break up the ice, and he resolved to attempt it.

For the length of seven marine miles he had hollowed in the ice a series of chambers, and in each of them was placed a kilogramme of dynamite. These were connected by a copper wire inclosed in gutta percha.

On the 30th of June, at eight o'clock in the morning, Erik from the deck of the "Alaska" pressed the button of the electrical machine, and a formidable explosion took place. The field of ice shook and trembled, and clouds of frightened sea-birds hovered around uttering discordant cries. When silence was restored, a long black train cut into innumerable fissures met their anxious gaze. The explosion of the terrible agent had broken up the ice field. There was, so to speak, a moment of hesitation, and then the ice acted as if it had only been waiting for some signal to move. Cracking in all parts it yielded to the action of the current, and they beheld here and there whole continents, as it were, gradually moving away from them. Some portions, however, were more slow to move; they seemed to be protesting against such violence. The next day the passage was clear, and the "Alaska" rekindled her fires.

Erik and his dynamite had done what it would probably have taken the pale arctic sun a month longer to accomplish.

On the 2d of July, the expedition arrived at Banks' Straits; on the fourth, she issued from the Arctic Sea properly speaking. From this time the route was open notwithstanding icebergs, fogs, and snow-storms. On the twelfth, the "Alaska" doubled Ice Cape; on the thirteenth, Cape Lisburne, and on the fourteenth she entered the Gulf of Kotzebue to the north of Behring's Straits and found there, according to instructions, the boat loaded with coal which had been sent from San Francisco.

Thus in two months and sixteen days they had accomplished the programme arranged by Erik before they left the coast of France.

The "Alaska" had hardly ceased to move, when Erik rushed into a small boat and hurried off to accost the officer who had charge of the boat loaded with coal.

"*Semper idem!*" said he, as he approached.

"Lisbon!" answered the Yankee.

"How long have you been waiting here for me?"

"Five weeks—we left San Francisco one month after the arrival of your dispatch."

"Have you heard any news of Nordenskiold?"

"At San Francisco they had not received any reliable information about him. But since I have been here I have spoken to several captains of whaling-vessels, who said that they had heard from the natives of Serdze-Kamen that an European vessel had been frozen in by the ice for nine or ten months; they thought it was the 'Vega.'"

"Indeed!" said Erik, with a joy which we can easily understand. "And do you believe that it has not yet succeeded in getting through the straits?"

"I am sure of it—not a vessel has passed us for the last five weeks, which I have not seen and spoken to."

"God be praised—our troubles will not be without recompense, if we succeed in finding Nordenskiold."

"You will not be the first who has done so!" said the Yankee, with an ironical smile—"an American yacht has preceded you. It passed here three days ago, and like you was inquiring for Nordenskiold."

"An American yacht?" repeated Erik, half stupefied.

"Yes—the 'Albatross,' Captain Tudor Brown, from Vancouver's Island. I told him what I had heard, and he immediately started for Cape Serdze-Kamen."

16

From Serdze-Kamen to Ljakow

Tudor Brown had evidently heard of the change in the route of the "Alaska." He had reached Behring's Straits before them. But by what means? It seemed almost supernatural, but still the fact remained that he had done so.

Erik was greatly depressed by this information, but he concealed his feelings from his friends. He hurried on the work of transporting the coal, and set out again without losing a moment.

Serdze-Kamen is a long Asiatic-promontory situated nearly a hundred miles to the west of Behring's Straits, and whaling-vessels from the Pacific visit it every year.

The "Alaska" reached there after a voyage of twenty-four hours, and soon in the bay of Koljutschin behind a wall of ice, they discovered the masts of the "Vega," which had been frozen in for nine months.

The barrier which held Nordenskiold captive was not more than ten kilometers in size. After passing around it, the "Alaska" came to anchor in a little creek, where she would be sheltered from the northerly winds. Then Erik with his three friends made their way overland to the establishment which the "Vega" had made upon the Siberian coast to pass this long winter, and which a column of smoke pointed out to them.

This coast of the Bay of Koljutschin consists of a low and slightly undulating plain. There are no trees, only some dwarf willows, marine grasses and lichens. Summer had already brought forth some plants, which Mr. Malarius recognized as a species which was very common in Norway.

The encampment of the "Vega" consisted of a large store-house for their eatables, which had been made by the orders of Nordenskiold, in case the pressure of the ice should destroy his ship, which so frequently

JULES VERNE & ANDRE LAURIE

happens on these dangerous coasts. It was a touching fact that the poor population, although always half starved, and to whom this depot represented incalculable wealth in the shape of food, had respected it, although it was but poorly guarded. The huts of skin of these Tschoutskes were grouped here and there around the station. The most imposing structure was the "Tintinjaranga," or ice-house, which they had especially arranged to use for a magnetic observatory, and where all the necessary apparatus had been placed. It had been built of blocks of ice delicately tinted and cemented together with snow; the roof of planks was covered with cloth.

The voyagers of the "Alaska" were cordially welcomed by the young astronomer, whom they found at the time of their arrival holding a consultation with the man in charge of the store-house. He offered with hearty goodwill to take them on board the "Vega" by the path which had been cut in the ice in order to keep open the means of communication between the vessel and the land, and a rope attached to stones served as a guide on dark nights. As they walked, he related to them their adventures since they had been unable to send home any dispatches.

After leaving the mouth of the Lena, Nordenskiold had directed his course toward the islands of New Siberia, which he wished to explore, but finding it almost impossible to approach them, on account of the ice which surrounded them, and the shallowness of the water in that vicinity, he abandoned the idea, and resumed his course toward the east. The "Vega" encountered no great difficulties until the 10th of September, but about that time a continuance of fogs, and freezing nights, compelled her to slacken her speed, besides the darkness necessitated frequented stoppages. It was therefore the 27th of September before she reached Cape Serdze-Kamen. They cast her anchor on a bank of ice, hoping to be able the next day to make the few miles which separated her from Behring's Straits and the free waters of the Pacific. But a north wind set in during the night, and heaped around the vessel great masses of ice. The "Vega" found herself a prisoner for the winter at the time when she had almost accomplished her work.

"It was a great disappointment to us, as you can imagine!" said the young astronomer, "but we soon rallied our forces, and determined to profit by the delay as much as possible, by making scientific investigations. We made the acquaintance of the 'Tschoutskes' of the neighborhood, whom no traveler has hitherto known well, and we have made a vocabulary of their language, and also gathered together a collection of their arms and utensils. The naturalists of the 'Vega' have also been diligent, and added many new arctic plants to their collection. Lastly, the end of the expedition has been accomplished, since we have doubled Cape Tchelynskin, and traversed the distance between it and the mouth of the Yenisei and of the Lena. Henceforth the north-east passage must become a recognized fact. It would have been more agreeable for us, if we could have effected it in two months, as we so nearly succeeded in doing. But provided we are not blocked in much longer, as the present indications lead us to hope, we will not have much to complain of, and we shall be able to return with the satisfaction of knowing that we have accomplished a useful work."

While listening to their guide with deep interest, the travelers were pursuing their way. They were now near enough to the "Vega" to see that her deck was covered over with a large canvas, and that her sides were protected by lofty masses of snow, and that her smoke-stacks had been carefully preserved from contact with the ice.

The immediate approach to the vessel was still more strange; she was not, as one would have expected, completely incrusted in a bed of ice, but she was suspended, as it were, in a labyrinth of lakes, islands, and canals, between which they had been obliged to throw bridges formed of planks.

"The explanation is very simple," said the young astronomer, in reply to a question from Erik. "All vessels that pass some months surrounded by ice form around them a bed of refuse, consisting principally of coal ashes. This is heavier than snow, and when a thaw begins, the bed around the vessel assumes the aspect which you behold."

The crew of the "Vega," in arctic clothing, with two or three officers, had already seen the visitors whom the astronomer was bringing with him. Their joy was great when they saluted them in Swedish, and when they beheld among them the well-known and popular physiognomy of Dr. Schwaryencrona.

Neither Nordenskiold nor Captain Palender were on board. They had gone upon a geological excursion into the interior of the country, and expected to be absent five or six days. This was a disappointment to the travelers, who had naturally hoped when they found the "Vega" to present their congratulations to the great explorer.

But this was not their only disappointment.[1]

They had hardly entered the officer's room, when Erik and his friends were informed that three days before the "Vega" had been visited by an American yacht, or rather by its owner, Mr. Tudor Brown. This

1   They returned sooner, for on the 18th of July the ice broke up, and after 264 days of captivity the "Vega" resumed her voyage. On the 20th of July she issued from Behring's Straits and set out for Yokohama.

gentleman had brought them news of the world beyond their settlement, which was very acceptable, they being confined to the limited neighborhood of the Bay of Koljutschin. He told them what had happened in Europe since their departure—the anxiety that Sweden and indeed all civilized nations felt about their fate, and that the "Alaska" had been sent to search for them. Mr. Tudor Brown came from Vancouver's Island, in the Pacific, and his yacht had been waiting there for him for three months.

"But," exclaimed a young doctor, attached to the expedition, "he told us that he had at first embarked with you, and only left you at Brest, because he doubted whether you would be able to bring the enterprise to a successful termination!"

"He had excellent reasons for doubting it," replied Erik, coolly, but not without a secret tremor.

"His yacht was at Valparaiso and he telegraphed for her to wait for him at Victoria, on the coast of Vancouver," continued the doctor; "then he took the steamer from Liverpool to New York, and the railroad to the Pacific. This explains how he was able to reach here before you."

"Did he tell you why he came?" asked Mr. Bredejord.

"He came to help us, if we stood in need of assistance, and also to inquire about a strange enough personage, whom I had incidentally mentioned in my correspondence, and in whom Mr. Tudor Brown seemed to take a great interest."

The four visitors exchanged glances.

"Patrick O'Donoghan—was not that the name?" asked Erik.

"Precisely—or at least it is the name which is tattooed on his body, although he pretends it is not his own, but that of a friend. He calls himself Johnny Bowles."

"May I ask if this man is still here?"

"He left us ten months ago. We had at first believed that he might prove useful to us by acting as interpreter between us and the natives of this coast, on account of his apparent knowledge of their language; but we soon discovered that his acquaintance with it was very superficial—confined, in fact, to a few words. Besides, until we came here, we were unable to hold any communications with the natives. This Johnny Bowles, or Patrick O'Donoghan, was lazy, drunken, and undisciplined. His presence on board would only have occasioned trouble for us. We therefore acceded without regret to his request to be landed on the large Island of Ljakow, as we were following the southern coast."

"What! did he go there? But this island is uninhabited!" cried Erik.

"Entirely; but what attracted the man appeared to be the fact that its shores are literally covered by bones, and consequently by fossil ivory. He had conceived the plan of establishing himself there, and of collecting, during the summer months, all the ivory that he could find; then when, in winter, the arm of the sea which connects Ljakow with the continent should be frozen over, to transport in a sleigh this treasure to the Siberian coast, in order to sell it to the Russian traders, who come every year in search of the products of the country."

"Did you tell these facts to Mr. Tudor Brown?" asked Erik.

"Assuredly, he came far enough to seek for them," replied the young doctor, unaware of the deep personal interest that the commander of the "Alaska" took in the answers to the questions which he addressed to him.

The conversation then became more general. They spoke of the comparative facility with which Nordenskiold had carried out his programme. He had not met with any serious difficulties, and consequently the discovery of the new route would be an advantage to the commerce of the world. "Not," said the officer of the "Vega," "that this path was ever destined to be much frequented, but the voyage of the 'Vega' would prove to the maritime nations of the Atlantic and Pacific that it was possible to hold direct communication with Siberia by water. And nowhere would these nations, notwithstanding the vulgar opinions, find a field as vast and rich."

"Is it not strange," observed Mr. Bredejord, "that they have failed completely during the last three centuries in this attempt that you have now accomplished without difficulty?"

"The singularity is only apparent," answered one of the officers. "We have profited by the experience of our predecessors, an experience often only acquired at the cost of their lives. Professor Nordenskiold has been preparing himself for this supreme effort during the last twenty years, in which he has made eight arctic expeditions. He has patiently studied the problem in all its aspects, and finally succeeded in solving it. Then we have had what our predecessors lacked, a steam vessel especially equipped for this voyage. This has enabled us to accomplish in two months a voyage that it would have taken a sailing vessel two years to do. We have also constantly been able not only to choose, but also to seek out, the most accessible route. We have fled from floating ice and been able to profit by the winds and tides. And still we have been overtaken by winter. How much more difficult it would have been for a mariner who was compelled to wait for favorable winds, and see the summer passing in the meantime."

In such conversation they passed the afternoon, and after accepting their invitation and dining on board the "Vega," they carried back with them to supper on board the "Alaska" all the officers who could be spared from duty. They mutually gave each other all the information and news in their power. Erik took care to inform himself exactly of the route followed by the "Vega," in order to utilize it for his own profit. After exchanging many good wishes and with the heartfelt desire that they would all soon return in safety to their country, they separated.

The next day at dawn Erik had the "Alaska" steering for the island of Ljakow. As for the "Vega" she had to wait until the breaking up of the ice would permit her to reach the Pacific.

The first part of Erik's task was now accomplished. He had found Nordenskiold. The second still remained to be fulfilled: to find Patrick O'Donoghan, and see if he could persuade him to disclose his secret. That this secret was an important one they were now all willing to admit, or Tudor Brown would never have committed such a dastardly crime to prevent them from becoming acquainted with it.

Would they be able to reach the Island of Ljakow before him?

It was hardly probable, for he was three days in advance of them: never mind—he would make the attempt.

The "Albatross" might lose her way, or meet with some unforeseen obstacles. As long as there was even a probability of success Erik determined to take the chances.

The weather was now mild and agreeable. Light fogs indicated an open sea, and a speedy breaking of the ice along the Siberian coast where the "Vega" had been held prisoner so long. Summer was advancing, and the "Alaska" could reasonably count upon at least ten weeks of favorable weather. The experience which they had acquired amongst the American ice had its value and would render this new enterprise comparatively easy. Lastly the north-east passage was the most direct way to return to Sweden, and besides the deep personal interest which induced Erik to take it, he had a truly scientific desire to accomplish in a reverse route the task which Nordenskiold had fulfilled. If he had succeeded, why should he not be able to do so?—this would be proving practically the experiment of the great navigator.

The wind favored the "Alaska." For ten days it blew almost constantly from the south-east, and enabled them to make from nine to ten knots at least without burning any coal. This was a precious advantage, and besides the wind drove the floating ice toward the north and rendered navigation much less difficult. During these ten days they met with very little floating ice.

On the eleventh day, it is true they had a tempestuous snow storm followed by dense fogs which sensibly retarded the progress of the "Alaska." But on the 29th of July the sun appeared in all its brilliancy, and on the morning of the 2d of August they came in sight of the Island of Ljakow.

Erik gave orders immediately to sail around it in order to see if the "Albatross" was not hidden in some of its creeks. Having done this they cast anchor in a sandy bottom about three miles from the southern shore. Then he embarked in his boat accompanied by his three friends and six of his sailors. Half an hour later they had reached the island.

Erik had not chosen the southern coast of the island to anchor his vessel without a reason. He had said to himself that Patrick O'Donoghan might have told the truth when he had stated that his object was to collect ivory; but if it was his intention to leave the island at the first opportunity which afforded, he would be sure to establish himself upon a spot where he would have a good view of the sea. He would undoubtedly choose some elevated place, and one as near as possible to the Siberian coast. Besides the necessity of sheltering himself against the polar winds would lead him to establish himself upon the southern coast of the island.

Erik did not pretend that his conclusions were necessarily incontrovertible, but he thought that, in any case, they would suffer no inconvenience from adopting them as the basis of a systematic exploration of the place. The results fully justified his expectations. The travelers had not walked along the shore for an hour, when they perceived on a height, perfectly sheltered by a chain of hills, facing the south, an object which could only be a human habitation. To their extreme surprise this little cottage, which was of a cubical form, was perfectly white, as if it had been covered with plaster. It only lacked green shutters to perfectly resemble a country home near Marseilles, or an American cottage.

After they had climbed the height and approached near to it, they discovered a solution of the mystery. The cottage was not plastered, it was simply built of enormous bones skillfully arranged, which gave it its white color. Strange as the materials were, they were forced to admit that the idea of utilizing them was a natural one; besides there was nothing else available on the island where vegetation was most meagre; but the whole place, even the neighboring hills were covered with bones, which Dr. Schwaryencrona recognized as the remains of wild beasts.

17

At Last

The door of the cottage was open. The visitors entered, and saw at a glance that the single room of which it consisted was empty, although it had been recently occupied. Upon the hearth, which was built of three large stones, lay some extinguished embers upon which the light ashes still lingered, although the lightest breeze would have been sufficient to carry them away. The bed, consisting of a wooden frame, from which was suspended a sailor's hammock, still bore the impress of a human figure.

This hammock, that Erik examined immediately, bore the stamp of the "Vega." On a sort of table formed from the shoulder-blade of some animal and supported by four thigh bones, lay some crumbs of ship's biscuit, a pewter goblet, and a wooden spoon of Swedish workmanship.

They could not doubt that they were in the dwelling-place of Patrick O'Donoghan, and according to all appearances he had only left it a short time ago. Had he quitted the island, or had he only gone to take a walk? The only thing they could do was to make a thorough exploration of the island.

Around the habitation excavations bore witness to the fact that a great amount of hard work had been done; on a sort of plateau that formed the summit of the hill, a great quantity of ivory had been piled up, and indicated the nature of the work. The voyagers perceived that all the skeletons of elephants and other animals had been despoiled of their ivory, and they arrived at the conclusion that the natives of the Siberian coast had been aware, long before the visit of Patrick O'Donoghan, of the treasure which was to be found upon the island, and had come and carried off large quantities of it. The Irishman, therefore, had not found the quantity of ivory upon the surface of the ground which he had expected, and had been compelled to make excavations and exhume it.

The quality of this ivory, which had been buried probably for a long time, appeared to the travelers to be of a very inferior quality.

Now the young doctor of the "Vega" had told them, as had the proprietor of the Red Anchor, in Brooklyn, that laziness was one of the distinguishing characteristics of Patrick O'Donoghan. It therefore seemed to them very improbable that he would be resigned to follow such a laborious and unremunerative life. They therefore felt sure that he would embrace the first opportunity to leave the Island of Ljakow. The only hope that still remained of finding him there was that which the examination of his cabin had furnished them.

A path descended to the shore, opposite to that by which our explorers had climbed up. They followed it, and soon reached the bottom, where the melting snows had formed a sort of little lake, separated from the sea by a wall of rocks. The path followed the shores of this quiet water, and going around the cliff they found a natural harbor.

They saw a sleigh abandoned on the land, and also traces of a recent fire; Erik examined the shore carefully, but could find no traces of any recent embarkation. He was returning to his companions, when he perceived at the foot of a shrub a red object, which he picked up immediately. It was one of those tin boxes painted outside with carmine which had contained that preserved beef commonly called "endaubage," and which all vessels carry among their provisions. It was not so great a prize, since the captain of the "Vega" had supplied Patrick O'Donoghan with food. But what struck Erik as significant, was the fact that there was printed on the empty box the name of Martinez Domingo, Valparaiso.

"Tudor Brown has been here," he cried. "They told us on board the 'Vega' that his vessel was at Valparaiso when he telegraphed them to wait for him at Vancouver. Besides, this box from Chili could not have been brought here by the 'Vega,' for it is evidently quite fresh. It can not be three days, perhaps not twenty-four hours since it has been opened!"

Dr. Schwaryencrona and Mr. Bredejord shook their heads, as if they hesitated to accept Erik's conclusions, when turning the box in his hands, he descried written in pencil the word "Albatross," which had doubtless been done by the person who had furnished the vessel with the beef. He pointed it out to his friends.

"Tudor Brown has been here," he repeated, "and why should he come except to carry off Patrick O'Donoghan. Let us go, it is evident they embarked at this creek. His men, while they were waiting for him, have taken breakfast around this fire. He has carried off the Irishman, either willingly or unwillingly. I am as certain of it as if I saw them embark."

Notwithstanding this firm belief, Erik carefully explored the neighborhood, to assure himself that Patrick O'Donoghan was no longer there. An hour's walk convinced him that the island was uninhabited. There was no trace of a path, nor the least vestige of a human being. On all sides valleys extended as far as his sight could reach, without even a bird to animate its solitude. And above all, the gigantic bones which they beheld lying around in every direction, gave them a feeling of disgust; it seemed as if an army of animals had taken refuge in this solitary island only to die there.

"Let us go!" said Dr. Schwaryencrona. "There is no use in making a more complete search of the island; we have seen sufficient to assure us that Patrick O'Donoghan would not require much urging to induce him to leave this place!"

Four hours later they were again on board of the "Alaska," and continuing their journey.

Erik did not hide the fact that his hopes had received a severe check. Tudor Brown had been ahead of him, he had succeeded in reaching the island first, and doubtless had carried off Patrick O'Donoghan. It was therefore hardly probable that they would succeed in finding him again. A man capable of displaying such ability in his fiendish attack upon the "Alaska," and who could adopt such energetic measures to carry off the Irishman from such a place, would assuredly exert himself to the utmost to prevent them from ever coming in contact with him. The world is large, and its waters were open to the "Albatross." Who could tell to what point of the compass Patrick O'Donoghan and his secret would be carried?

This is what the captain of the "Alaska" said to himself, as he walked the deck of his vessel, after giving orders to steer to the westward. And to these doleful thoughts was added a feeling of remorse that he had permitted his friends to share the dangers and fatigue of his useless expedition. It was doubly useless, since Tudor Brown had found Nordenskiold before the "Alaska," and also preceded them to the Island of Ljakow. They must then return to Stockholm, if they ever succeeded in reaching it, without having accomplished one of the objects of the expedition. It was indeed a great disappointment. But at least their returning in a contrary direction to the "Vega" would prove the feasibility of the northeast passage. At any risk he must reach Cape Tchelynskin, and double it from east to west. At any risk he must return to Sweden by way of the Sea of Kara. It was this redoubtable Cape Tchelynskin, formerly considered impassable, that the "Alaska" crowded on steam to reach. They did not follow the exact route of the "Vega," for Erik had no occasion to descend the Siberian coast.

Leaving to starboard the islands of Stolbovvi and Semenoffski, which they sighted on the 4th of August, they sailed due west, following closely the 76th degree of latitude, and made such good speed that in eight days they had made 35 degrees of longitude, from the 140th to the 105th degree east of Greenwich. It is true that they had to burn a great deal of coal to accomplish this, for the "Alaska" had had contrary winds almost all the time. But Erik thought rightly that everything was subordinate to the necessity of making their way out of these dangerous passes as speedily as possible. If they could once reach the mouth of the Yenisei, they could always procure the necessary fuel.

On the 14th of August, at midday they were unable to make a solar observation on account of a thick fog, which covered the whole sky. But they knew that they were approaching a great Asiatic promontory, therefore Erik advanced with extreme caution, while at the same time he had the speed of the vessel slackened.

Toward night he gave orders to have the vessel stopped. These precautions were not useless. The following morning at daylight they made soundings and found that they were in only thirty fathoms of water, and an hour afterward they came in sight of land; and the "Alaska" soon reached a bay in which she could cast anchor. They resolved to wait until the fog dispersed before going on land, but as the 15th and 16th of August passed without bringing about this desired result, Erik determined to start accompanied by Mr. Bredejord, Mr. Malarius, and the doctor. A short examination showed them that the "Alaska" was at the extreme north of the two points of Cape Tchelynskin; on two sides the land lay low toward the sea, but it rose gradually toward the south, and they perceived that it was about two or three hundred feet in height. No snow or ice was to be seen in any direction, except along the borders of the sea where there was a little band, such as is commonly seen in all arctic regions. The clayey soil was covered with abundant vegetation, consisting of mossy grasses and lichens. The coast was enlivened by great numbers of wild geese and walruses. A white bear displayed himself on top of a rock. If it had not been for the fog which cast a gray mantle over everything, the general aspect of this famous Cape Tchelynskin was not particularly disagreeable; certainly there was nothing to justify the name of Cape Severe, which it had borne for three centuries.

As they advanced to the extreme point at the west of the bay, the travelers perceived a sort of monument that crowned a height, and natu-

JULES VERNE & ANDRE LAURIE

rally pressed forward to visit it. They saw, as they approached, that it was a sort of "cairn," or mass of stones supporting a wooden column made out of a post. This column bore two inscriptions; the first read as follows:

"On the 19th of August, 1878, the 'Vega' left the Atlantic to double Cape Tchelynskin, en route for Behring's Straits."

The second read:

On the 12th of August, 1879, the 'Albatross,' coming from Behring's Straits, doubled Cape Tchelynskin, en route for the Atlantic."

Once again Tudor Brown had preceded the "Alaska." It was now the 16th of August.

He had written this inscription only four days previously.

In Erik's eyes it appeared cruel and ironical; it seemed to him to say: "I will defeat you at every turn. All your efforts will be useless. Nordenskiold has solved the problem. Tudor Brown, the counter proof."

As for himself he would return humiliated and ashamed, without having demonstrated, found or proved anything. He was going without adding a single word to the inscriptions on the column. But Dr. Schwaryencrona would not listen to him, and taking out his knife from his pocket he wrote on the bottom of the post these words:

"On the 16th of August, 1879, the 'Alaska' left Stockholm, and came here across the Atlantic and the Siberian Sea, and has doubled Cape Tchelynskin, en route to accomplish the first circumpolar periplus."

There is a strange power in words. This simple phrase recalled to Erik what a geographical feat he was in hopes of accomplishing, and without his being conscious of it restored him to good humor. It was true, after all, that the "Alaska" would be the first vessel to accomplish this voyage. Other navigators before him had sailed through the arctic-American seas, and accomplished the northwest passage. Nordenskiold and Tudor Brown had doubled Cape Tchelynskin; but no person had as yet gone from one to the other, completely around the pole, completing the three hundred and sixty degrees.

This prospect restored every one's ardor, and they were eager to depart. Erik thought it best, however, to wait until the next day and see if the fog would lift; but fogs appeared to be the chronic malady of Cape Tchelynskin, and when next morning the sun rose without dissipating it, he gave orders to hoist the anchor.

Leaving to the south the Gulf of Taymis—which is also the name of the great Siberian peninsula of which Cape Tchelynskin forms the extreme point—the "Alaska," directing her course westward, sailed un-interruptedly during the day and night of the 17th of August.

On the eighteenth, at day-break, the fog disappeared at last and the atmosphere was pure and enlivened by the sunshine. By midday they had rounded the point, and immediately descried a distant sail to the south-west.

The presence of a sailing-vessel in these unfrequented seas was too extraordinary a phenomenon not to attract special attention. Erik, with his glass in his hand, ascended to the lookout and examined the vessel carefully for a long time. It appeared to lie low in the water, was rigged like a schooner and had a smoke-stack, although he could not perceive any smoke. When he descended from the bridge the young captain said to the doctor:

"It looks exactly like the 'Albatross!'" Then he gave orders to put on all steam possible. In less than a quarter of an hour he saw that they were gaining on the vessel, whose appointments they were now able to discern with the naked eye. They could see that the breeze had slack-ened, and that her course was at right angles with that of the "Alaska."

But suddenly a change took place in the distant vessel; Clouds of smoke issued from her smoke-stack, and formed behind her a long black cloud. She was now going by steam and in the same direction as the "Alaska."

"There is now no doubt of it. It is the 'Albatross,'" said Erik.

He gave orders to the engineer to increase the speed of the "Alaska," if possible. They were then making fourteen knots, and in a quarter of an hour they were making sixteen knots. The vessel that they were pursuing had not been able to attain a like rate of speed, for the "Alaska" continued to gain upon her. In thirty minutes they were near enough to her to distinguish all her men who were maneuvering her. At last they could see the moldings and letters forming her name, "Albatross."

Erik gave orders to hoist the Swedish flag. The "Albatross" immedi-ately hoisted the stars and stripes of the United States of America.

In a few minutes the two vessels were only separated by a few hun-dred yards. Then the captain of the "Alaska" took his speaking-trumpet and hailed the vessel in English:

"Ship ahoy! I wish to speak with your captain!"

In a few moments some one made his appearance on the bridge of the "Albatross." It was Tudor Brown.

"I am the proprietor and captain of this yacht," he said. "What do you want?"

"I wish to know whether Patrick O'Donoghan is on board!'"

"Patrick O'Donoghan is on board and can speak for himself," answered Tudor Brown.

He made a sign, and a man joined him on the bridge.

"This is Patrick O'Donoghan," said Tudor Brown. "What do you want with him?"

Erik was desirous of this interview so long, he had come so far in search of this man, that when he found himself unexpectedly in his presence and recognized him by his red hair and broken nose, he was at first taken aback and scarcely knew what to say to him. But gathering his ideas together, he at last made an attempt.

"I have been wishing to talk to you confidentially for several years," he said. "I have been seeking for you, and it was to find you that I came into these seas. Will you come on board of my vessel?"

"I do not know you, and I am very well satisfied to stay where I am," answered the man.

"But I know you. I have heard through Mr. Bowles that you were on board when the 'Cynthia' was wrecked, and that you had spoken to him about the infant who was tied to a buoy. I am that infant, and it is about this matter that I wish you to give me all the information in your power."

"You must question somebody else, for I am not in the humor to give any."

"Do you wish me to suppose that the information is not to your credit?"

"You can think what you like; it is a matter of perfect indifference to me," said the man.

Erik resolved to betray no irritation.

"It would be better for you to tell me what I wish to know of your own free will than to be compelled to do so before a court of justice," he said, coolly.

"A court of justice! They will have to catch me first," answered the other, mockingly.

Here Tudor Brown interposed.

"You see it is not my fault if you have not obtained the information that you desired," said he to Erik. "The best thing is now for us both to resume our course and go where we desire."

"Why should we each go our way?" answered the young captain. "Would it not be better for us to keep together until we reach some civilized country where we can settle these matters."

"I have no business with you, and do not want any one's company," answered Tudor Brown, moving as if he was about to leave the bridge.

Erik stopped him by a sign.

"Proprietor of the 'Albatross,'" he said, "I bear a regular commission from my government, and am besides an officer of the maritime police. I therefore ask you to show me your papers immediately!"

Tudor Brown did not make the slightest answer, but descended the bridge with the man whom he had called. Erik waited a couple of minutes, and then he spoke again:

"Commander of the 'Albatross,' I accuse you of having attempted to shipwreck my vessel on the rocks of Sein, and I now summon you to come and answer this accusation before a marine tribunal. If you refuse to answer this summons it will be my duty to compel you to do so!"

"Try it if you like," cried Tudor Brown, and gave orders to resume his journey.

During this colloquy his vessel had insensibly tacked, and now stood at right angles with the "Alaska." Suddenly the wheel commenced to revolve and beat the water which boiled and foamed around it. A prolonged whistle was heard, and the "Albatross" carrying all the steam she could raise sped over the waters in the direction of the North Pole.

Two minutes later, the "Alaska" was rushing after her.

18

Cannon-Balls

At the same time that he gave orders to pursue the "Albatross," Erik also desired his men to get the cannon in readiness. The operation took some time, and when they had everything in order the enemy was beyond their reach. Doubtless they had taken advantage of the time occupied by their stoppage to increase their fires, and they were two or three miles ahead. This was not too great a distance for a Gatling gun to carry, but the rolling and speed of the two vessels made it probable that they would miss her; and they thought it better to wait, hoping that the "Alaska" would gain upon the enemy. It soon became evident, however, that the two vessels were equally matched, for the distance between them remained about the same for several hours.

They were obliged to burn an enormous amount of coal—an article which was becoming very scarce on board the "Alaska"—and this would be a heavy loss if they could not succeed in overtaking the "Albatross" before night set in. Erik did not think it right to do this without consulting his crew. He therefore mounted the bridge, and frankly explained to them the position in which he was placed.

"My friends," he said, "you know that I am anxious to seize and deliver up to justice this rascal who attempted to shipwreck our vessel on the rocks of Sein. But we have hardly coal enough left to last us for six days. Any deviation from our route will compel us to finish our voyage under sail, which may make it very long and toilsome for all of us, and may even cause us to fail in our undertaking. On the other hand, the 'Albatross' counts upon being able to get away from us during the night. To prevent this we must not slacken our speed for a moment, and we must keep her within the range of our electric light. I feel sure, however, that we will eventually overtake her, but it may take us some time to do so. I did not feel willing to continue this pursuit without laying the facts plainly before you, and asking you if you were willing to risk the dangers which may arise for us."

The men consulted together in a low tone, and then commissioned Mr. Hersebom to speak for them:

"We are of opinion that it is the duty of the 'Alaska' to capture this rascal at any sacrifice!" he said, quietly.

"Very well, then, we will do our best to accomplish it," answered Erik.

When he found that he had the confidence of his crew, he did not spare fuel, and in spite of the desperate efforts of Tudor Brown, he could not increase the distance between them. The sun had scarcely set when the electric light of the "Alaska" was brought to bear unpityingly upon the "Albatross," and continued in this position during the night. At daybreak the distance between them was still the same, and they were flying toward the pole. At midday they made a solar observation, and found that they were in 78, 21', 14" of latitude north, by 90 of longitude east.

Floating ice, which they had not encountered for ten or fifteen days, now became very frequent. It was necessary to ward it off, as they had been compelled to do in Baffin's Bay. Erik, feeling sure that they would soon reach fields of ice, was careful to steer obliquely to the right of the "Albatross" so as to bar the way toward the east if she should attempt to change her course, finding her path toward the north obstructed. His foresight was soon rewarded, for in two hours a lofty barrier of ice casts its profile on the horizon. The American yacht immediately steered toward the west, leaving the ice two or three miles on its starboard. The "Alaska" immediately imitated this maneuver, but so obliquely to the left of the "Albatross" as to cut her off if she attempted to sail to the south.

The chase became very exciting. Feeling sure of the course which the "Albatross" would be compelled to take, the "Alaska" tried to push her more toward the ice. The yacht's course becomes more and more wavering, every moment they made some change, at one time steering north at another west. Erik, mounted aloft, watched every movement she made, and thwarted her attempts to escape by appropriate maneuvers. Suddenly she stopped short, swung round and faced the "Alaska." A long white line which was apparent extending westward told the reason of this change. The "Albatross" found herself so close to the ice-banks that she had no recourse but to turn and face them.

The young captain of the "Alaska" had scarcely time to descend, before some missile whistled past his head. The "Albatross" was armed, and relied upon being able to defend herself.

"I prefer that it should be so, and that he should fire the first shot," said Erik, as he gave orders to return it.

His first attack was not more successful than that of Tudor Brown—for it fell short two or three hundred yards. But the combat was now begun, and the firing became regular. An American projectile cut the large sail yards of the "Alaska," and it fell upon the deck killing two men. A small bomb from the Swedish vessel fell upon the bridge of the "Albatross," and must have made great havoc. Then other projectiles skillfully thrown lodged in various parts of the vessel.

They had been constantly approaching each other, when suddenly a distant rumbling mingled with the roar of artillery, and the crews raising their heads saw that the sky was very black in the east.

Was a storm with its accompanying fog and blinding snow, coming to interpose between the "Albatross" and the "Alaska," to permit Tudor Brown to escape?

This Erik wished to prevent at any price. He resolved to attempt to board her. Arming his men with sabers, cutlasses, and hatchets, he crowded on all the steam the vessel could carry and rushed toward the "Albatross."

Tudor Brown tried to prevent this. He retreated toward the banks of ice, firing a shot from his cannon every five minutes. But his field of action had now become too limited; between the ice and the "Alaska" he saw that he was lost unless he made a bold attempt to regain the open sea. He attempted this after a few feigned maneuvers to deceive his adversary.

Erik let him do it. Then at the precise moment when the "Albatross" tried to pass the "Alaska," she made a gaping hole in the side of the yacht which stopped her instantly, and rendered her almost unmanageable; then she fell quickly behind and prepared to renew the assault. But the weather, which had become more and more menacing, did not give him time to do this.

The tempest was upon them. A fierce wind from the south-east, accompanied by blinding clouds of snow, which not only raised the waves to a prodigious height, but dashed against the two vessels immense masses of floating ice. It seemed as if they were attacked at all points at once. Erik realized his situation, and saw that he had not a minute to lose in escaping, unless he wished to be hemmed in perhaps permanently. He steered due east, struggling against the wind, the snow, and the dashing ice.

But he was soon obliged to confess that his efforts were fruitless. The tempest raged with such violence that neither the engine of the "Alaska" nor her steel buttress were of much use. Not only did the vessel advance very slowly, but at times she seemed to be fairly driven backward. The snow was so thick that it obscured the sky, blinded the crew, and covered the bridge a foot in depth. The ice driven against the "Alaska" by the fierce wind increased and barred their progress, so that at length they were glad to retreat toward the banks, in the hope of finding some little haven where they could remain until the storm passed over.

The American yacht had disappeared, and after the blow it had received from the "Alaska" they almost doubted if it would be able to resist the tornado.

Their own situation was so perilous that they could only think of their own safety, for every moment it grew worse.

There is nothing more frightful than those arctic tempests, in which all the primitive forces of nature seem to be awakened in order to give the navigator a specimen of the cataclysms of the glacial period. The darkness was profound although it was only five o'clock in the afternoon. The engine had stopped, and they were unable to light their electric light. To the raging of the storm was added the roars of thunder and the tumult made by the floating blocks of ice dashing against each other. The ice-banks were continually breaking with a noise like the roar of a cannon.

The "Alaska" was soon surrounded by ice. The little harbor in which she had taken refuge was soon completely filled with it, and it commenced to press upon and dash against her sides until she began to crack, and they feared every moment that she would go to pieces.

Erik resolved not to succumb to the storm without a combat with it, and he set the crew to work arranging heavy beams around the vessel so as to weaken the pressure as much as possible, and distribute it over a wider surface. But, although this protected the vessel, it led to an unforeseen result which threatened to be fatal.

The vessel, instead of being suddenly crushed, was lifted out of the water by every movement of the ice, and then fell back again on it with the force of a trip-hammer. At any moment after one of these frightful falls they might be broken up, crushed, buried. To ward off this danger there was only one resource, and this was to re-enforce their barrier by heaping up the drift ice and snow around the vessel to protect her as well as they could.

Everybody set to work with ardor. It was a touching spectacle to see this little handful of men taxing their pygmy muscles to resist the forces of nature—trying with anchors, chains, and planks to fill up the fissures made in the ice and to cover them with snow, so that there might be a uniformity of motion among the mass. After four or five hours of almost superhuman exertions, and when their strength was exhausted, they were in no less danger, for the storm had increased.

Erik held a consultation with his officers, and it was decided that they should make a depot on the ice-field for their food and ammunition in case the "Alaska" should be unable to resist the powerful shocks to which she was being subjected. At the first moment of danger every man had received provisions enough for eight days, with precise instructions in case of disaster, besides being ordered to keep his gun in his belt even while he was working. The operation of transporting twenty tons of provisions was not easy of accomplishment, but at last it was done and the food was placed about two hundred yards from the ship under a covering of tarred canvas, which was soon covered by the snow with a thick white mantle.

This precaution, having been taken, everybody felt more comfortable as to the result of a shipwreck, and the crew assembled to recruit their strength with a supper supplemented with tea and rum.

Suddenly, in the midst of supper, a more violent shock than any that had as yet agitated the vessel, split the bed of ice and snow around the "Alaska." She was lifted up in the stern with a terrible noise, and then it appeared as if she were plunging head-foremost into an abyss. There was a panic, and every one rushed on deck. Some of the men thought that the moment had come to take refuge on the ice, and without waiting for the signal of the officers they commenced clambering over the bulwarks.

Four or five of these unfortunate ones managed to leap on a snow-bank. Two others were caught between the masses of floating ice and the beams of the starboard, as the "Alaska" righted herself.

Their cries of pain and the noise of their crushed bones were lost in the storm. There was a lull, and the vessel remained motionless. The lesson which the sailors had been taught was a tragical one. Erik made use of it to enforce on the crew the necessity of each man's retaining his presence of mind, and of waiting for positive orders on all occasions.

"You must understand," he said to his men, "that to leave the ship is a supreme measure, to which we must have recourse only at the last extremity. All our efforts ought to be directed toward saving the 'Alaska.' Deprived of her, our situation will be a very precarious one on the ice. It is only in case of our vessel becoming uninhabitable that we must desert it. In any case such a movement should be made in an orderly manner to avoid disasters. I therefore expect that you will return quietly to your supper, and leave to your superior officers the task of determining what is best to do!"

The firmness with which he spoke had the effect of reassuring the most timid, and they all descended again. Erik then called Mr. Herse-bom and asked him to untie his good dog Kaas, and follow him without making any noise.

"We will go on the field of ice," he said, "and seek for the fugitives and make them return to their duty, which will be better for them than wandering about."

The poor devils were huddled together on the ice, ashamed of their escapade, and at the first summons were only too glad to take the path toward the "Alaska."

Erik and Mr. Hersebom having seen them safely on board, walked as far as their depot of provisions, thinking that another sailor might have taken refuge there. They went all around it but saw no one.

"I have been asking myself the last few moments," said Erik, "if it would not be better to prevent another panic by landing part of the crew?"

"It might be better perhaps," answered the fisherman. "But would not the men who remained on board feel jealous and become demoral-ized by this measure?"

"That is true," said Erik. "It would be wiser to occupy them up to the last moment in struggling against the tempest, and it is in fact the only chance we have of saving the ship. But since we are on the ice we may as well take advantage of it, and explore it a little. I confess all these crack-ings and detonations inspire me with some doubt as to its solidity!"

Erik and his adopted father had not gone more than three hundred feet from their depot of provisions before they were stopped short by a gigantic crevasse which lay open at their feet. To cross it would have re-quired long poles, with which they had neglected to supply themselves. They were therefore compelled to walk beside it obliquely toward the west, in order to see how far it reached.

They found that this crevasse extended for a long distance, so long that after they had walked for half an hour they could not see the end of it. Feeling more secure about the extent of this field of ice upon which they had established their depot of provisions, they turned to retreat their steps.

After they had walked over about half of the distance a new vibra-tion occurred, followed by detonations and tumultuous heavings of ice. They were not greatly disturbed by this, but increased their speed, being anxious to discover whether this shock had had done the "Alaska" any mischief.

The depot was soon reached, then the little haven that sheltered the vessel.

Erik and Mr. Hersebom rubbed their eyes, and asked each other whether they were dreaming, for the "Alaska" was no longer there.

Their first thought was that she had been swallowed up by the waters. It was only too natural that they should think this after such an evening as they had just passed.

But immediately they were struck by the fact that no *debris* was visible, and that the little harbor had assumed a new aspect since their departure. The drift ice which the tempest had piled up around the "Alaska" had been broken up, and much of it had drifted away. At the same time Mr. Hersebom mentioned a fact which had not struck him while they were hurrying along, and this was that the wind had changed and was now blowing from the west.

Was it not possible that the storm had carried away the floating ice in which the "Alaska" had become embedded. Yes, evidently it was possible; but it remained for them to discover whether this supposition was true. Without delaying a moment, Erik proceeded to reconnoiter, followed by Mr. Hersebom.

They walked for a long time. Everywhere the drift was floating freely, the waves came and went, but the whole aspect of things around them looked strange and different.

At length Erik stopped. Now he understood what had befallen them. He took Mr. Hersebom's hand and pressed it with both his own.

"Father," said he, in a grave voice, "you are one of those to whom I can only speak the truth. Well, the fact is that this ice-field has split; it has broken away from that which surrounded the 'Alaska,' and we are on an island of ice hundreds of yards long, and carried along by the waters, and at the mercy of the storm."

19

Gunshots

About two o'clock in the morning Erik and Mr. Hersebom, exhausted with fatigue, laid down side by side between two casks, under the canvas that protected their provisions. Kaas, also, was close to them and kept them warm with his thick fur. They were not long in falling asleep. When they awoke the sun was already high in the heavens, the sky was blue and the sea calm. The immense bank of ice upon which they were floating appeared to be motionless, its movement was so gentle and regular. But along the two edges of it which were nearest to them enormous icebergs were being carried along with frightful rapidity. These gigantic crystals reflected like a prism the solar rays, and they were the most marvelous that Erik had ever beheld.

Mr. Hersebom also, although but little inclined in general, and especially in his present situation, to admire the splendor of Nature in the arctic regions, could not help being impressed with them.

"How beautiful this would look were we on a good ship!" he said, sighing.

"Bah!" answered Erik, with his usual good humor. "On board a ship one must be thinking only how to avoid the icebergs so as not to be crushed to pieces, whilst on this island of ice we have none of these miseries to worry us."

As this was evidently the view of an optimist, Mr. Hersebom answered with a sad smile. But Erik was determined to take a cheerful view of things.

"Is it not an extraordinary piece of good luck that we have this depot of provisions?" he said. "Our case would, indeed, be a desperate one if we were deprived of everything; but, with twenty casks of biscuits, preserved meats, and, above all, our guns and cartridges, what have we to fear? At the most, we will only have to remain some weeks without seeing any land that we can reach. You see, dear father, that we have happened upon this adventure in the same manner as the crew of the 'Hansa.'"

"Of the 'Hansa'?" asked Mr. Hersebom, with curiosity.

"Yes, a vessel that set out in 1869 for the arctic seas. Part of her crew were left, as we are, on a floating field of ice, while they were occupied in transporting some provisions and coal. The brave men accommodated themselves as well as they could to this new life, and after floating for six mouths and a half over a distance of several thousand leagues, ended by landing in the arctic regions of North America."

"May we be as fortunate!" said Mr. Hersebom, with a sigh. "But it would be well I think for us to eat something."

"That is also my opinion!" said Erik. "A biscuit and a slice of beef would be very acceptable."

Mr. Hersebom opened two casks to take out what they required for their breakfast, and as soon as his arrangements were completed they did ample justice to the provisions.

"Was the raft of the crew of the 'Hansa' as large as ours?" asked the old fisherman, after ten minutes conscientiously devoted to repairing his strength.

"I think not—ours is considerably larger. The 'Hansa's' became gradually much smaller, so that the unfortunate shipwrecked men were at last compelled to abandon it, for the waves began to dash over them. Fortunately they had a large boat which enabled them, when their island was no longer habitable, to reach another. They did this several times before they at last reached the main-land."

"Ah, I see!" said Mr. Hersebom, "they had a boat—but we have not. Unless we embark in an empty hogshead I do not see how we can ever leave this island of ice."

"We shall see about it when the time comes!" answered Erik. "At the present moment I think the best thing that we can do is to make a thorough exploration of our domain."

He arose, as did Mr. Hersebom, and they commenced climbing a hill of ice and snow—a hummock is the technical name—in order to obtain a general idea of their island.

They found it from one end to the other lying and floating insensibly upon the polar ocean. But it was very difficult to form a correct estimate either of its size or shape; for a great number of hummocks intercepted their view on all sides. They resolved, however, to walk to the extremity of it. As far as they could judge from the position of the sun, that end of the island which extended toward the west had been detached from the mass of which it had formerly been a part, and was now turning to the north. They therefore supposed that their ice raft was being carried toward the south by the influence of the tide and breeze, and the fact that they no longer saw any trace of the long barriers of ice, which are very extensive in the 78, fully corroborated this hypothesis.

Their island was entirely covered with snow, and upon this snow they saw distinctly here and there at a distance some black spots, which Mr. Hersebom immediately recognized as "ongionks," that is to say, a species of walrus of great size. These walruses doubtless inhabited the caverns and crevasses in the ice, and believing themselves perfectly secure from any attack, were basking in the sunshine.

It took Erik and Mr. Hersebom more than an hour to walk to the extreme end of their island. They had followed closely the eastern side, because that permitted them to explore at the same time both their raft and the sea. Suddenly Kaas, who ran ahead of them, put to flight some of the walruses which they had seen in the distance. They ran toward the border of the field of ice in order to throw themselves into the water. Nothing would have been more easy than to have killed a number of them. But what would have been the use of their doing so, since they could not make a fire to roast their delicate flesh? Erik was occupied about other matters. He carefully examined the ice-field, and found that it was far from being homogeneous. Numerous crevasses and fissures, which seemed to extend in many cases for a long distance, made him fear that a slight shock might divide it into several fragments. It was true that these fragments might in all probability be of considerable size; but the possibility of such an accident made them realize the necessity of keeping as close as possible to their depot of provisions, unless they wished to be deprived of them. Erik resolved to examine carefully their whole domain, and to make his abode on the most massive portion; the one that seemed capable of offering the greatest resistance. He also determined to transport to this spot their depot of provisions.

It was with this resolve that Mr. Hersebom and Erik continued their exploration of the western coast, after resting a few minutes at the northerly point. They were now following that portion of the ice-field where they had attacked the American yacht.

Kaas ran on before them, seeming to enjoy the freshness of the air, and being in his true element on this carpet of snow, which doubtless reminded him of the plains of Greenland.

Suddenly Erik saw him sniff the air and then dart forward like an arrow, and stop barking beside some dark object, which was partially hidden by a mass of ice.

"Another walrus, I suppose!" he said, hurrying forward.

It was not a walrus which lay extended on the snow, and which had so excited Kaas. It was a man, insensible, and covered with blood, whose clothing of skins was assuredly not the dress worn by any seamen of the "Alaska." It reminded Erik of the clothing worn by the man who had passed the winter on the "Vega." He raised the head of the man; it was covered with thick red hair, and it was remarkable that his nose was crushed in like that of a negro.

Erik asked himself whether he was the sport of some illusion.

He opened the man's waistcoat, and bared his chest. It was perhaps as much to ascertain whether his heart still beat as to seek for his name.

He found his name tattooed in blue, on a rudely designed escutcheon. "Patrick O'Donoghan, 'Cynthia,'" and his heart still beat. The man was not dead. He had a large wound in his head, another in his shoulder, and on his chest a contusion, which greatly interfered with his respiration.

"He must be carried to our place of shelter, and restored to life," said Erik, to Mr. Hersebom.

And then he added in a low tone as if he was afraid of being overheard.

"It is he, father, whom we have been seeking for such a long time without being able to find him—Patrick O'Donoghan—and see he is almost unable to breathe."

The thought that the secret of his life was known to this bloody object upon which death already appeared to have set his seal, kindled a gloomy flame in Erik's eyes. His adopted father divined his thoughts, and could not help shrugging his shoulders—he seemed to say:

"Of what use would it be to discover it now. The knowledge of all the secrets in the world would be useless to us."

He, however, took the body by the limbs, while Erik lifted him under the arms, and loaded with this burden they resumed their walk.

The motion made the wounded man open his eyes. Soon the pain caused by his wounds was so great that he began to moan and utter confused cries, among which they distinguished the English word "drink!"

They were still some distance from their depot of provisions. Erik, however, stopped and propped the unfortunate man against a hummock, and then put his leathern bottle to his lips.

It was nearly empty, but the mouthful of strong liquor that Patrick O'Donoghan swallowed seemed to restore him to life. He looked around him, heaved a deep sigh and then said:

"Where is Mr. Jones?"

"We found you alone on the ice," answered Erik. "Had you been there long?"

"I do not know!" answered the wounded man, with difficulty. "Give me something more to drink." He swallowed a second mouthful and then he recovered sufficiently to be able to speak.

"When the tempest overtook us the yacht sunk," he explained. "Some of the crew had time to throw themselves into the boats, the rest perished. At the first moment of peril Mr. Jones made a sign for me to go with him into a life-boat, which was suspended in the stern of the yacht and that every one else disdained on account of its small dimensions, but which proved to be safe, as it was impossible to sink it. It is the only one which reached the ice island—all the others were upset before they reached it. We were terribly wounded by the drift ice which the waves threw into our boat, but at length we were able to draw ourselves beyond their reach and wait for the dawn of day. This morning Mr. Jones left me to go and see if he could kill a walrus, or some sea-bird, in order that we might have something to eat. I have not seen him since!"

"Is Mr. Jones one of the officers of the 'Albatross'?" asked Erik.

"He is the owner and captain of her!" answered O'Donoghan, in a tone which seemed to express surprise at the question.

"Then Mr. Tudor Brown is not the captain of the 'Albatross'?"

"I don't know," said the wounded man, hesitatingly, seeming to ask himself whether he had been too confidential in speaking as freely as he had done.

Erik did not think it wise to insist on this point. He had too many other questions to ask.

"You see," he said to the Irishman, as he seated himself on the snow beside him, "you refused the other day to come on board of my ship and talk with me, and your refusal has occasioned many disasters. But now that we have met again, let us profit by this opportunity to talk seriously and like rational men. You see you are here on a floating ice-bank, without food, and seriously wounded, incapable by your own efforts of escaping the most cruel death. My adopted father and myself have all that you need, food, fire-arms, and brandy. We will share with you, and take care of you until you are well again. In return for our care, we only ask you to treat us with a little confidence!"

The Irishman gave Erik an irresolute look in which gratitude seemed to mingle with fear—a look of fearful indecision.

"That depends on the kind of confidence that you ask for?" he said, evasively.

"Oh, you know very well," answered Erik, making an effort to smile, and taking in his hands those of the wounded man. "I told you the other day; you know what I want to find out and what I have come so far to discover. Now, Patrick O'Donoghan, make a little effort and disclose to me this secret which is of so much importance to me, tell me what you know about the infant tied to the buoy. Give me the faintest indication of who I am, so that I may find my family. What do you fear? What danger do you run in satisfying me?"

O'Donoghan did not answer, but seemed to be turning over in his obtuse brain the arguments that Erik had used.

"But," he said at last, with an effort, "if we succeed in getting away from here, and we reach some country where there are judges and courts, you could do me some harm?"

"No, I swear that I would not. I swear it by all that is sacred," said Erik, hotly. "Whatever may be the injuries you have inflicted upon me or upon others, I guarantee that you shall not suffer for them in any way. Besides, there is one fact of which you seem to be ignorant, it is that there is a limit to such matters. When such events have taken place more than twenty years ago, human justice has no longer the right to demand an accounting for them."

"Is that true?" asked Patrick O'Donoghan, distrustfully. "Mr. Jones told me that the 'Alaska' had been sent by the police, and you yourself spoke of a tribunal."

"That was about recent events—an accident that happened to us at the beginning of our journey. You may be sure that Mr. Jones was mocking you, Patrick. Doubtless he has some interest of his own for wishing you not to tell."

"You may be sure of that," said the Irishman, earnestly. "But how did you discover that I was acquainted with this secret?"

"Through Mr. and Mrs. Bowles of the Red Anchor in Brooklyn, who had often heard you speak of the infant tied to the buoy."

"That is true," said the Irishman. He reflected again. "Then you are sure that you were not sent by the police?" he said, at length.

"No—what an absurd idea. I came of my own accord on account of my ardent desire, my thirst, to discover the land of my birth and to find out who my parents were, that is all."

O'Donoghan smiled, proudly:

"Ah, that is what you want to know," he said. "Well, it is true that I can tell you. It is true that I know."

"Tell me—tell me!" cried Erik, seeing that he hesitated. "Tell me and I promise you pardon for all the evil that you have done, and my everlasting gratitude if I am ever in a position to show it!"

The Irishman gave a covetous look at the leathern bottle.

"It makes my throat dry to talk so much," he said, in a faint tone. "I will drink a little more if you are willing to give it to me."

"There is no more here, but we can get some at our depot of provisions. We have two large cases of brandy there," answered Erik, handing the bottle to Mr. Hersebom.

The latter immediately walked away, followed by Kaas.

"They will not be gone long," said the young man, turning toward his companion. "Now, my brave fellow, do not make merchandise of your confidence. Put yourself in my place. Suppose that during all your life you had been ignorant of the name of your country, and that of your mother, and that at last you found yourself in the presence of a man who knew all about it, and who refused the information which was of such inestimable value to you, and that at the very time when you had saved him, restored him to consciousness and life. I do not ask you to do anything impossible. I do not ask you to criminate yourself if you have anything to reproach yourself with. Give me only an indication, the very slightest. Put me on the track, so that I can find my family; and that is all that I shall ask of you."

"By my faith, I will do you this favor!" said Patrick, evidently moved. "You know that I was a cabin-boy on board the 'Cynthia'?"

He stopped short.

Erik hung upon his words. Was he at last going to find out the truth? Was he going to solve this enigma and discover the name of his family, the land of his birth? Truly the scene appeared to him almost chimerical. He fastened his eyes upon the wounded man, ready to drink in his words with avidity. For nothing in the world would he have interfered with his recital, neither by interruption nor gesture. He did not even observe that a shadow had appeared behind him. It was the sight of this shadow which had stopped the story of Patrick O'Donoghan.

"Mr. Jones!" he said, in the tone of a school-boy detected in some flagrant mischief.

Erik turned and saw Tudor Brown coming around a neighboring hummock, where until this moment he had been hidden from their sight.

The exclamation of the Irishman confirmed the suspicion which during the last hour had presented itself to his mind.

Mr. Jones and Tudor Brown were one and the same person.

He had hardly time to make this reflection before two shots were heard.

Tudor Brown raised his gun and shot Patrick O'Donoghan through the heart, who fell backward.

Then before he had time to lower his rifle, Tudor Brown received a bullet in his forehead, and fell forward on his face.

"I did well to come back when I saw suspicious footprints in the snow," said Mr. Hersebom, coming forward, his gun still smoking in his hands.

20

The End of the Voyage

Erik gave a cry and threw himself on his knees beside Patrick O'Donoghan, seeking for some sign of life, a ray of hope. But the Irishman was certainly dead this time, and that without revealing his secret.

As for Tudor Brown, one convulsion shook his body, his gun fell from his hands, in which he had tightly held it at the moment of his fall, and he expired without a word.

"Father, what have you done?" cried Erik, bitterly. "Why have you deprived me of the last chance that was left to me of discovering the secret of my birth? Would it not have been better for us to throw ourselves upon this man and take him prisoner?"

"And do you believe that he would have allowed us to do so?" answered Mr. Hersebom. "His second shot was intended for you, you may be sure. I have avenged the murder of this unfortunate man, punished the criminal who attempted to shipwreck us, and who is guilty perhaps of other crimes. Whatever may be the result, I do not regret having done so. Besides of what consequence is the mystery surrounding your birth, my child, to men in our situation? The secret of your birth before long, without doubt, will be revealed to us by God."

He had hardly finished speaking, when the firing of a cannon was heard, and it was re-echoed by the icebergs. It seemed like a reply to the discouraging words of the old fisherman. It was doubtless a response to the two gunshots which had been fired on their island of ice.

"The cannon of the 'Alaska!' We are saved!" cried Erik, jumping up and climbing a hummock to get a better view of the sea that surrounded them.

He saw nothing at first but the icebergs, driven by the wind and sparkling in the sunshine. But Mr. Hersebom, who had immediately reloaded his gun, fired into the air, and a second discharge from the cannon answered him almost immediately.

Then Erik discovered a thin streak of black smoke toward the west, clearly defined against the blue sky. Gunshots, answered by the cannon, were repeated at intervals of a few minutes, and soon the "Alaska" steamed around an iceberg and made all speed toward the north of the island.

Erik and Mr. Hersebom, weeping for joy, threw themselves into each other's arms. They waved their handkerchiefs and threw their caps into the air, seeking by all means to attract the attention of their friends.

At length the "Alaska" stopped, a boat was lowered, and in twenty minutes it reached their island.

Who can describe the unbounded joy of Dr. Schwaryencrona, Mr. Bredejord, Mr. Malarius, and Otto when they found them well and safe; for through the long hours of that sad night they had mourned them as lost.

They related all that had befallen them—their fears and despair during the night, their vain appeals, their useless anger. The "Alaska" had been found in the morning to be almost entirely clear of the ice, and they had dislodged what remained with the assistance of their gunpowder. Mr. Bosewitz had taken command, being the second-officer, and had immediately started in search of the floating island, taking the direction in which the wind would carry it. This navigation amidst floating icebergs was the most perilous which the "Alaska" had as yet attempted; but thanks to the excellent training to which the young captain had accustomed his crew, and to the experience which they had acquired in maneuvering the vessel, they passed safely among these moving masses of ice without being crushed by them. The "Alaska" had had the advantage of being able to travel more swiftly than the icebergs, and she had been able to benefit by this circumstance. Kind Providence had willed that her search should not prove fruitless. At nine o'clock in the morning the island had been sighted. They recognized it by its shape, and then the two shots from the guns made them hopeful of finding their two shipwrecked friends.

All their other troubles now appeared to them as insignificant. They had a long and dangerous voyage before them, which they must accomplish under sail, for their coal was exhausted.

"No," said Erik, "we will not make it under sail. I have another plan. We will permit the ice island to tow us along, as long as she goes toward the south or west. That will spare us incessantly fighting with the icebergs, for our island will chase them ahead of her. Then we can collect here all the combustibles that we will require in order to finish the voyage, when we are ready to resume it."

"What are you talking about?" asked the doctor, laughing. "Is there an oil-well on this island?"

"Not exactly an oil-well," answered Erik, "but what will answer our purpose nearly as well, multitudes of fat walruses. I wish to try an experiment, since we have one furnace especially adapted for burning oil."

They began their labors by performing the last rites of the two dead men. They tied weights to their feet and lowered them into the sea. Then the "Alaska" made fast to the ice bank in such a manner as to follow its movements without sustaining any injury to herself. They were able, with care, to carry on board again the provisions which they had landed, and which it was important for them not to lose. That operation accomplished, they devoted all their energies to the pursuit of the walrus.

Two or three times a day, parties armed with guns and harpoons and accompanied by all their Greenland dogs landed on the ice bank, and surrounded the sleeping monsters at the mouth of their holes. They killed them by firing a ball into their ears, then they cut them up, and placed the lard with which they were filled in their sleighs, and the dogs drew it to the "Alaska." Their hunting was so easy and so productive, that in eight days they had all the lard that they could carry. The "Alaska," still towed by the floating island, was now in the seventy-fourth degree; that is to say, she had passed Nova Zembla.

The ice island was now reduced at least one-half, and cracked by the sun was full of fissures, more or less extensive, evidently ready to go to pieces. Erik resolved not to wait until this happened, and ordering their anchor to be lifted, he sailed away westward.

The lard was immediately utilized in the fire of the "Alaska," and proved an excellent combustible. The only fault was that it choked up the chimney, which necessitated a daily cleaning. As for its odor, that would doubtless have been very disagreeable to southern passengers, but to a crew composed of Swedes and Norwegians, it was only a secondary inconvenience.

Thanks to this supply, the "Alaska" was able to keep up steam during the whole of the remainder of her voyage. She proceeded rapidly, in spite of contrary winds, and arrived on the 5th of September in sight of Cape North or Norway. They pursued their route with all possible speed, turned the Scandinavian Peninsula, repassed Skager-Rack, and reached the spot from which they had taken their departure.

On the 14th of September they cast anchor before Stockholm, which they had left on the tenth of the preceding February.

Thus, in seven months and four days, the first circumpolar periplus had been accomplished by a navigator of only twenty-two years of age.

This geographical feat, which so promptly completed the great expedition of Nordenskiold, would soon make a prodigious commotion in the world. But the journals and reviews had not as yet had time to expatiate upon it. The uninitiated were hardly prepared to understand it, and one person, at least, reviewed it with suspicion—this was Kajsa. The supercilious smile with which she listened to the story of their adventures was indescribable.

"Was it sensible to expose yourself to such dangers?" was her only comment.

But the first opportunity that presented itself she did not fail to say to Erik:

"I suppose that now you will do nothing more about this tiresome matter, since the Irishman is dead."

What a difference there was between these cold criticisms and the letters full of sympathy and tenderness that Erik soon received from Noroe.

Vanda told him in what a state of anxiety she and her mother had passed these long months, how the travelers had been ever present in their thoughts, and how happy they were when they heard of their safe return. If the expedition had not accomplished all that Erik hoped, they begged him not to worry himself too much about it. He must know that if he never succeeded in finding his own family he had one in the poor Norwegian village, where he would be tenderly cared for like one of themselves. Would he not soon come and see them, could he not stay with them one little month. It was the sincere desire of his adopted mother and of his little sister Vanda, etc., etc.

The envelope also contained three pretty flowers, gathered on the borders of the fiord, and their perfume seemed to bring back vividly to Erik his gay and careless childhood. Ah, how sweet these loving words were to his poor disappointed heart, and they enabled him to fulfill more easily the concluding duties appertaining to the expedition. He hoped soon to be able to go and tell them all he felt. The voyage of the "Alaska" had equaled in grandeur that of the "Vega." The name of Erik was everywhere associated with the glorious name of Nordenskiold. The journals had a great deal to say about the new periplus. The ships of all nations anchored at Stockholm united in doing honor to this national victor. The learned societies came in a body to congratulate the commander and crew of the "Alaska." The public authorities proposed a national recompense for them.

All these praises were painful to Erik. His conscience told him that the principal motive of this expedition on his part had been purely a personal one, and he felt scrupulous about accepting honors which appeared to him greatly exaggerated. He therefore availed himself of the first opportunity to state frankly that he had gone to the polar seas to discover if possible the secret of his birth, and of the shipwreck of the "Cynthia," that he had been unsuccessful in doing so.

The occasion was offered by a reporter of one of the principal newspapers of Stockholm, who presented himself on board of the "Alaska" and solicited the favor of a private interview with the young captain. The object of this intelligent gazeteer, let us state briefly, was to extract from his victim the outlines of a biography which would cover one hundred lines. He could not have fallen on a subject more willing to submit to vivisection. Erik had been eager to tell the truth, and to proclaim to the world that he did not deserve to be regarded as a second Christopher Columbus. He therefore related unreservedly his story, explaining how he had been picked up at sea by a poor fisherman of Noroe, educated by Mr. Malarius, taken to Stockholm by Dr. Schwaryencrona; how they had found out that Patrick O'Donoghan probably held the key to the mystery that surrounded him. They discovered that he was on board of the "Vega;" they had gone in search of him. He related the accident which had induced them to change their route. Erik told all this to convince the world that he was no hero. He told it because he felt ashamed of being so overwhelmed with praises for a performance that only seemed to him natural and right.

During this time the pen of the delighted reporter, Mr. Squirrelius, flew over the paper with stenographic rapidity. The dates, the names, the least details were noted with avidity. Mr. Squirrelius told himself with a beating heart that he had obtained matter not only for one hundred lines, but that he could make five or six hundred out of it. And what a story it would be—more interesting than a novel!

The next day Erik's revelations filled the columns of the most largely circulated newspaper in Stockholm, and indeed in all Sweden. As is usually the case, Erik's sincerity, instead of diminishing his popularity, only increased it, on account of his modesty, and the romantic interest attached to his history. The press and the public seized upon it with avidity. These biographical details were soon translated into all languages, and made the tour of Europe. In this way they reached Paris, and penetrated in the form of a French newspaper into a modest draw-ing-room on Varennes Street.

There were two persons in this room. One was a lady dressed in black, with white hair, although she still appeared to be young, but her whole appearance betrayed profound sorrow. Seated under a lighted lamp she worked mechanically at some embroidery, which at times fell from her thin fingers, while her eyes, fixed on vacancy, seemed to be thinking of some overwhelming calamity.

On the other side of the table sat a fine-looking old gentleman, who took the newspaper abstractedly which his servant brought in.

It was Mr. Durrien, the honorary consul-general of the geographi-cal society, the same person who had been at Brest when the "Alaska" reached that place.

This was doubtless the reason why Erik's name attracted his notice, but while reading the article carefully which contained the biography or the young Swedish navigator, he was startled. Then he read it again carefully, and little by little an intense pallor spread over his face, which was always pale. His hands trembled nervously, and his uneasiness be-came so evident that his companion noticed it.

"Father, are you suffering?" she asked with solicitude.

"I believe it is too warm here—I will go to the library and get some fresh air. It is nothing; it will pass off," answered Mr. Durrien, rising and walking into the adjoining room.

As if by accident, he carried the paper with him.

If his daughter could have read his thoughts, she would have known that amidst the tumults of hopes and fears that so agitated him was also a determination not to let her eyes rest upon that paper.

A moment later she thought of following him into the library, but she imagined that he wished to be alone, and discreetly yielded to his desire. Besides she was soon reassured by hearing him moving about and opening and closing the window.

At the end of an hour, she decided to look in, and see what Mr. Durrien was doing. She found that he was seated before his desk writing a letter. But she did not see that us he wrote his eyes filled with tears.

21

A Letter From Paris

Since his return to Stockholm, Erik had received every day from all parts of Europe a voluminous correspondence. Some learned society wished for information on some point, or wrote to congratulate him; foreign governments wished to bestow upon him some honor or recompense; ship-owners, or traders, solicited some favor which would serve their interests.

Therefore he was not surprised when he received one morning two letters bearing the Paris postmark.

The first that he opened was an invitation from the Geographical Society of France, asking him and his companions to come and receive a handsome medal, which had been voted in a solemn conclave "to the navigators of the first circumpolar periplus of the arctic seas."

The second envelope made Erik start, he looked at it. On the box which closed it was a medallion upon which the letters "E.D." were engraved, surrounded by the motto "Semper idem."

These initials and devices were also stamped in the corner of the letter enclosed in the envelope, which was that from Mr. Durrien.

The letter read as follows:

"MY DEAR CHILD,

Let me call you this in any case. I have just read in a French newspaper a biography translated from the Swedish language, which has overcome me more than I can tell you. It was your account of yourself. You state that you were picked up at sea about twenty-two years ago by a Norwegian fisherman in the neighborhood of Bergen; that you were tied to a buoy, bearing the name of 'Cynthia;' that the especial motive of your arctic voyage was to find a survivor of the vessel of that name—ship wrecked in October, 1858; and then you state that you have returned from the voyage without having been able to gain any information about the matter.

"If all this is true (oh, what would I not give if it is true!), I ask you not to lose a moment in running to the telegraph office and letting me know it. In that case, my child, you can understand my impatience, my anxiety, and my joy. In that case you are my grandson, for whom I have mourned so many years, whom I believed lost to me forever, as did also my daughter, my poor daughter, who, broken-hearted at the tragedy of the 'Cynthia,' still mourns every day for her only child—the joy and consolation at first of her widowhood, but afterward the cause of her despair.

"But we shall see you again alive, covered with glory. Such happiness is too great, too wonderful. I dare not believe it until a word from you authorizes me to do so. But now it seems so probable, the details and dates agree so perfectly, your countenance and manners recall so vividly those of my unfortunate son-in-law. Upon the only occasion when chance led me into your society, I felt myself mysteriously drawn toward you by a deep and sudden sympathy. It seems impossible that there should be no reason for this.

"One word, telegraph me one word. I do not know how to exist until I hear from you. Will it be the response that I wait for so impatiently? Can you bring such happiness to my poor daughter and myself as will cause us to forget our past years of tears and mourning?

"E. DURRIEN, HONORARY CONSUL-GENERAL,
"*104 Rue de Varennes, Paris.*"

To this letter was added one of explanation, that Erik devoured eagerly. It was also in Mr. Durrien's handwriting, and read as follows:

"I was the French consul at New Orleans when my only daughter, Catherine, married a young Frenchman, Mr. George Durrien, a distant connection, and, like ourselves, of Breton origin. Mr. George Durrien was a mining engineer. He had come to the United States to explore the recently discovered mines of petroleum and intended to remain several years. I received him into my family—he being the son of a dear friend—and when he asked for my daughter's hand, I gave her to him with joy. Shortly after their marriage I was appointed consul to Riga; and my son-in-law being detained by business interests in the United States, I was obliged to leave my daughter. She became a mother, and to her son was given my Christian name, united to that of his father—Emile Henry Georges.

"Six months afterward my son-in-law was killed by an accident in the mines. As soon as she could settle up his affairs, my poor daughter, only twenty years of age, embarked at New York on the 'Cynthia' for Hamburg, to join me by the most direct route.

"On the 7th of October, 1858, the 'Cynthia' was shipwrecked off the Faroe Islands. The circumstances of the shipwreck were suspicious, and have never been explained.

"At the moment of the disaster, when the passengers were taking their places one by one in the boat, my little grandson, seven months old—whom his mother had tied to a buoy for safety—slipped or was pushed into the sea, and was carried away by the storm and disappeared. His mother, crazed by this frightful spectacle, tried to throw herself into the sea. She was prevented by main force and placed in a fainting condition in one of the boats, in which were three other persons, and who had alone escaped from the shipwrecked vessel. In forty-nine hours this boat reached one of the Faroe Islands. From there my daughter returned to me after a dangerous illness which lasted seven weeks, thanks to the devoted attentions of the sailor who saved her and who brought her to me. This brave man, John Denman, died in my service in Asia Minor.

"We had but little hope that the baby had survived the shipwreck. I, however, sought for him among the Faroe and Shetland Islands, and upon the Norwegian coast north of Bergen. The idea of his cradle floating any further seemed impossible, but I did not give up my search for three years; and Noroe must be a very retired spot, or surely some inquiries would have been made there. When I had given up all hope I devoted myself exclusively to my daughter, whose physical and moral health required great attention. I succeeded in being sent to the Orient, and I sought, by traveling and scientific enterprises, to draw off her thoughts from her affliction. She has been my inseparable companion sharing all my labors, but I have never been able to lighten her incurable grief. We returned to France, and we now live in Paris in an old house which I own.

"Will it be my happiness to receive there my grandson, for whom we have mourned so many years? This hope fills me with too much joy, and I dare not speak of it to my daughter, until I am assured of its truth; for, if it should prove false, the disappointment would be too cruel.

"To-day is Monday: they tell me at the post-office that by next Saturday I can receive your answer."

Erik had hardly been able to read this, for the tears would obscure his sight. He also felt afraid to yield too quickly to the hope which had been so suddenly restored to him. He told himself that every detail coincided—the dates agreed; all the events down to the most minute particulars. He hardly dared to believe, however, that it could be true. It was too much happiness to recover in a moment his family, his own mother, his country. And such a country—the one that he could have chosen above all because she possessed the grandeur, the graces, the supreme gifts of humanity—because she had fostered genius, and the civilization of antiquity, and the discoveries and inventions of modern times.

He was afraid that he was only dreaming. His hopes had been so often disappointed. Perhaps the doctor would say something to dispel his illusions. Before he did anything he would submit these facts to his cooler judgment.

The doctor read the documents attentively which he carried to him, but not without exclamations of joy and surprise.

"You need not feel the slightest doubt!" he said, when he had finished. "All the details agree perfectly, even those that your correspondent omits to mention, the initials on the linen, the device engraved on the locket, which are the same as those on the letter. My dear child, you have found your family this time. You must telegraph immediately to your grandfather!"

"But what shall I tell him?" asked Erik, pale with joy.

"Tell him that to-morrow you will set out by express, to go and embrace him and your mother!"

The young captain only took time to press the hands of this excellent man, and he ran and jumped into a cab to hasten to the telegraph office.

He left Stockholm that same day, took the railroad to Malmo on the north-west coast of Sweden, crossed the strait in twenty minutes, reached Copenhagen, took the express train through to Holland and Belgium, and at Brussels the train for Paris.

On Saturday, at seven o'clock in the evening, exactly six days after Mr. Durrien had posted his letter, he had the joy of waiting for his grandson at the depot.

As soon as the train stopped they fell into each other's arms. They had thought so much about each other during these last few days that they both felt already well acquainted.

"My mother?" asked Erik.

"I have not dared to tell her, much as I was tempted to do so!" answered Mr. Durrien.

"And she knows nothing yet?"

"She suspects something, she fears, she hopes. Since your dispatch I have done my best to prepare her for the unheard-of joy that awaits her. I told her of a track upon which I had been placed by a young Swedish officer, the one whom I had met at Brest, and of whom I had often spoken to her. She does not know, she hesitates to hope for any good news, but this morning at breakfast I could see her watching me, and two or three times I felt afraid that she was going to question me. One can not tell, something might have happened to you, some other misfortune, some sudden mischance. So I did not dine with her to-night, I made an excuse to escape from a situation intolerable to me."

Without waiting for his baggage, they departed in the *coup* that Mr. Durrien had brought.

Mme. Durrien, alone in the parlor in Varennes Street, awaited impatiently the return of her father. She had had her suspicions aroused, and was only waiting until the dinner hour arrived to ask for an explanation.

For several days she had been disturbed by his strange behavior, by the dispatches which were continually arriving, and by the double meaning which she thought she detected beneath all he said. Accustomed to talk with him about his lightest thoughts and impressions, she could not understand why he should seek to conceal anything from her. Several times she had been on the point of demanding a solution of the enigma, but she had kept silence, out of respect for the evident wishes of her father.

"He is trying to prepare me for some surprise, doubtless," she said to herself. "He is sure to tell me if anything pleasant has occurred."

But for the last two or three days, especially that morning, she had been impressed with a sort of eagerness which Mr. Durrien displayed in all his manner, as well as the happy air with which he regarded her, insisting in hearing over and over again from her lips, all the details of the disaster of the "Cynthia," which he had avoided speaking of for a long time. As she mused over his strange behavior a sort of revelation came to her. She felt sure that her father must have received some favorable intelligence which had revived the hope of finding her child. But without the least idea that he had already done so, she determined not to retire that night until she had questioned him closely.

Mme. Durrien had never definitely renounced the idea that her son was living. She had never seen him dead before her eyes, and she clung mother-like to the hope that he was not altogether lost to her. She said that the proofs were insufficient, and she nourished the possibility of his sudden return. She might be said to pass her days waiting for him. Thousands of women, mothers of soldiers and sailors, pass their lives under this touching delusion. Mrs. Durrien had a greater right than they had to preserve her faith in his existence. In truth the tragical scene enacted twenty-two years ago was always before her eyes. She beheld the "Cynthia" filling with water and ready to sink. She saw herself tying her infant to a large buoy while the passengers and sailors were rushing for the boats. They left her behind, she saw herself imploring, beseeching that they would at least take her baby. A man took her precious burden, and threw it into one of the boats, a heavy sea dashed over it, and to her horror she saw the buoy floating away on the crest of the waves. She gave a dispairing cry and tried to jump after him, then came unconsciousness. When she awoke she was a prey to despair, to fever, to delirium. To this succeeded increasing grief. Yes, the poor woman recalled all this. Her whole being had in fact received a shock from which she had never recovered. It was now nearly a quarter of a century since this had happened, and Mrs. Durrien still wept for her son as on the first day. Her maternal heart so full of grief was slowly consuming her life. She sometimes pictured to herself her son passing through the successive phases of infancy, youth, and manhood. From year to year she represented to herself how he would have looked, how he was looking, for she obstinately clung to her belief of the possibility of his return.

This vain hope nothing had as yet had the power to shake—neither travels, nor useless researches, nor the passage of time.

This is why this evening she awaited her father with the firm resolution of knowing all that he had to tell.

Mr. Darrien entered. He was followed by a young gentleman, whom he presented to her in the following words:

"My daughter, this is Mr. Erik Hersebom, of whom I have often spoken to you, and who has just arrived at Paris. The Geographical Society wish to bestow upon him a grand medal, and he has done me the honor to accept our hospitality."

She had arisen from her arm-chair, and was looking kindly at him. Suddenly her eyes dilated, her lips trembled, and she stretched out her hands toward him.

"My son! you are my son!" she cried.

Then she advanced a step toward Erik.

"Yes, you are my child," she said. "Your father lives over again in you!"

When Erik, bursting into tears, fell on his knees before her, the poor woman took his head in her hands, and fainted from joy and happiness as she tried to press a kiss on his forehead.

22

At Val-Feray

A month later at Val-Feray, an old homestead of the family, situated half a league from Brest, Erik's adopted family were assembled, together with his mother and grandfather. Mrs. Durrien had, with the delicacy of feeling habitual to her, desired that the good, simple-hearted beings who had saved her son's life should share her profound and inexpressible joy. She had insisted that Dame Katrina, and Vanda, Mr. Hersebom, and Otto should accompany Doctor Schwaryencrona, Kajsa, Mr. Bredejord, and Mr. Malarius, and they held a great festival together.

Amidst the rugged natural scenery of Breton and near the sea, her Norwegian guests felt more at their ease than they could have done in Varennes Street. They took long walks in the woods together, and told each other all they knew about Erik's still somewhat obscure history, and little by little many hitherto inexplicable points became clear. Their long talks and discussions cast light upon many obscure circumstances.

The first question they asked each other was, Who was Tudor Brown? What great interest did he have in preventing Patrick O'Donoghan from telling who Erik's relations were? The words of that unfortunate man had established one fact, viz., that Tudor Brown's real name was Jones, as it was the only one that the Irishman had known him by. Now, a Mr. Noah Jones had been associated with Erik's father in working a petroleum mine, that the young engineer had discovered in Pennsylvania. The simple announcement of this fact gave a sinister aspect to many events which had so long appeared mysterious: the suspicious wreck of the "Cynthia," the fall of the infant into the sea, perhaps the death of Erik's father. A document that Mr. Durrien found among his papers elucidated many of these perplexing questions.

"Several months before his marriage," he said to Erik's friends, "my son-in-law had discovered, near Harrisburg, a petroleum well. He lacked the capital necessary to purchase it, and he saw that he was in danger of losing all the advantages which the possession of it would secure to him. Chance made him acquainted with Mr. Noah Jones, who represented himself as a cattle dealer from the far West. But in reality, as he found out afterward, he was a slave-trader.

"This individual agreed to advance the sum necessary to purchase and work the petroleum mine, which was called the Vandalia. He made my son-in-law sign, in exchange for this assistance, an agreement which was very profitable to himself. I was ignorant of the terms of this contract at the time of his marriage to my daughter, and according to all appearances he thought but little of it. Unusually gifted, and understanding chemistry and mechanics, yet he was entirely ignorant of business matters, and already had to pay dearly for his inexperience. No doubt he had trusted all the arrangements to Noah Jones, according to his usual habit. Probably he signed with closed eyes the contract which was laid before him. These are the principle articles agreed upon:

"ART. III.   The Vandalia shall remain the sole property of Mr. George Durrien, the discoverer, and Mr. Noah Jones, his silent partner.

"ART. IV.   Mr. Noah Jones will take charge of moneys, and pay out what is necessary for the exploration of the mine, he will also sell the product, take charge of the receipts, and have a settlement with his partner every year, when they will divide the net profits.

"ART. V.   If either of the partners should wish to sell his share, the other would have the first right to purchase it, and he should have three months in which to make arrangements to do so. He might then become sole proprietor by paying the capital and three per cent. on the net revenue, according to what it had been proved to be at the last inventory.

"ART. VI.   Only the children of the two partners could become inheritors of these rights. In case one of the partners should die childless, or his children should not live until they were twenty-one years of age, the entire property to revert to the survivor, to the exclusion of all other heirs of the dead partner.

"N.B.   The last article is on account of the different nationalities of the two partners, and because of the complications that could not fail to arise in case of the death of either of them without issue."

"Such," continued Mr. Durrien, "was the contract which my future son-in-law had signed at the time, when he had no thought of marrying, and when everybody, except, perhaps, Mr. Noah Jones, was ignorant of what immense value the Vandalia mine would become in the course of time. They had then hardly commenced operations, and they met with the usual discouragements incident to all new undertakings. Perhaps Noah Jones hoped that his associate would become disgusted with the whole business and retire, leaving him sole proprietor. The marriage of George with my daughter, the birth of his son, and the well becoming suddenly prodigiously fruitful, must have modified his plans by degrees. He could no longer hope to purchase for a trifling sum this splendid property; but before it came into the possession of Noah Jones, first George himself, and then his only child, must disappear from the world. Two years after his marriage and six months after the birth of my grandson, George was found dead near one of the wells—asphyxiated, the doctors said, by gas. I had left the United States upon my nomination as consul to Riga. The business relating to the partnership was left to an attorney to settle. Noah Jones behaved vert well, and agreed to all the arrangements that were made for the benefit of my daughter. He agreed to continue the work, and pay every six months into the Central Bank of New York that part of the net profits which belonged to the infant. Alas! he never made the first payment. My daughter took passage in the 'Cynthia' in order to join me. The 'Cynthia' was lost with her crew and freight under such suspicious circumstances that the insurance company refused to pay; and in this shipwreck the sole heir of my son-in-law disappeared.

"Noah Jones remained the sole proprietor of the Vandalia, which has yielded him at the least since that event an annual income of one hundred and eighty thousand dollars a year."

"Did you never suspect that he had had some hand in these successive catastrophies?" asked Mr. Bredejord.

"I have certainly suspected him; it was only too natural. Such an accumulation of misfortunes, and all tending to his private enrichment, seemed to point him out as the author only too clearly. But how could I prove my suspicions, particularly in a court of justice? They were only vague, and I knew too well that they would have but little weight in an international contest. And then, besides I had my daughter to console, or at least to try and draw away her thoughts from this tragedy, and a lawsuit would only have revived her grief. Briefly I resigned myself to silence. Did I do wrong? Is it to be regretted?"

"I think not, for I feel convinced that it would have produced no results. You see how difficult it is even today, after we have related all the facts in our possession, to arrive at any definite conclusion!"

"But how can you explain the part which Patrick O'Donoghan has taken in this matter?" asked Dr. Schwaryencrona.

"On this point, as on many others, we are reduced to conjectures, but it seems to me that there is one which is plausible enough. This O'Donoghan was cabin-boy on board of the 'Cynthia,' in the personal service of the captain, and consequently in constant communication with the first-class passengers, who always eat at the captain's table. He therefore certainly knew the name of my daughter, and her French origin, and he could easily have found her again.

"Had he been commissioned by Noah Jones to perform some dark mission? Had he a hand in causing the shipwreck of the 'Cynthia,' or simply in pushing the infant into the sea? this they could never know for a certainty since he was dead. One thing was evident, he was aware how important the knowledge of this fact was for Noah Jones. But did this lazy drunken man know that the infant was living? Had he any hand in saving it? Had he rescued it from the sea to leave it floating near Noroe?

"This was a doubtful point. In any case he must have assured Noah Jones that the infant had survived. He was doubtless proud of knowing the country which had received him, and he had probably taken precautions to know all about the child, so that if any misfortune happened to him—O'Donoghan—Noah Jones would be obliged to pay him well for his silence. He was doubtless the person from whom he received money every time he landed in New York."

"All this appears to me to be very probable," said Mr. Bredejord, "and I think that subsequent events confirm it. The first advertisements of Doctor Schwaryencrona disturbed Noah Jones, and he believed it to be an imperative necessity to get rid of Patrick O'Donoghan, but he was obliged to act prudently. He therefore contented himself with frightening the Irishman, by making him believe that he would be brought before a criminal court. The result of this we know from Mr. and Mrs. Bowles, of the Red Anchor, who told us of the haste with which Patrick O'Donoghan had taken flight. He evidently believed that he was in danger of being arrested, or he would not have gone so far, to live among the Samoyedes, and under an assumed name, which Noah Jones had doubtless advised him to do.

"But the announcement in the newspapers about Patrick O'Donoghan must have been a severe blow to him. He had made a journey to Stockholm expressly to assure us that the Irishman was dead, and doubtless to discover if possible how far we had pushed our inquiries. The publication of the correspondence of the 'Vega, and the departure of the 'Alaska,' must have made Noah Jones, or Tudor Brown, as he called himself, feel that he was in imminent peril, for his confidence in Patrick O'Donoghan could be only very limited, and he would have revealed his secret to any one who would have assured him that he would not be punished. Happily as affairs have turned out, we may congratulate ourselves upon having escaped pretty well."

"Who knows?" said the doctor, "perhaps all the danger we have encountered has only helped to bring us to the knowledge of the truth. But for running on the rocks of the Basse-Froide, we would probably have pursued the route through the Suez Canal, and then we should have reached Behring's Strait too late to meet the 'Vega.' It is at least doubtful whether we would have undertaken the voyage to the Island of Ljakow, and more doubtful still whether we would have been able to extract any information from Patrick O'Donoghan if we had met him in company with Tudor Brown.

"So, although our entire voyage has been marked by tragical events, it is due to the fact of our having accomplished the periplus in the 'Alaska, and the consequent celebrity which has been the result for Erik, that he has at last found his family."

"Yes," said Mrs. Durrien, laying her hand proudly on the head of her son, "it is his glory which has restored him to me."

And immediately she added:

"It was a crime that deprived me of you, but your own goodness which has restored you to me!"

"And the rascality of Noah Jones has resulted in making our Erik one of the richest men in America," cried Mr. Bredejord.

Every one looked at him with surprise.

"Doubtless," answered the eminent lawyer. "Erik is his father's heir, and has a share in the income, derived from the Vandalia mine. Has he not been unjustly deprived of this for the last twenty-two years?

"We have only to give proofs of his identity, and we have plenty of witnesses, Mr. Hersebom, Dame Katrina and Mr. Malarius, besides ourselves. If Noah Jones has left any children, they are responsible for the enormous arrears which will probably consume all their share of the capital stock.

"If the rascal has left no children, by the terms of the contract which Mr. Durrien has just read, Erik is the sole inheritor of the entire property; and according to all accounts he ought to have in Pennsylvania an income of one hundred and fifty to two hundred thousand dollars a year!"

"Ah, ah," said the doctor, laughing. "Behold the little fisherman of Noroe become an eligible *parti!* Laureate of the Geographical Society, author of the first circumpolar periplus, and afflicted with the modest income of two hundred thousand dollars. There are not many such husbands to be met with in Stockholm. What do you say Kajsa?"

The young girl blushed painfully at being thus addressed, but her uncle had no suspicion that he had made a cruel speech.

Kajsa had felt that she had not acted wisely in treating Erik as she had done, and she resolved for the future to show him more attention.

But it was a singular fact that Erik no longer cared for her, since he felt himself elevated above her unjust disdain. Perhaps it was absence, or the lonely hours which he had spent walking the deck at night, which had revealed to him the poverty of Kajsa's heart; or it might be the satisfaction he felt that she could no longer regard him as "a waif"; he only treated her now with the most perfect courtesy, to which she was entitled as a young lady and Dr. Schwaryencrona's niece.

All his preference now was for Vanda, who indeed grew every day more and more charming, and was losing all her little village awkwardness under the roof of an amiable and cultivated lady. Her exquisite goodness, her native grace, and perfect simplicity, made her beloved by all who approached her. She had not been eight days at Val-Fray, when Mrs. Durrien declared positively that it would be impossible for her ever to part with her.

Erik undertook to arrange with Mr. Hersebom and Dame Katrina that they should leave Vanda behind them, with the express condition that he would bring her himself every year to see them. He had tried to keep all his adopted family with him, even offering to transport from Noroe the house with all its furniture where he had passed his infancy. But this project of emigration was generally regarded as impracticable. Mr. Hersebom and Katrina were too old to change their habits. They would not have been perfectly happy in a country of whose language and habits they were ignorant. He was obliged, therefore, to permit them to depart, but not before making such provision for them as would enable them to spend the remainder of their days in ease and comfort, which, notwithstanding their honest, laborious lives, they had been unable to accomplish.

Erik would have liked to have kept Otto at least, but he preferred his fiord, and thought that there was no life preferable to that of a fisherman. It must also be confessed that the golden-haired and blue-eyed daughter of the overseer of the oil-works had something to do with the attractions which Noroe had for him. At least we must conclude so, since it was soon made known that he expected to marry her at the next "Yule," or Christmas.

Mr. Malarius counted upon educating their children as he had educated Erik and Vanda. He modestly resumed his position in the village school, after sharing in the honor of the decorations bestowed by the Geographical Society of France upon the captain of the "Alaska." He was also busily occupied in correcting the proofs of his magnificent work on the "Flora of the Arctic Regions." As for Dr. Schwaryencrona, he has not quite finished his "Treatise on Iconography," which will transmit his name to posterity.

The latest legal business of Mr. Bredejord has been to establish Erik's claim as sole proprietor of the Vandalia mine. He gained his case in the first instance, and also on appeal, which was no small success.

Erik took advantage of this, and of the enormous fortune thus accruing to him, to purchase the "Alaska," which he converted into a pleasure yacht. He uses it every year to go to Noroe in company with Mme. Durrien and Vanda, to visit his adopted family. Although his civil rights have been accorded to him, and his legal name is Emile Durrien, he has added that of Hersebom, and among his relatives he is still called only Erik.

The secret desire of his mother is to see him some day married to Vanda, whom she already loves as a daughter, and, as Erik evidently shares this desire, we may suppose that it will be realized one of these days.

Kajsa still remains single, with the knowledge that she has lost her opportunity.

Dr. Schwaryencrona, Mr. Bredejord, and Professor Hochstedt still play innumerable games of whist.

One evening the doctor, having played worse than usual, Mr. Bredejord, as he tapped his snuff-box, had the pleasure of recalling to his mind a circumstance which had too long been forgotten.

"When do you intend to send me your Pliny?" he asked, with a wicked gleam in his eye. "Certainly you can no longer think that Erik is of Irish origin?"

The doctor was thunder-struck for a moment by this speech, but he soon recovered himself.

"Bah! an ex-president of the French Republic was a direct descendant of one of the Irish kings," he said, seriously. "I should not be at all surprised if Mr. Durrien belongs to the same family!"

"Evidently," replied Mr. Bredejord. "In fact it is so extremely probable that out of sport I will send you my Quintilian!"

The End